FALSE
CONFESSION

by Sylvie Grayson

GREAT WESTERN PUBLISHING c/o sylviegraysonauthor@gmail.com

Copyright © 2017 by Sylvie Grayson

All rights reserved.

For information contact

sylviegraysonauthor@gmail.com

www.sylviegrayson.com

ISBN: 978-1-7750405-0-7

Great Western Publishing is a registered trademark of Sylvie Grayson.

Cover art by Steven Novak   novakillustration@gmail.com

Books by Sylvie Grayson

<u>Contemporary romantic suspense</u>

Suspended Animation

The Lies He Told Me

Legal Obstruction

My Best Mistake

Moon Shine

<u>Sci-fi/fantasy</u>

Khandarken Rising,
The Last War: Book One

Son of the Emperor,
The Last War: Book Two

Truth and Treachery,
The Last War: Book Three

Weapon of Tyrants,
The Last War: Book Four

Prince of Jiran,
The Last War: Book Five

Praise for Sylvie Grayson's books

I've been reading Sylvie Grayson - can't seem to put them down. How do you come up with these exciting mysteries? Very fun reading!!

Suspended Animation

Wow! This book is amazing, its very well written and the characters are very well developed. This is my first book by Sylvie Grayson and it won't be my last. I was hooked from the first page and this book was very hard to put down.

Interesting characters, family conflicts and divided loyalties make this a book that kept me up half the night

Legal Obstruction

I loved this book! I've found my new favorite author. Emily is a fiercely professional woman who is on her own and determined to protect her little family. Joe is a solitary guy who often doesn't deal with problems until they are front and center. But boy does Emily wake him up and does he take notice. Add in a wildcard assistant and a few unsavory characters and I was up all night finishing the book to find out what happens.

The Lies He Told Me

If you are a fan of the heartwarming craftiness and domesticity of a Debbie McComber romance, and the intense intrigues of Danielle Steele, you'll enjoy the writing style of Sylvie Grayson; where the bad guys are not heartless, and the good guys are virtually flawless.

Just a quick note to let you know how much I enjoyed your book. You drew on your vast experience as a result of being a female, a wife, lover, mother, business woman, lawyer, friend, gardener, homeowner, compassionate and caring individual. It was an intriguing read which kept me guessing and very interested. Well done, Sylvie.

The Last War: Book One, Khandarken Rising

The General of Khandarken sends his son, Dante, to investigate the situation. When Dante meets the lovely Beth she eyes him with suspicion. But he won't stop until he solves the tangle of motives, fueled by greed, which threaten Beth and her family. I enjoyed this book very much. The well-developed characters and sensuous love scenes make this a page turner. I look forward to reading Book Two and Book Three

… this story is one of a kind in its own and couldn't be truly compared to anything but itself. It has so many unique characteristics to it. The personal relationships are intriguing and different from many other fictional relationships. The names are cool, the plot gets thicker with each page, and I loved the author's style. It became evident that I was addicted to reading the book once I was sad to be finished. I'm going to give this a strong recommendation. It's my kind of book.

The Last War: Book Two, Son of the Emperor

I am a big fan of The Last War series. I loved Book One, the story of Major Dante Regiment and Beth Farmer. The dystopian world Grayson has created, where women are scarce and Clones are used to replace them, where the Emperor has finally been defeated but his son takes up the fight, just gets better in this second book. …Thrills abound on the race to freedom and home. I really enjoyed this book and can't wait for Book Three. Grayson has great imagination, the fantasy series is awesome.

Truth and Treachery, The Last War: Book Three

4 stars - Format: Paperback

Ok, this series is just getting better and better. The increasing complexity of the characters and the development of lead characters is a pleasure to read. The plot, with its twists and turns, intrigue and adventure, is a real joy. If you liked the first two books in The Last War series (and, seriously, that's the place to start before reading this book - it's worth doing) then you will love this book.

Weapon of Tyrants, The Last War: Book Four

4 stars - ByThe Mysterious Amazon Customeron March 17, 2017 Format: Kindle Edition

The Last War has been a truly excellent series so far, and Weapon of Tyrants is staying strong. Exciting, full of intrigue and adventure, wonderfully developed strong lead characters with a great supporting cast, neat world-building and excellent writing. I mean, what more can you ask for? You do need to start with book 1 in this series, but it too was excellent so you can't go wrong, and I can guarantee you'll have a ball with this one when you reach it.

DEDICATION

I am blessed with wonderful support that has enabled me to write. To my husband, who is always ready to listen, read and lend a hand with difficult passages. To my children who had faith in me and helped with their interest, support and practical suggestions.

To my critique group: You know who you are. Your help with polishing and editing is invaluable.

Any errors or omissions are mine alone.

Sylvie Grayson
www.sylviegrayson.com *or*

sylviegraysonauthor@gmail.com

FALSE CONFESSION

CHAPTER ONE

Whates *she* doing here?" Alex Vecchio glared around the dim upstairs storage room, which was theirs one night a week for band practice. The bar had cases of wine and hard liquor stacked against the far wall. Barrels of beer had been lugged in and placed near the elevator. A single light bulb illuminated the space, the walls dingy with age and the floor boards bare and unpainted.

He spotted his brother's shaggy head. "Ryan? What's going on?" His voice was low and fierce. "What's she *doing* here?"

Ryan grinned as he pulled his drums from the case. "Hey, Alex. Have you met Glory?" His sandy bangs fell forward as he motioned toward the young woman on the other side of the room. She was bent over a keyboard, unfolding the legs and snapping the braces into place.

Alex lowered his brows and kept his face turned toward his younger brother, his voice a growl. "What's going on? Why is she here?"

"Glory!" As she straightened, Ryan waved the young woman over. "This is my brother, Alex. He plays lead."

Alex turned toward her. "Hi," was all he managed, his body stiff with outrage. Her smile was sunny as she beamed up at him.

"Hi, Alex. Nice to meet you." She thrust her hand out, and he was forced to give it a reluctant shake. "I didn't know you were his brother. What a coincidence!" She was still smiling as she turned to Ryan. "Alex lives right next door at the townhouse complex. I've seen him a few times when I go off to work in the morning."

Alex filed that comment away for further scrutiny. She'd been going off to work? In that getup? At five in the morning, her hair was up in a messy pony tail. She wore purple stretch shorts and a little pink tube top. He'd thought she was leaving fresh from the new neighbour's bed. It was how her hair was kind of all every which way that had put that thought into his head. Well, and the time of day.

He was suddenly irritated by the idea that he'd rushed to judgement without much prompting. He grunted and slung his guitar case to the floor, going down on one knee to unsnap the buckles.

"So," Ryan continued blithely, "Glory is going to try out with the band tonight, she's thinking of joining us."

Alex's head snapped up. "Joining us?" he barked, then felt his face flush. That sounded just a touch unfriendly, even to his own ears.

"Yeah," said Ryan. "We need a keyboard. Pete plays sometimes but his strength is in the strings. This should round us out the way I've imagined the band sounding. I thought we'd give it a try tonight and find a few songs to work on that we can all play." He waved at the other band members who were busy setting up. Pete nodded distractedly at their new member as he pulled his fiddle from the case and began to tune it.

Alex looked over at Glory. She was chatting with Eddie and laughing at something he'd said. That didn't surprise him. Eddie loved women, all women. No wonder Corrie had left him. Again.

This woman was trouble. As she moved back to her keyboard, Eddie's dark eyes followed, focussed tightly on her ass clad in a snug pair of jeans.

She positioned her bench so she could see the other band members and settled down to play a few scales.

Alex noted the skinny legs on her pants and the high heels of her strappy shoes. Nothing but trouble. He shook his head and walked over to plug in. The air resounded with strings being tuned and keys pounded. He heard the thud of Ryan's big drum as he snapped it into place in the harness.

His brother thumped a few drum rolls and silence fell. "Guys," he said, "I thought we'd try a few suggestions from Glory. She's got a sheet of numbers she likes to play, and we can just follow along to see how we sound."

Glory nodded and immediately began the intro to one of Adelle's old songs, *Rolling in the Deep*. Alex groaned silently. Not a bunch of chick songs! He so did not want to…

But as she played and the others joined in, the song began to hang together. They worked their way to the finale and she struck a chord to finish. Then she started the song again. This time she sang. Alex watched and listened, eyes narrowed as she got to the chorus. *We could have had it all*, she sang, then finished with— *You played it, you played it to the beat.*

When they stopped, the other guys clapped enthusiastically and he saw the pink flush on her cheeks as she laughed and waved them away.

Alex didn't clap, but suddenly he felt like it. She was good, he'd give her that. He looked over at Ryan and saw him flash a smile. Little bugger, he was always trying to put something together, something bigger, something better. He just might have done it this time.

~~***~~

CHAPTER TWO

By the end of the session, Ryan had pulled together a half dozen new songs that Glory would lead, and run through a large part of their own repertoire to which she'd begun to add her own contributions. They were all tired but jubilant at the possibilities of the new sound.

Glory folded the legs of her keyboard and left it on the floor. She thanked everyone and waved goodbye. "I work pretty early," she called. "I need to get home, so I won't hang around tonight. Thanks, it was fun."

After she left, the guys went downstairs and settled round a small table at the back of the sparsely populated bar. The waitress dropped their beers. It had become a tradition to end their practices this way, a drink or two, then home.

"So, guys. What do you think?" Ryan began.

Before Alex could open his mouth, the others had chimed in. "Corrie ain't gonna like it," Eddie remarked in his deep voice, his heavy mustache bristling. "You know how suspicious she is of other women." He shook his head mournfully.

"Well," Pete shot back, "that won't matter, will it? You told us Corrie's already moved out." What was left unsaid was Corrie probably had good reason to be suspicious.

Eddie shook his head. "That's just temporary. You know that. She'll be back in a day or two. But," and he brightened noticeably, "that little girl sure can play. She can sing, too."

"I told you," said Pete, addressing Ryan. "I told you she was good."

"You know her?" Alex stared at him in disbelief.

Pete blushed. "I don't *know* her. She was in a band in high school, but she was a few years ahead of us. Right? And Ryan had a crush on her."

Ryan frowned at his friend but the colour crept up his cheeks. "Yeah, well. I did like her. We used to go hear them play. It was her band. She chose the songs, sang lead and played keyboard. It was a girl band, but still." He must have seen Alex's mouth tighten in disapproval.

"I know you don't like girls right now, big bro. But she's good, and she said she misses playing in a band. So, I invited her to come and give it a try. What do you guys think? Will this make sense, can we work with her?" He looked around the table expectantly.

Everyone muttered in agreement except Alex. He was still steaming over the *don't like girls* gibe from his brother.

"That's what I thought." Ryan sat back with satisfaction. "I vote we take her on. What do you say?"

Alex looked around as the others nodded their heads, then turned as one to stare at him. He shrugged in feigned disinterest. "Ryan, it's your band. Do as you please."

"Nope, you can't get off that easy. Everyone has to agree, everyone has to buy in. That's how this works. So what do you say? Shall we ask her to join us? You have to admit, she knows what she's doing. She even made our songs better, with the keyboard and backup singing, and she's only just started with what she can contribute. Come on, jump in with both feet." Ryan made an encouraging motion with his hand that nearly knocked his beer over. He had to make a quick grab for the glass as it tipped dangerously. There was a round of loud laughter. He joined in but still stared expectantly at his brother, waiting for an answer.

Eddie leaned to clap Alex on the shoulder with a beefy hand. "Come on, bud. Like Ryan says, it's time to tune this band up. It'll be more fun, and we can get out of our rut, try some new stuff. What do you say?"

Alex nodded reluctantly. "Okay. I say, okay."

Ryan cheered and raised his glass. "Way to go. All right. So there will be some new songs, and some new arrangements. But that's good. We were getting stale anyway. We'll stick to our list with her add-ons from tonight, at least for a few weeks. Give us time to get cohesive. Then we can start to branch out and add material as we go along." He was crackling with energy and enthusiasm.

Alex gave a reluctant chuckle and grabbed his younger brother around the neck in a chokehold. "Okay, Ryan. We get it. We'll do it and we'll even like it."

They all guffawed.

~~*~~

As Ryan helped him drag the equipment out to the pickup parked on the street in the pouring rain, Alex glanced at the keyboard in its case stuck awkwardly under one arm. "So, do we have to lug her equipment around as well? Is that part of the deal?"

Ryan gave him a stern look. "Calm down, Alex. She just has a little car and it's hard to fit that keyboard in. Besides, we're driving to your place anyway, which is right next to hers. So what's the big deal?"

"No big deal. Just wondering. How did you decide to ask her to join us?"

Ryan turned an innocent face in his direction. "I was sitting on your step waiting for you to get home the other day and I heard someone on a piano. It sounded good. Then this guy knocked at her door. When she opened it, I recognized her. So later, as I was leaving your place, I rapped on her door and introduced myself. She said she remembered me." The colour climbed his neck and he jerked his head forward, intent on placing the drums carefully on the floor of the truck bed. "From high school, you know. I'm not sure I believe her, but anyway. I told her about the band, and that we needed a keyboard."

"Humph." Alex grunted as he lifted the rest of the cases into the bed of the truck, and closed the tailgate, securing the cap. If they'd needed a keyboard, he hadn't been aware of it. And weren't there guys out there that could play the keys? Finding musicians had never been a problem before.

"Yeah, she was really enthusiastic," Ryan continued. "She said she'd been looking for a band to join, had been thinking about starting her own again because she couldn't find anything that worked for her. Good timing. That's what Josie always says about me." He grinned impudently at his older brother. "I have good timing."

Alex laughed and cuffed him on the back of the head. "Don't let Mum hear you say that. Or your girlfriend, for that matter."

Ryan snickered.

"Did you really have a crush on her in high school?"

Ryan stilled for a second, then moved around to open the passenger door of Alex's black truck. "Maybe," he said, as he climbed in and buckled his seat belt. "But I'm over that now."

"You better not let Josie hear you say that, either," Alex said as he slammed the door and jammed the key in the ignition.

~~***~~

CHAPTER THREE

The first time Alex laid eyes on Glory, he'd been arriving home in the early morning hours. Trudy had called in the middle of the night. She'd been in a real state and he couldn't get a word in edgewise over her shrieking and crying on the other end of the phone. He'd eventually gone over to see what he could do.

The last time she'd said they were through was almost a year ago. It became the last time because he had finally declared it so. The back and forth in their relationship had been going on too long for his stability and peace of mind, so he dug in his heels and called it quits.

But she didn't understand 'quits'. Pretended not to understand, anyway.

Alex knew in his heart and his gut that it was over, had been finished for a long time. But he'd ignored that fact, rolling with her punches as she called it off then repeatedly reinstated their relationship. This time he swore he wasn't going back, not for anything. He'd moved out of the house they'd shared since graduating from high school, gotten his own place in the townhouse complex and settled in. They were done.

But when she called and continued to call as the hours wore on, all broken and weepy on the phone, he couldn't pretend he hadn't cared at one time. He climbed out of bed and threw on some clothes.

Trudy had been his girlfriend back in grade twelve when they'd met in a body-building competition. She was buff and fit, nearly as tall as he and almost as strong. The relationship was rocky from the start. She was temperamental and he'd soon learned that things could change between them at the drop of a hat.

When he drove up to the familiar house this time, pulled into the curb and sat with the engine running, he tried to decide what to do next. Her boyfriend's car wasn't anywhere in sight, which was a good thing. Cautiously he turned the engine off, climbed out and looked around before knocking on the door. The last thing he wanted was to run into Rolf in the middle of the night outside Trudy's place.

When the door opened, she rushed into his arms where he stood on the step, clinging to the front of his shirt. As she wept into his neck, he tried to hold her back from wrapping herself around him.

"Hold on, Trudy. Hold on." He held his arms out to the sides. "Come on. If big boy Rolf comes in here he's going to be pissed to see you holding onto me like this."

"He won't be coming back. He's left me!" Her eyes glistened wetly in the dim light, blond strands of hair glued to her red cheeks.

He sighed and seized her arm, pulling her inside and slamming the door. He dragged her to the couch and tugged her down beside him. As he slung one arm around her shoulders, he noticed she was wearing a nightie that was dammed near transparent. He groaned as she sobbed against his chest.

Her guy had left her? What was he supposed to do about that? And wasn't that why they'd broken up that final time, because she already had a new man?

He tried to be sympathetic. He really did care, just not in that way anymore. But she was hurt and he hung in there, patting her back and making reassuring comments.

Yet he didn't want to be here, and he certainly didn't want to encounter the boyfriend if he should decide to return. Rolf was a body builder, too. Alex had done it for sport in high school and since. It was a hobby that he enjoyed and that kept him in shape for his real job.

But Rolf did it professionally. Not that he was a fighter, but he was strong. More importantly, he was aggressive. Alex didn't want to get into a fight over his ex-girlfriend, no matter how long they'd gone together before Rolf intervened in the relationship.

~~*~~

By the time Trudy calmed down and he left for home, the sky was getting light in the east. Alex pulled his truck to the curb in front of his place just as a young woman bounded down the front steps of the townhouse complex. At first he'd thought she came out of his unit, and a shot of alarm aided him out of the cab of his truck. But then he remembered seeing the movers at the suite across from him. A new guy had apparently moved in.

And this must be his girlfriend. She was pretty, her long light-brown hair up in a ponytail. She was spilling out of a tiny tank top and a tight pair of elastic shorts. He looked his fill. Nice, very nice. As she jogged down the sidewalk to a little red car, shirt tails flapping as she ran, she jiggled in all the right places.

Then he frowned. The guy'd been there one day and already she was staying over?

Now he realized it had been Glory jogging down the sidewalk. She'd joined the band at Ryan's invitation and he was stuck with her as a neighbour and a band member. What was he supposed to do with that?

Another foolish female running around at all hours, without a care for her own safety. And where the hell was she going at five in the morning in that getup?

~~***~~

CHAPTER FOUR

Ryan hit the last beat on his drums. The song ended and the band fell silent. All except Glory. To her embarrassment, she'd managed to hit an extra couple of keys before she brought the song to a full stop. Oblivious, the crowd in the nightclub shouted and clapped.

She sank reflexively down on the bench, her head drooping between her shoulder blades. She hoped the sound had been drowned out by the loud noise from the audience. The rest of the band dropped their instruments and moved toward the two steps that led down from the small stage at *Rooster's* nightclub. Heaving herself from the bench, she searched against the spotlights for the table where her friends were sitting.

Pippa stood from her chair and waved wildly. Glory spotted them and excitedly waved back. There they all were, Pippa, Mercedes, Greg. Amazingly even Cliff had shown up. She sidestepped between crowded tables and grabbed the chair they'd saved for her. Pippa had a tall cranberry and soda waiting, the ice only slightly melted.

Everyone leaned over to give her a hug, until Cliff was forced to join the sentiment. He had a slightly sardonic look on his face, as if he were above this kind of thing.

Glory swatted him on the shoulder as she grabbed her glass. "Don't give me that superior look," she demanded above the noise. "I know you want to hug me just as much as Greg does."

He looked amused and Greg burst out laughing. "Don't worry, Glory. He doesn't get jealous. Not of women anyway." He raised expressive brows at her. "The music was pretty good," he conceded.

"Pretty good?" Mercedes sounded indignant. "I thought it was great. Glory, you're really on top of it tonight, and I can't believe how the sound's come together. That tall guy on the drums is cute."

Glory grinned. "I thought you'd notice him. That's Ryan. It's his band. He's the one who asked me to join them."

Mercedes' mouth rounded in an O of surprise. "Hmmm. I thought the boss might be that guy at the front, the lead guitar. He's built. And he has a look about him. Kind of in control of things."

Glory stored that thought away. That might be true. Ryan was eager about the music, the playing, the gigs they got, and he promoted like crazy. But Alex was in control. Of himself at least, if not the band. And she got the impression that Ryan didn't stray too far from his brother's approval. Might be a big-bro, little-bro situation, but certainly he carried a lot of weight in the opinion of the guys in the group.

"Anyway," said Pippa. "It was really good, I've been enjoying the music. Who's suggestion was it to call the band, *Hot to Trot?*"

Glory laughed. "I don't know for sure, but it has to be Ryan's idea. It's his band."

Her friend nodded. "Is it fun, being up on the stage again?"

Glory felt that old leap of adrenaline, and had to smile. She'd loved having her own band. "Not yet. I'm still getting used to the guys. But it's going to be good once I'm more comfortable. Then it'll be exciting."

~~*~~

When the musicians gathered on stage again, the second set worked much better. The crowd was loud and they were excited. She felt she was just starting to gel with the group. She was glad it was a Thursday night, Friday was her last shift at the bakery this week.

At the end of the last set, everyone left their equipment on stage and trooped to a corner near the bar where a tiny table had been held for them.

They fended off the fan routine of high fives, half hugs, congratulations, then Ryan conducted a windup as the waiters went around for last call from the bar. He recapped the songs that worked best, where they needed to adjust things, winking at Glory as he reminded them to quit playing when he signalled it.

Her face burned but she kept the smile on her face.

Eddie wrapped a beefy consoling arm around her shoulders. "Don't worry, little girl. I still do that every now and then. Ryan is always giving me shit." He squeezed her lightly and let his hand slide casually down her arm as he let go.

Uncomfortable, she shifted her chair toward Alex on her other side, hoping to be unobtrusive.

"Eddie." Ryan leaned forward to gain his attention and began to dissect the last number.

Alex slid a draft beer in front of Glory and gazed at her over the glass. "Do you drink beer?" he asked. It wasn't that his voice was cold exactly, just cool.

"Yes, thank you." She picked up the draft and took a small sip. She smiled at Pete. "I think it went pretty well tonight, don't you?"

Pete nodded, obviously still tongue-tied in her presence.

"Should be better tomorrow." Alex's statement fell flat between them. Glory turned to look at him. Was he as unfriendly as he sounded?

But Pete didn't seem to notice. He bobbed his head in agreement. "That's right. This was likely our worst night. And it wasn't bad. So the next time will be even better. We're coming along fine."

"Do you work again tomorrow morning?" Alex was still looking at her, examining her actually. At least that's what it felt like.

She nodded her head and made the effort to smile. "Yep. Monday to Thursday usually. But I promised to take a shift tomorrow."

After a few more minutes of conversation, Glory excused herself and headed out of the club. Most of the patrons were gone and the crowd was thin. When she escaped onto the sidewalk, she paused to button her jacket against the chill in the air as a group of nightclub customers burst onto the street behind her.

"Where did you park?"

She glanced around in surprise to see Alex a step behind her. "Uh, sorry?"

"Just wondering where you parked." He gestured toward the sidewalk.

"Oh, yes." She looked blankly down the street for a minute, caught off guard. "Umm, in the parkade." She pointed.

"Okay. I'm near there. I'll walk you."

"Oh. You don't have to. I'm fine, really."

He just looked at her, then reached to take her arm. "I'm going that way, anyway." He released his grip as soon as she began to move. They walked for half a block in total silence.

Glory took a deep breath, smiled and tried another comment. "Well, what did you think?"

He looked her in the eyes, then surveyed her hair hanging straight down her back. "I think that guy with the suspenders really had the hots for you. I wondered if he might be waiting out here."

18

"Who?" She frowned in confusion, then burst out laughing. "Oh, you mean Greg. Uh, no, not Greg. He's just an old friend."

"Really? From the way he never took his eyes off you, I would have thought more than just old friends. Maybe you misunderstand his intentions."

"His what?" She choked on the thought, and he tapped her lightly between the shoulder blades. "No, Greg doesn't have those kinds of intentions, not toward me at any rate. I'm positive. And if he'd been waiting out here, I would have been safe as houses with him."

Alex said nothing further but pointed the way into the parking lot. "Which level?"

"Right here." She indicated her little red car at the back of the first floor of parking. "And you?"

"I'm not far. Maybe next time we can travel together, given we leave from the same front step, save on parking fees."

"Okay." She was surprised but doubtful. "Sure, sounds great. Talk to you tomorrow."

She slid into the driver's seat and he walked away as she slammed the door and locked it. She took a deep breath and let her smile fade. It was a tired smile. It was hard to keep smiling when no one smiled back

~~***~~

CHAPTER FIVE

Alex climbed into his truck. He sat there, keys in hand, waiting for Glory's shiny red Mini to come down the ramp onto the street. No, he wasn't going to tail her home, even though they lived in the same building. He wouldn't go that far. But still, a single girl didn't wander around downtown at night by herself. Not on his watch. Not when she looked like Glory and had just left a nightclub where she was the focus of most of the male attention.

He'd spied her again this morning, running down the sidewalk to her car at some ungodly hour. Wearing next to nothing, stretch workout shorts and halter top with a shirt pulled over it, the tails trailing as she ran. He'd just gotten back from Trudy's. Again.

He scrubbed his hands over his face and forced the key into the ignition. Trudy was going to be the death of him.

It was over. She'd declared it over. So, he'd said, *Fine, I'm finished.* It was a relief to move on and that was ages ago. But she wouldn't let it go. Phone calls in the middle of the night, screaming matches at his front door, demands that he get over there and clean up the mess he'd left. Fuck! Whatever he'd left, it had been ten months ago. How bad could it be? And why did it have to be addressed in the small hours of the morning?

He was bone tired. He shoved the truck into gear and eased out of his parking spot. He could just see Glory's taillights winking as she turned the corner up ahead.

He'd had a good time tonight, and he was excited about it. He loved to play and it was obvious the band was just going to get better. He hadn't figured out yet how to handle their new member, but she was going to liven things up. Having a woman in the band got the attention of all the men in the joint. That really picked up the pace, as well.

There'd been a couple of yokels who hooted every time Glory shook her hair. She'd smiled and kept on singing, but they got louder.

One tried to climb onto the stage but Ryan signalled the staff and the bartender called the bouncer. The guy was dragged back onto the dance floor and warned he'd get tossed if he did it again. He had to be content to ogle her from afar and eventually gave up, finding someone else to dance with.

Alex sighed and braked for the corner. He had to work tomorrow. That alarm went pretty early and he was usually the first man on the construction site.

~~*~~

Manx Construction was building a townhouse complex that was going to be a real challenge. It was a bigger job than they usually took on, but Alex had assured everyone he could manage it without any problem. Jim Manx had clapped him on the back and said they were going to count on that.

As Alex slapped off his alarm, he heard the door to the next townhouse bang shut. He parted the blinds in time to see Glory dash down the steps and onto the sidewalk, looking madly around for her car.

Did the woman not know where she parked? And why did she leave so damn early? She turned right and broke into a jog heading up the block. He leaned closer to the window, watching the enticing sight of her tight shorts and slim legs as she quickly crossed the street and beeped her car lock. She climbed in and was lost from view.

He huffed out a breath he hadn't been conscious of holding and threw the covers back. A good night's sleep for once. Just in time, too, because the building inspector was making his first official visit to the site this morning and he needed to be ready.

An hour later, he strode the construction project, trying to keep pace with the inspector from city hall. The fellow was long and lean and he walked like a machine, over ditches, through shrubs and up inclines without stopping as he spouted his conclusions. Alex needed to hear those conclusions and it was a tough job with the wind whistling across the water.

"Hold it a minute," he said. He halted on the nearest point of land and held up his hand to stop their progress.

The inspector looked startled. Impatiently he drew up beside him and frowned down the slope. "What's the matter?"

Alex gave an internal sigh. "Listen, you say there's too much grade for townhouses to work on this site. We've got the engineer's specs to show that isn't a problem." He pointed up the bank to the construction trailer parked at the side of the driveway. "Why don't we go have a look at those, before we make any decisions?"

The inspector braced his narrow shoulders in his padded jacket and gazed across to the small island in the middle of the bay, just visible through the heavy mist. "I've seen those specs," he said.

Alex raised his brows. "Well, what seems to be the issue, then? Henny Manx is the chief engineer and there isn't anyone more reliable. He has a good reputation. Why are you questioning the grade?"

Mouth tight, the inspector turned back to survey the wall of mud behind them. "Do you see a set of townhouses sticking to that slope?" he muttered.

"Yeah, I do." Alex reined in his impatience. "We've done all the drilling, found bedrock and begun excavating to pour the foundation. You know that as well as I do. There was a similar one built just down the coast a few miles. No problems with any of it."

"Humph." The guy turned and climbed the hill toward the driveway, mud caking beneath the tread of his boots. "Okay. But I'll expect complete compliance with all safety and construction procedures and I'll nail your hide to my office door if I don't get it."

"Of course." Alex trod after him, jamming his hands in his pockets to keep from strangling the man. "That won't be a problem. Manx Construction is a reputable business and we always do everything by the book. Thanks for working with us. Can you sign off on the plans?"

Why did they have to get the inspector from hell? Just the luck of the draw, he figured.

~~***~~

CHAPTER SIX

The next week, Glory closed her apartment door and listened for the lock to catch. Running lightly down the steps to the sidewalk, she glanced up and down the street. Where did she park last night? She'd been working late at the Music Conservatory and the street was crowded when she got home. Okay, there it was, her little red car at the end of the block. She jogged toward it, ponytail bouncing.

Today was her first shift of the week at the bakery. The hours were very early at one job and sometimes late at the other. She tried to take an occasional nap during the day just to keep her energy levels high, but didn't always manage it.

Well, she liked the bakery. Bagels were her thing and they made good ones at Benjamin's. Besides, she liked the staff and the owners. They'd been good to her, allowing the freedom to arrange her shifts while accommodating her music and that was a rare concession from any employer.

She clicked her key ring and heard the car unlock with a cheerful chirping sound. She had another practice with the band tonight. Their first few nights in the club last week had gone well. She was already hyped about it, thrilled to be back performing and playing something more exciting than musical scales.

It was pretty obvious Ryan's brother, Alex, wasn't too ecstatic about the whole idea. She'd been able to read it in his body language, if not his purposely blank expression when he looked her way. But that could be just because he didn't know her like Ryan and his friend Pete did. She'd give him time to get used to the idea of a female in a rock band.

Alex had been a surprise. Ryan was tall and lean, his long skinny legs encased in low-slung jeans. But his brother seemed to be a body builder. A little shorter than Ryan, he was about six feet tall and looked like someone off a billboard with a lean square jaw, wide shoulders and muscular arms, slim waist and powerful thighs. He must do a lot of workouts or else his job was very physical to maintain a physique like that.

The band practice sessions had turned out to be fun. First they spent time jamming. Someone would play the opening bars of a song and the others would join, or a voice would call out the name of a number and the rest dove into it. It gave her a better sense of the strengths and talents of the group, and they began to let her in to contribute her sound to the combined effort.

Eddie had begun giving her soulful looks, and she laughed it off. She'd met guys like him before, and they were seldom serious. Often, it seemed to be habit to come on to any new female. Plus she had overheard enough comments from the other band members to know that he had a wife, Corrie. And Corrie had just left him. It seemed to be a common occurrence, according to the off-the-cuff remarks that were made. Everyone fully expected her back any day now.

Glory turned the key in the ignition and the little engine sprang to life. She twisted to grab her seatbelt and caught the image of a black pickup truck with lettering on the cab door pulling up to the sidewalk a half block behind her. She recognized that vehicle.

Alex Vecchio climbed out and carelessly slung the door closed. He looked haggard, his eyes dark rimmed.

She leaned forward to keep his face in the mirror, but lost him so cranked her neck around to gaze behind her. This was almost exactly like the first time she'd seen him outside their common townhouse entrance. He'd been pulling up just as she was leaving for work. He'd looked rumpled, his hair showing signs of fingers having plowed through it many times. His eyes had been red, his expression strained.

What did he do that kept him out all night? Must be a woman. Unless he had some huge gambling problem or boozing habit. But she'd passed him on the walkway that first time and he hadn't reeked of liquor, didn't look shaky or drugged. She'd bet it was a woman. As far as she knew from her short time here, he'd be heading out to work in about an hour. Must be some girlfriend to keep him out all night.

~~*~~

Glory arrived at the bakery just as Ben was unlocking the front door. "Morning, Glory," he said, as he struggled with the lock, finally putting his shoulder to the panel and forcing it open.

She laughed. Ben never tired of the pun. "Morning, Ben. Must be time to get that door fixed."

He gave a low chuckle. "I promise. I'll call the landlord about it today."

Glory grinned and walked in behind him as Tom, the head baker, lumbered up the sidewalk to the entrance. She followed the men around the front counter into the kitchens at the back.

Ben grabbed yeast packets and dumped them into a row of stainless steel bowls on the counter, adding sugar and warm water. He was a control freak about some things, and this was one of them. Once the yeast was set to rise, he left them to get started on the first batch of bagels.

Glory turned on the beaters and poured in water, slowly adding flour. As she worked, she noticed Tom seemed more taciturn than usual this morning. She gave him a nudge in his thick ribs with her elbow on her way past. "How are you this morning, my fine friend?"

His fair skin flushed darker and his gaze slid sideways. "You know. Could be better." He stirred the yeast mixture, set the spoon aside and poured water into the boiling pot. He heaved it onto the burner.

"Come on, Tom. It's been a while. Things must be improving," she admonished.

"Why would they?" The soulful look he gave her from under his blond bangs tugged at her heartstrings. "She's not coming back."

"No, maybe not. But it's still not the end of the world." She gave an encouraging smile. *Who was she to decide that?* She winced and went back to the beaters. The memory of how she and her boyfriend had parted still burned at the back of her brain. Men weren't for her. It was a good decision and one she'd stuck to ever since. *Why put herself out there just to get hurt?*

"Anyway, life goes on," she muttered. *Not very encouraging.* Tom was a good guy, he had just made a bad choice in a girlfriend. Now he was lonely. *Well, join the club.*

"You could come hear my new band this weekend," she offered.

His doleful expression brightened. "You're in a new band?"

"Yeah. Well, it's not my band. But we play at *Rooster's* Thursday to Sunday for the next month. It's fun. My friend Greg was there last time."

"Greg?" Tom had met Greg before. They ran with some of the same crowd that biked the trails around town.

"Yes, and his buddy Cliff came once, so anything is possible."

Tom laughed. "I see. Well, maybe I'll come Friday night."

Glory nodded and turned the beaters up to blend the batter. She dumped in the yeast mix and added flour as it ground between the blades. The water in the pot was just simmering and they were almost ready to boil the first rounds.

She gave the high sign to Tom and went over to turn the ovens on, smiling to herself. It was nice to cheer someone up, even if she couldn't help hanging onto her own bad memories.

~~***~~

CHAPTER SEVEN

Eddie dialed the number and waited. This was the third time he'd called, and Trudy must be one busy girl, because she didn't answer her cell phone. He'd gotten the number off Alex's phone the other night at practice when Alex went off to order another round of beers. His cell had been sitting right there on the table.

The first thing he noticed on the screen was Alex had Glory's number in there under three different designations—Glory, neighbour, townhouse. Did that mean he didn't know her last name? it certainly seemed to indicate he wanted to be able to find the number.

Trudy clicked on, and Eddie felt his whole body snap to attention. "Hello," she drawled. "Who is this? Would you please stop phoning me."

"Hi Trudy. How are you? This is Eddie, Alex's buddy. I've been wanting to get together with you."

"Get together?" She sounded like she didn't have a clue what that could mean.

"Yeah. Have a drink, go for dinner. Sit down for a chat. What do you say?"

There was a drawn out pause, then she said, "Well, I'm pretty busy right now."

"Yeah? Then why not do lunch? I can be in your neighbourhood around noon tomorrow. Why don't we meet for a quick bite?"

She giggled, and he grew all warm inside. It sounded promising, he might be getting somewhere with her. "I can pick you up, how would that be?"

"No, don't pick me up. Listen, I'll call you around eleven to let you know if I can make it."

Eddie nodded to himself. He knew she'd be up for something. "Great. I'll wait for you call. Don't disappoint me."

~~*~~

Glory was getting dressed for the performance at the club when her doorbell rang. The cheery *dingdong* startled her and she dropped one of her crystal earrings. It skittered across the floor.

That must be Alex. They were supposed to travel together tonight, but he was damned early. She yanked the door open, only to be confronted by Greg. His usual trendy clothing hung loosely on his lean frame, his shirt buttoned awkwardly. And he looked like he'd been crying.

"What is it? Greg, get in here. What's wrong?" She grabbed his arm and pulled him through the doorway.

"Here, sit down and I'll get you something." She threw a frantic glance in an effort to locate her missing earring, then marched to her tiny kitchenette and grabbed a beer from the half-sized fridge. Twisting the cap off, she handed the bottle to him and dragged up a chair for herself. "Drink this."

Greg took the beer, but just held it in his hand as he gazed at her. "Cliff left me. He's gone."

"Gone? Gone where?" Cliff was a strange bird but he hadn't moved in with Greg, so he must still be at his own apartment.

"He left town."

"Wow." Her mouth stayed open in a moment of surprise. "Really? He's moved away?"

Greg nodded.

She nudged his hand upward and he finally took a swallow from the bottle, then another.

"That was fast." She pursed her lips. "I never liked him, anyway," she added.

Greg gave a weak grin. "You're a good friend, Glory. I never liked him either." He gave an unsteady chuckle. "Not much, anyway."

She responded with a gentle laugh. "Listen, I have to get ready. We're playing tonight and I'm getting a lift from Alex. But there's no rush, you can stay here as long as you like."

"Okay." He sniffed and straightened his shoulders. "I won't be there tonight. Just don't feel up to it, you know?"

Glory wrapped her arms around his shoulders. "I don't expect you to come. Just know I'm thinking of you, and try not to take it too hard. Was he a keeper?" She scrutinised his expression.

Greg shook his head and she nodded knowingly. "I didn't think so."

When her friend left she closed the door with a sigh and darted into the bathroom to finish her hair. She'd just started to put on her makeup when there was another rap at her door. She made a face in the mirror. This was starting to feel like a merry-go-round.

It was Alex, and he was dressed to kill. His wide shoulders had been jammed into a tight cotton shirt, most of the buttons left undone. The chest that showed through the gap was all muscle with a light dusting of hair. His waist was lean and his blue jeans tight enough to leave little to the imagination.

"Ready?"

Her gaze darted north to meet his dark eyes. *Had he noticed where her stare was riveted?* She hoped not. "Almost. Come in. I'll just be a minute."

She went back in the bathroom and began applying eyeliner, but her hand was shaking. *Men aren't for me, remember?* She'd have to repeat that mantra, because tonight there suddenly seemed to be a serious problem with her concentration.

"Okay," she said when she finally emerged from the bathroom. "I think I'm ready."

She attempted a smile, but his expression was sober. He pointed. "What about your other earring?"

"Oh!" She grabbed both ears, clasping the one earring that was there. "Damn. I dropped it and couldn't find it again." She shuffled over near her bed and peered around the floor.

"Here it is." Alex held the dangling crystal jewellry between his fingers. His gaze seemed pinned to the bed and he gave the covers a long scrutiny before he looked back at her. "Must have fallen off in the night."

Heat rushed to her cheeks as she took the earring from his grasp and fitted the hook through her ear. "Thank you."

She wouldn't be embarrassed. Just because she hadn't made her bed today, she wouldn't be embarrassed. Back stiff, she marched through the door ahead of Alex.

~~***~~

CHAPTER EIGHT

Rooster's was jammed to capacity and the dance floor seethed with bodies. Ryan hit a drum roll and the song came to a halt. Even Glory had remembered to stop playing at his signal. Alex felt his mouth quirk at the corner. He caught his brother's eye and they exchanged a humourous look.

He hadn't felt much like smiling tonight. Watching Glory say good-bye in her doorway to Mr Suspenders this afternoon wasn't his idea of fun. The guy had been at the club the first night they played, and the way he hugged her then had fired his imagination. But to see him coming out of her place today, his clothes hastily slung on, didn't make Alex feel great. Not when he'd finally admitted to himself that he was interested in her.

Once he managed to get inside her suite, he'd been set back on his heels. The bed was unmade and her earring lay half-hidden under one of the blankets dragging on the floor. It couldn't be clearer what had taken place. His shoulder blades itched. His neck was hot.

He straightened as Glory followed Pete off the stage. In the dim light, he'd just caught sight of Corrie at a table in the corner, sitting with two other women. His head swung around as he looked for Eddie, who'd obviously seen her as well.

Alex propped his guitar on the stand and took a step to intercept him, but Eddie could be fast in spite of his bulk. He was already off the stage, heading for his wife. At least she wasn't with another man, that would have triggered a fight for sure. Eddie stopped at the table, and appeared to be talking to Corrie. She listened but shook her head at her husband and motioned to her friends.

Alex turned away and moved toward the table reserved for the band, leaving Eddie to sort out his own business. Glory was already seated beside Ryan, with Pete on her other side. He had to work pretty hard to get anywhere near her, it seemed.

Before he even got to the table, someone hailed him from the dance floor. "Hi, Alex."

He raised his head and peered against the glare of the stage lights, but he already knew who it was. *Could this night get any more complicated?*

Trudy surged through the crowd and broke free, landing flat against his chest. He put his hands up to ward her off but it was too late. She planted a wet kiss square on his mouth, clinging to the front of his shirt with her talons. She didn't have to stand on tiptoes to reach him either, because she was nearly as tall as he was.

Alex took a breath. "Hi, Trudy. Is Rolf with you?"

Her face went a dull red. "I told you, he's gone. Come back home, Alex. I need you." Her eyes filled with tears and he looked away uncomfortably. He wasn't going back, and that wasn't his home.

She glared at him. "When did you get a girl to join the band? Why is she here?"

He shrugged. "Ryan's decision, it's his band."

"Yeah, but she's not here for Ryan. She's here for you." Her expression hardened.

"Calm down." He tried to step back to disengage but hit a wall of bodies behind him. She pressed closer. "Ryan asked her to join," he added in desperation. "He knew her from high school."

"I'll bet." Her gaze swung back to his. "Dance with me, Alex. I love how you dance."

"Trudy, let it go."

There was nowhere to escape. He glanced over to the table where the band was ensconced and gave Ryan a nod. This might be the shortest set break in band history, but he needed to get back on stage. Anything to escape her clutches. Might be good for Eddie, too. It didn't look like he was making much progress with Corrie tonight. Probably best for both of them to cut their losses.

Ryan took the steps to the small stage. The others trailed behind, Pete still clutching his drink. He hit a couple of strokes on the drum to signal the bar to cut the canned music. Alex peeled Trudy's fingers from his shirtfront and gratefully returned to pick up his guitar.

~~*~~

Glory climbed into the high seat of the truck as Alex shut the door and walked around the back. Ryan had left earlier with Pete, aiming for an after-hours club to wind down. They were alone.

"There's room if you want to give your girlfriend a lift. I don't mind." Glory turned an innocent face in his direction as he stepped in and stuffed the key in the ignition.

He looked surprised, then his frown darkened. "I don't have a girlfriend," he said and started the engine. As he backed out of the parking space, he shot her a guarded look.

Maybe not, but the lipstick stain is still spread across your mouth. She smirked and turned back to look out the front window. "Up to you," she said smugly.

There was silence as he drove into the Fairfield neighbourhood. Then he offered, "Your boyfriend didn't come to the club tonight."

Her eyes darted sideways. "What boyfriend?"

"The one with the suspenders. He called by your house earlier today, but didn't show to hear the band." He had a self-satisfied grin on his face that she wanted to wipe off with the palm of her hand.

"He's not my boyfriend," she said mildly. "Don't worry, when I get one, I'll let you know."

He gave her a penetrating look, then concentrated on the light traffic.

When he pulled up in front of their townhouse complex, she had the door open before he got the engine shut off. She jumped neatly to the sidewalk.

As Alex walked around the vehicle and stepped onto the walkway, she swung around and left him standing there. The sound of his footsteps trailed hers up the steps as she pulled her keys out of her purse and fumbled for the right one.

"And if she isn't your girlfriend," Glory tossed over her shoulder as she opened the door, "You shouldn't kiss her. That shade of red doesn't suit you."

She stepped inside her flat and slammed the door on his muffled curse.

~~*~~

Trudy waved good-bye to Eddie who stood at the cash to pay their bill, and marched out of the café before he could stop her. No, she wouldn't let him see her home before he went back to work, because it was too dangerous. But she was feeling better already, having a friend of Alex showing interest in her, even if just for a little fun. Eddie was good-looking, not in the same shape as Rolf or Alex, but still tall and well-built. He wasn't a serious guy, but why not have a little fling? Alex had made it clear he wasn't ever coming back. Her eyes watered suddenly. Must be the bright sun shining directly into her face.

She walked faster, past the wool shop, the muffin bakery, around the corner in the direction of her house.

Rolf wasn't there any longer. The last time he got rough with her, she'd determined it was time to stand up to him. She'd threatened to call the police if he didn't leave. To her relief, he'd thrown some clothes into a duffel bag. Then he left, but not before he threatened her again.

So was he gone, or not? It was hard to tell. He'd taken most of his things, and she hadn't heard from him since. A frisson of fear snaked down her spine. If he wasn't gone, this was a dangerous route to take. But she got so lonely when there was no one else there. She rattled around the house in a desperate funk.

Eddie might be just the answer. He wasn't going to hang around long. In fact, didn't he have a wife? She was sure he'd been married soon after high school. Whatever, this was a short-term solution maybe, but a solution.

~~***~~

CHAPTER NINE

Ryan opened the front door to his family's home. It was in an established neighbourhood of medium sized stucco-clad houses, most of which had been built in the fifties. "Mum?"

Maybe she wasn't here. She was one busy woman, with her church committees and bridge club. His university class had been cancelled. A short nap should do the trick, because the band was playing again tonight.

The wave of satisfaction felt bone deep. They were good, and even better now with the keyboard added. *Rooster's* had just offered to add another month to the contract -- every Thursday, Friday and Saturday night. It was almost more than he'd hoped for, maybe more than he could manage with his university studies. The classes were all over the map in terms of days and times. It was a challenge to manage.

As he eased his bedroom door open, he heard footsteps on the stairs to the basement and Mum appeared in the hall, a basket of laundry in her arms.

"Ryan Vecchio. You aren't usually home this time of day."

He turned and stooped to plant a kiss on her plump cheek. "Hi Mum. Yeah, class cancelled and I thought I'd take a nap. I'm beat."

"I'm not surprised." She set the basket on the kitchen table and began to fold the pillow cases. "You're playing a lot of nights, more than usual."

"It's good though." He dipped a hand into the basket, came out with a bunch of dish towels and stacked them on the table. "The band is really getting a following. We've been offered another contract."

Her eyes lit up. "I heard."

"You did?" He looked his surprise. "Did Alex tell you?"

"Trudy."

Ryan slapped a hand to his forehead. "Has Trudy been here?"

Mum looked grim. "She came this morning, I thought she'd never leave." She snapped the sides of a sheet together and gave it a forceful fold. "She wants Alex back."

Ryan shrugged. "Yeah, that's what I thought. She was at the club last night."

His mother laid the sheet down and leaned on the table with one hand, planting the other on a well-rounded hip. "Why can't she leave him alone? Is he interested?"

"No. Not at all. He got back on the stage as fast as possible to get away from her." He gazed out the kitchen window. "But she clings like velcro. He had to peel her off." He gave her a questioning look. "Did you know she calls him at night?"

"What for?" Then Mum shook her head. "As if I don't know. Where's Rolf?"

"She said her boyfriend left and she needs his help."

Mum looked dumbfounded.

"So he went over to comfort her."

"You're joking! Has he got rocks in his head?" She grabbed another dish towel and gave it a savage snap.

Ryan shuffled toward his bedroom. "He didn't go last time, if it's any consolation. He turned his phone off."

~~*~~

Glory turned the kettle off and poured boiling water into her teapot. *Something herbal*, Mum said, *something spicy*. Well, she had three kinds of tea. The choice was limited.

She glanced at her mother, seated in one of two chairs that fit around her half table in the bachelor suite. At least she'd put the bed up today before her visitor arrived, so the place didn't look quite so small. It was tucked against the wall and disguised as a big cupboard between the two windows.

"Here you go, Mum." Glory poured tea and passed her mother a cup.

"Jean," her mother said.

She could have predicted that. Mum wasn't mother to anyone any more. She had reinvented herself while Glory was still in high school, about the same time her parents ended their marriage. New wardrobe, new hairstyle with blond highlights, new slim body. She was Jean now, a friend who called by for a chat. Glory sighed and sat in the chair opposite.

"What do you think of my place?" she asked.

"It's small," Jean said. "But I guess that's no surprise. You don't earn enough money to get yourself a decent apartment." Her mouth puckered in disapproval.

Glory took a sip of tea. It didn't taste too bad, a mix of rooibos and chamomile. "It was time to move out, Mum."

"Jean," her mother said.

"And," Glory continued, ignoring the nudge, "I'm working with music because that's my dream. When I decide I can't afford it any longer, I'll get a different job. Meanwhile, this is it. I like it." She shot her mother a challenging look and took a piece of gingerbread from the plate on the table. "Thanks for the cookies."

Jean pursed her pink-painted lips and sipped her tea. Then she rose to leave. "Thank you, dear. Good to see you. Not that you make much of an effort. You haven't been by the house for weeks. Ever since you moved out, in fact."

There was a good reason for that, one Glory decided not to pursue at the moment. After all, this visit was a little like an olive branch, extended in peace. She reached for the door handle. "Bye, Mum. Take care."

"Jean," her mother said as she grabbed her purse.

~~***~~

CHAPTER TEN

Alex strolled over to the bar and leaned against the counter to chat with the guy on the end stool while he waited for the frazzled bartender to take his order.

Glory admired that trim muscular build before turning back to the table. Pete was still on stage tuning his fiddle, and Eddie had gone to circle the room.

"Is he looking for his wife?" she asked, watching as the bass player faded into the darkness over by the far wall.

Ryan nodded. "Probably. Not likely she's here though. She's a nurse, does a lot of night shifts. That's why it worked so well for them, having Eddie in the band."

Glory took in Ryan's shaggy hair and lean build. Not a lot like his older brother. "Do your parents come to hear you play?"

"Uh." Ryan gave a grin. "Mum has been a few times, but she prefers a community hall or something. She doesn't really do nightclubs."

Glory laughed. "And your dad?"

"Dead," he said shortly. "Died when I was still in high school. Heart attack on the worksite."

"Oh, my." Glory put her hand to her mouth. "I'm sorry. That's sad, Ryan."

"Yeah." He shook his head. "He was a great dad, a really good man. What about you?"

"Me?" She looked confused.

"Yeah, your mum and dad still in town?"

"Yes, actually." She nodded her thanks to Alex as he slid a glass of beer in front of her. "My parents are divorced, but they both live here."

Alex sat next to her and leaned an elbow on the table. "Was that your mother I saw leaving your place this afternoon?"

Glory pressed her lips together. "Is there no privacy?"

"Afraid not." Alex sipped his beer. "I stopped by home to get changed before the gig. Just caught her as she came down the steps. You look a bit like her." He peered at her over the glass.

"Have you got brothers and sisters?" Ryan asked.

Glory took a breath and met his gaze. *What was with all the questions?* But maybe she had started it. "No, sorry. Just me."

"Yeah, that's tough." Ryan kicked Alex under the table. "Having a brother can be a good thing—I guess," he added and rolled his eyes. "Sometimes."

She had to laugh. These two were so different, the one very serious, the other full of enthusiasm and goofiness. Yet they obviously cared a great deal for each other.

Pete gave up on his fiddle and came down the stage steps to take a chair. He grabbed a glass just as Eddie returned.

"We have a new engagement for the band," Ryan said over the noise of the canned music.

"Really?" Glory inhaled her beer and coughed heavily into her elbow. She felt a hard hand rub her back.

"Take a breath," a deep voice said in her ear.

She glanced at Alex bending over her. "I'm fine," she gasped. "There, that's better."

He removed his hand and she sat back, trying to recover from the heat of his touch. It had seemed like some kind of electrical charge.

Pete had already finished his beer and was waving to the waitress for another round.

"What's this about?" said Eddie. "*Rooster's* has already booked us for the next month."

Ryan waved at his brother. "Tell them, Alex."

Alex nodded. "My buddy, Coop, is getting married and he wants us to play at the wedding dance afterward. You remember Coop, Eddie. He was in school with us. The thing is, the event will take place up in northern BC, way past Fort St John."

He took a sip of beer and leaned back in the chair. "Ryan says he can manage time from classes and I've booked off work. What do you think? Will you all be able to come? It'll take two days to get there, but I sort of owe him. It should be fun."

Glory listened as the band members hashed out what might happen and when. The place was called Big Smokey, apparently, and sounded like it was way out in the wilderness somewhere. She had no experience with that kind of territory.

Pete had already agreed to go. When Ryan turned to her, she regretfully shook her head. "I don't think I can do that, Ryan. I could get the time off work, that wouldn't be a problem. But I can't afford the flight up there and back. Then how do we get to Big Smokey from the airport?"

Ryan just nodded and exchanged a knowing look with Alex before changing the topic. They sorted out the routine for next week and left in a group.

"Eddie will drive you home, Glory. I've got a stop to make on my way." Alex shot a fierce look at Eddie. Glory watched him take off up the street in the other direction. *Must be the girlfriend again, the one he doesn't have. That red lipstick must taste pretty good, after all.*

Yet, why should she care? She wasn't into men right now.

~~*~~

Alex strode the length of the worksite, water running off his hardhat. Two excavators were busy at the other end digging down to bedrock, with the prospect of having foundation framing in place by week's end. If that happened, they'd be ready to pour concrete the following week.

It was almost lunch time and the whistle would go shortly. He backed out of the way as a dump truck eased up the slope and lumbered onto the muddy drive. It was slow going, the track slippery with rain. He glanced up at the sky, wishing the weather would clear.

Jim Manx should be here any minute. They were expecting Henny's engineer this afternoon and everything had to be ready. His cell phone shrilled and he dug beneath his wet jacket to tug it out of his shirt pocket.

"Vecchio." The noise level was loud, he was having trouble hearing.

"Alex, it's Ryan. Have you got a minute?"

He headed back to the truck, watching the nearest machine shut down. Time for a break. "Yeah. Go ahead. What's up?"

"I thought we should nail down dates for this wedding dance up north. I have to buy the airline tickets. Are you still thinking of driving up with the equipment?"

Alex reached his truck and yanked the driver's door open. "Hold on." He threw his hardhat on the passenger seat, climbed in and slammed the door. Immediately it became quiet, the rain a distant patter on the roof overhead.

"Okay, I can hear you now. Yeah, the dates. Let me have a look." He stabbed the calendar on his phone and pulled up the details. "Are we all going?"

Ryan hesitated. "Everyone but Glory."

"Have you specifically asked her to come? It would be great, the band is better with her there."

Ryan snuffled a laugh. "A huge step forward, bro, to admit that."

Alex grinned, knowing his brother couldn't see it. "Just facing facts," he barked.

"Not to mention," Ryan added, "She makes us look good on stage."

His breath caught in his throat. She looked great on stage, there was no getting around it. "It would be nice if she came," he said almost wistfully.

"Mmm." Ryan was silent for a moment. "I've been thinking about that. What if we were to tell her the band is paying for the trip? She might be more interested."

"The band is paying? You can't afford it, Ryan. And if I pay, I doubt she'll accept that."

"We don't tell her. The band buys her ticket. She doesn't have to know who actually paid for it."

Alex gazed at the water running down his windshield. "I wonder if it would work. I mean, Coop asked us because it would bring me up for the wedding, but we'd do a stand-up job playing for the dance with her there."

"Let's give it a shot."

Ryan sounded excited, and for once Alex wanted to have that same feeling of anticipation. He wanted to believe that if he went for it, something like this could happen. "I'm in," he said. "You ask her, I'll pay for it. Thanks, Ryan."

~~***~~

CHAPTER ELEVEN

lex watched Eddie take hold of Glory's arm to help her down the steps from the stage. *What was it about the man, that he couldn't leave any woman alone?* Eddie laid a heavy hand on her shoulder and leaned in to speak in her ear. She looked startled and stepped back but he slid his arm around her waist and tugged her closer in an attempt to talk.

Just then, the canned music kicked in and noise flooded the room. Glory pulled away and turned to walk around the bar to find the ladies room, where a long lineup usually formed between sets.

Alex walked with purpose toward the table, catching Eddie by the elbow before he could settle into his seat. "Leave her alone," he said, his voice a low growl. "You've got a wife. You don't need another woman and Glory doesn't welcome your attentions. Got it?"

The bartender glanced over as his voice rose above the din.

Ryan leaped from his chair. "Hey, guys. Come on." He waved to the bartender that everything was under control, and dragged Alex by the arm to a seat next to Pete who was carefully sipping at an overflowing glass of beer.

"Sit down. I mean it, no disruptions. I've worked too hard…"

Alex sank into the chair. "Right." He glared across the table as Eddie's mustache bristled in outrage. Then he leaned forward. "Find Corrie and patch things up," he hissed. "But leave Glory alone."

Ryan frowned and Eddie left the table to patrol the room. "What are you doing?" He glowered at his older brother. "We need this gig. Don't blow it for me."

Alex shrugged his shoulders. "Sorry, Ryan. He just can't keep his hands to himself."

Ryan raised his brows. "Glory's a big girl. She can tell him to take a hike. She doesn't need you acting as her bodyguard."

He felt his face flush. What *was* he doing? Watching Eddie with her had just pushed him over some edge, the very same edge he seemed to walk whenever he was in Glory's presence. She was too attractive to remain single. Mr Suspenders hadn't been back to her townhouse or the club, not that Alex had noticed. She said she didn't have a boyfriend, but still…

He went into the *Men's* room in an effort to calm down, and splashed his face from the cold water tap. When he wiped it off, he glanced in the mirror and spotted Ryan standing behind him.

"If you like her, Alex, then ask her out."

He stared at his goofy brother. *The little shit, why does he think he has all the answers?* That's exactly what he planned to do.

~~*~~

Alex drove home, easing his truck to the side of the street in front of his townhouse. Glory grabbed her bag and opened the door in preparation to jump.

"Wait, Glory. Just a minute. Let me get parked so I can talk to you."

"Talk?" She gave him a skeptical look, as if they'd never have anything to say to each other.

He jammed the truck into park and turned off the ignition, pressing his foot on the emergency brake. "Yeah, I wanted to ask you something."

"Oh." She eased the door closed and he heard the lock click.

"That's better." He turned toward her, his arm going along the back of the seat. She stilled for a moment, then moved slightly forward so they didn't touch. She was one twitchy woman. Was she afraid of all men, or just him? He wouldn't know until he asked.

"What is it you wanted to say?" She glanced sideways at him.

"Not much." He moved his hand an inch and his fingers landed lightly on her shoulder. She froze.

"I wondered if you'd like to go out sometime. Nothing big, I know you're busy. Maybe dinner Sunday night? That's one day neither of us works."

"Uh, dinner?" She looked confused by the idea.

"Yeah, I like just about any kind of food. The Fireside Bistro is usually pretty good and not too crowded. Or the dining room at the James Bay Plaza. I've had good food there." Both places served great steaks.

"The James Bay Plaza? I don't think…"

"We don't have to go there," he added quickly. "Do you have a favourite place we can try?"

She gave him a long look. "I eat Vietnamese," she said. "I often go to Saigon Palace. The owner does a great job, and I like the food."

He grinned. He'd never heard of Saigon Palace. "Sounds great," he said. "I'd like that. How about it?" He took a strand of that long light-brown hair that he watched swing down her back every night when they played, mesmerizing him. He rubbed it gently between his fingers. It was thick, and soft as down. It smelled good, too. He wanted to lean forward and bury his nose just about anywhere she'd let him, but he knew the chances were slim she'd find that charming.

"How about this Sunday?" he urged.

She seemed to be thinking it over, because she stopped moving restlessly and sat still for a moment. Then she bowed her head, looking at her hands entwined in her lap. "I don't date much, Alex. Never seems to work out for me. Perhaps another time?"

His heart hitched and the breath caught in his throat. He hurried his words. "This isn't a date. We live next door to each other and I like to eat out now and then. It's more fun with a companion, right? Are you free Sunday night?"

"Well, I guess I am." She blinked and gazed at him like a deer in the headlights. "I suppose I could."

As his lungs started to function again, Alex didn't give her another chance to change her mind. "Great."

He opened his door and climbed out, slamming it behind him. Walking around the back of the truck, he got there in time to grab the handle on Glory's door and pull it open. She stepped out.

She wasn't tall, but she sure filled out her clothes in all the right places. He gazed over her head as if there was something in the truck that caught his attention. No need to let her see the interest that just got deeper with each encounter.

He walked up the path behind her, lost for words but fascinated by the sight as she climbed the steps. He fished for his key, but she already had hers in the lock. "Night, Alex."

"Uh, good night, Glory. Thanks for agreeing to go to dinner." The door closed quietly in his face.

He stood there a moment, keys in hand as he stared at the dark panel. Lights went on, glowing through the privacy sidelight. He needed to think of a way to get in there.

~~***~~

CHAPTER TWELVE

Glory hit the last key and the band fell silent. Their practices had really been improving, each time the sound became clearer and more cohesive. Alex had a great voice for the rock songs, deep and powerful, and his lead guitar presence was commanding. Eddie, on bass, sang backup and sometimes led on his own songs. Pete didn't sing, but his fiddle music was magical in the numbers they were working on.

She was surprised they'd let her into the group, given how talented they were. But she felt like she was contributing, too. It was amazing to be performing again. She loved it.

Ryan laid his drum sticks down and walked over to grab his jacket. "I only have time for one beer," he called. "I'm into term papers in a big way. Let's get to it." The band members took the elevator down from the store room, stepping past a stack of beer barrels, and found a table in the downstairs bar.

"Glory, you'll have one?" Ryan raised his brows, his forehead wrinkling. "Please stay, we need to sort out the trip north."

"Okay," she said. "But I wasn't going up there with you."

"That's what we have to figure out." He glanced at Alex, then quickly away, turning to wave five fingers at the bartender.

Glory gave a big sigh as the beers appeared. She was thirsty. Alex grabbed one and pushed it toward her, then took another for himself. He seemed to always be looking after her. She slid a sideways glance at him.

They were supposed to go for dinner this Sunday. *Did he remember?* He was staring at her and when she looked his way, his expression grew intense. Maybe he did.

Ryan drank deeply, then set his glass aside. "Listen up, guys. Here are the dates." He opened his music case and dragged out a wall calendar, with dates in December circled. "We need two days to get there. I'm flying to Fort St John as I have exams right up until then. Alex leaves the day before in his truck with the band equipment. Eddie, are you riding with him?"

Eddie nodded and Pete raised a finger. "I'm riding up with him too, I've got the time off, and he says there's room."

Ryan took that in and continued. "That means just Glory and I are flying. We rent a truck at the airport and drive north. We stay with Coop's folks, I think. We should get in a practice at the hall."

"What kind of hall?" Glory was intrigued in spite of herself. "Like a church hall?"

"Uh." Ryan looked at Alex.

Alex shook his head. "The community hall. It's in the village along with the general store, the church and the two-room school."

She felt let down. "Oh, so it will be small, maybe thirty people in a little hall like that."

Alex laughed. "No, the hall isn't small and the crowd won't be either. They're expecting a hundred or a hundred fifty people."

"Oh, my gosh!" She fell back in her chair in amazement. "Really? It sounds so exciting."

He grinned. "Yeah, it should be a lot of fun. Our band is in great shape, we'll do a good job and they're amazed that we're coming. All the folks from around Big Smokey will attend the dance."

She grinned at his enthusiasm. He didn't look at all like the disgruntled man who'd been playing lead guitar the first night she joined the band practice.

"And," Ryan leaned forward so they all turned toward him. "The band is paying for the travel. So, we're hoping you can come, Glory. It would round out the sound nicely."

"The band is paying for the airline tickets?" She glanced around at the men. "Really? Are you sure you can afford it? Come on, guys. None of you is made of money."

"We're sure." Ryan's voice was firm. "We voted on it." Pete glanced away and Eddie couldn't hide a little smirk that perked his mustache up in one corner.

"I don't know what to say. Of course I'll go." She felt flushed and a little off balance. These were such nice guys, she was just lucky to fall in with a group like this. "Let me get a pen, and I'll write down the dates."

"Right." Ryan became all business again. "Alex, Eddie and Pete leave Wednesday with the gear. We fly up Thursday and they'll meet us in Fort St John. We pick up the second truck and drive north, get to Big Smokey late Thursday, early Friday. Practice Friday afternoon. A shindig Friday night. Then the wedding is Saturday and the dance that night. We head home Sunday, which means the flights will likely be out of Fort St John Monday morning. How does that sound? Everyone clear?"

"It'll be late Tuesday before I'm back on the job." Alex rubbed his chin. "Jim has already said he's fine with that but I'll check again."

"Good." Ryan downed the rest of his beer and grabbed his jacket from the back of the chair. "Gotta leave, study time."

Eddie clapped him on the shoulder. "Way to go, little bro. You're almost as pushy as your older brother."

There was laughter around the table, and Ryan's neck went red.

Glory smiled. These guys cared about each other. It was nice to see. And this trip was going to be a lot of fun. Northern British Columbia in December? She'd never been past Prince George and that had been once with her father on a camping trip in the summertime. She remembered the swarms of mosquitoes. This was all new territory for her. She couldn't wait.

She looked up to meet Alex's gaze. He gave a slow grin and she smiled back.

~~***~~

CHAPTER THIRTEEN

By Friday the weather had turned and bright sunshine showed clumps of dried mud dotting the construction site. Alex made a grab for the phone vibrating in his shirt pocket. It was Jim Manx with news on changes the building inspector had just handed down. He listened and made a note with his carpenter's pencil on the nearest two-by-four, then bellowed above the whine of the saw. "Stuart. New specs, it sounds like."

His carpenter's helper was cutting boards for the foundation framing. He flipped the switch on the saw and the noise died. "What is it?"

"The reinforcement for the floors," Alex said. He tugged a sheet of paper out of his pocket with a list of suppliers. "They're saying we have to lay down rebar every twelve inches instead of eighteen."

Stuart nodded. "Okay. That means we'll be delayed at least a couple of days for the first concrete pour."

Alex nodded. "Right, and it means more rebar and ties. I'll put in the order and get it trucked out this afternoon. How are we doing on sixteen footers?" He glanced at a pile of two-by-fours covered with a tarp on the ground. "Looks like we're still okay."

Stuart flipped the tarp back and counted the stacks. "Enough for now," he said. "We'll need more, middle of next week."

Alex made another notation. "Okay, I'll make the call and then we'll finish framing this side."

As he worked with Stuart laying boards and nailing them in place, Alex went over in his mind what needed to be done. He didn't want to be the cause of any delays. With this trip north, he'd be off-site for close to a week, so it would be a stretch.

His neck got hot and he stood to take a deep breath. He was taking Glory to dinner Sunday. His chest grew tight. He'd been looking forward to this with an intensity that he hoped wasn't obvious.

Stuart flipped another board into place and they both bent to nail it to the studs. He couldn't remember the last time he'd been this excited about a date. A dinner date, a first date.

He shrugged. It had been him and Trudy on and off since grade twelve. Even through trade school, she'd been there – either building him up or dragging him the hell down. But he was through with all that.

This was entirely different and it felt darned good. He grinned.

~~*~~

Alex knocked at the next-door townhouse and waited. No answer, but he knew she was in because the lights were on, and her little red car was parked right out front. He knocked again, then rang the bell. He heard it *dingdong* inside the tiny unit. He'd already seen the size of it, there wasn't much room in there.

Just then the door opened, and she stepped into view. He caught his breath. She looked beautiful, a pair of tight jeans and a low-cut blouse, a jacket thrown over her shoulders. Her hair was brushed back on one side and held there with a glittery comb, little baubles swung from her earlobes. She smiled up at him.

"Uh." He stuttered and took a step back. She always knocked him off balance. "Are you ready? I don't know if I'm early or…"

She pulled the door closed and pocketed the key. "Right on time. I'm ready."

"Okay, good." He couldn't help the smile that crept across his face. "You look great." Was that a blush? In the fading light he couldn't tell if her cheeks were unusually rosy.

He took her to Saigon Palace, totally prepared to silently grin and bear the food, given he was a meat and potatoes man. To his surprise, he liked it. The flavours were quite different from what he was used to.

Glory obviously knew what she liked, so he let her go ahead and order for both of them. That was a whole new experience. He usually made the decisions, and he grinned to himself. He got the feeling he'd be doing that a lot, letting her decide, if he was lucky enough to spend much time with her.

She ordered him a Vietnamese beer, which wasn't quite as interesting as the food turned out to be. He switched to a local brew.

"You told me you don't have a girlfriend," Glory said.

Alex sat up straight. "I don't." He gave her a stubborn look, his meal immediately forgotten.

"Then who was that woman at *Rooster's* who spread the lipstick on your face?" she said, a gleam in her eye.

His lips flattened. "That was Trudy."

"Yeah. Eddie says Trudy is your girlfriend."

Alex gritted his teeth and filed that away to deal with Eddie later. "She's not my girlfriend. She was, but that ended a long time ago, nearly a year."

She twirled some noodles around her chopsticks. "That's not what it looked like," she said, and took a bite.

Alex laid down his fork, not having progressed to the chopsticks yet. "I can't help how it looked," he said grimly. "We used to live together and when we broke up I moved out. I've been at that townhouse since January. Alone."

"Oh." Glory glanced away, then back. "Then why do you go out at night and stay out? I've seen you coming home just about the time I leave for work in the morning."

Alex felt unease creep up his spine. She didn't seem to be buying the fact that he was single. "I don't have a girl, Glory. I wouldn't have asked you out if I did."

"I see." She picked at a prawn and put it back in her bowl.

"What do you want me to say?" He gave her a desperate look.

She sipped tea from a tiny cup and set it back on the table. "I don't do well with men who are unfaithful. I don't expect you to be faithful," she added hastily, blushing a lovely rose. "We aren't really dating, so that's not what I mean."

He opened his mouth to protest. If they weren't dating, what were they doing out for dinner together? On the other hand, he had assured her this wasn't a date.

"I just mean…"

He reached to take her hand and she stopped talking mid-sentence. "Glory, I don't two-time and I don't cheat. I'm single, Trudy and I were finished a long time ago."

"Okay," she said. She might have believed him but she didn't raise her gaze above his chin.

The waiter arrived with a dish of dumplings and he let go of her hand to sit back while they were served.

"How long have you been a carpenter?" she asked.

Surprise hit him in the gut. "How do you know I'm a carpenter?"

She smiled. "Eddie said…"

He groaned. "I'll sort Eddie out later. I've only been a carpenter for about five or six years. I did trades school, then apprenticed two years for my ticket."

By the time dinner was over, he was enjoying himself. She'd pried a lot of information out of him and he didn't know much more about her than he had at the start of the evening.

"Would you like to go for a drink somewhere?" He waved the waiter over to get the bill.

"Oh, no thanks. I'm ready to go home. I've got some preparation to do for my students tomorrow." She stifled a yawn with her hand.

"Your students?" He eyed her guardedly. *What else didn't he know about her?*

"Music students," she said. "At the Conservatory."

"Wow, we have a teacher from the Conservatory in our band. Does Ryan know that?"

She laughed. "I'm not sure. Probably."

"If he does, it'll be on the next batch of *Hot to Trot* posters he has printed. Ryan is nothing if not a promoter." He grinned.

He'd known she'd mix things up for him. He just hadn't known how personal it would become. Because he was damned determined to get a lot closer to her than this.

~~*~~

Alex held the restaurant door for her, then took her hand in his as they walked to his truck in the light rain. Her fingers felt small and defenceless in his grip.

"Here you go." He held the door as she climbed up, then slammed it behind her. He rounded the vehicle to the driver's side.

"Do you mind if we make a stop on the way back? I have to pick up some stuff at my Mum's house."

"No, I don't mind." She gave him a curious look, then grabbed her seatbelt to fasten it. She stared out the windshield as he flipped on the wipers. "It won't take long, will it?"

"Nope." He didn't really have to stop at the house. There was nothing there he needed to pick up right now. But Mum was a friendly soul and had a remarkable effect on people.

He'd take backup wherever he could get it.

~~***~~

CHAPTER FOURTEEN

S o I won't be able to make it tomorrow night." Trudy glanced in the mirror as she talked, phone pressed to the side of her head. The sight was alarming. One eye was swollen and turning purple as she watched. The red splotch on her cheek could be hidden with makeup, but the eye would need dark glasses and no one went to dinner at a fancy restaurant wearing those.

Eddie crooned into the phone. "That's too bad. Did this competition just come up suddenly?"

She attempted a girlish laugh. "I've known about it for a long time. It had just slipped my mind when I talked to you last. I'll be leaving in the morning on the ferry. So sorry. But another time, for sure. Shall I call you?"

She heard his low chuckle. "Yes, please. Call me. But if I don't hear, then I'll call you. Good luck in the show. I want to hear all about it."

"Thank you, Eddie." She disconnected and whirled at a sound behind her, but there was no one there. Now she was getting unhinged. Rolf was making this a war of nerves as well as fists. She went silently down the stairs, straight for the front door and threw the bolt. That should slow him down. She'd check the back door as well. Were the windows all locked? Just one more thing to worry about.

She pressed her fingers over the eyelid and caught her breath at the pain. Should she see a doctor? What if she lost some sight in that eye? Damn the man. He'd left! What the hell was he doing back, making all kinds of claims on her?

~~*~~

Glory surveyed the clothes strewn on the unmade bed. She organized them hurriedly—tops, pants, sweaters. Socks, underwear, shoes. She didn't have boots, but decided she'd better get some. She wrote it on her list. Grabbing the outfit she'd wear to play for the wedding dance, she folded it neatly and added it to the stack.

What about jackets? She'd need something like a ski jacket. It would be cold up there. Add that to the list. Maybe long underwear, although the ski gear should cover that.

She'd Googled Big Smokey but hadn't come up with much, other than a dot on the north end of the British Columbia map. No help there. But even the information on Fort St John told her it was well below freezing all winter, and Big Smokey was farther north.

She'd checked Fort Nelson. From the info she found, the place was east of there.

Did the weather differ much from place to place? She'd always imagined once a person passed Prince George they were darned near in the Yukon Territories. She snickered to herself. She really didn't have any idea what it would be like.

She'd have to go back to the house to get her ski clothes. Glory shivered at the thought. She'd been avoiding the place, ever since the day she'd walked in to find her mother standing in the living room, in the tight embrace of Glory's boyfriend, his mouth on hers. It had taken months for her to recover enough to pull things together and move out. In the meantime she'd spent as little time as possible at home.

She ran her fingers through her hair and tugged handfuls out each side, trying to get her feelings under control. Had she been in love with Randall? To be honest, no. *But he was her boyfriend. What did Jean think she was doing?*

She bundled the clothes haphazardly into the open suitcase on the floor. She'd deal with this later. She was out of time.

Shrugging into her pea jacket, she buttoned it hurriedly, grabbed her purse and pushed her feet into a pair of shoes at the door. Music time, her students were waiting. And she wasn't into men right now.

~~*~~

Trudy sounded delighted to hear Eddie's voice but she didn't exactly invite him over to her house. In the end, she agreed to meet him at Tony's Steakhouse downtown. When she finally arrived, he was waiting at a fancy cloth-covered table, with a candle in the centre. She looked fabulous. He stood to pull out her chair.

Trudy was not a beautiful woman. Her features were too strong and well defined. She was lean and trim, her limbs muscled. Her body was a picture of healthy aggression. He wondered just what that might translate to in the bedroom. Alex knew, and he didn't, it was that simple. But not for long. Eddie was determined to find his way in there.

She wore a tight sleeveless top that showed off firm arms and great cleavage, and a very short skirt leaving little to his imagination. Her legs were one of her best features, long, slim and toned.

He grinned and leaned toward her. "You look fantastic. But then, you always did look good."

She gave him a slow smile and settled in the chair.

He waved at the waiter. "What will you have to drink?" This was going to be fun. He'd had the hots for Trudy for years, since shortly after Alex started going with her in high school. Finally the field was open. Although not entirely open, apparently. She hadn't let him pick her up at the house. He wasn't sure what that meant.

"Some white wine, chardonnay, I think," she said and hung her purse on the back of the chair. Then she crossed those long legs, letting her high-heeled sandal hang from one toe. Who wore sandals in December, even in Victoria? Yet, she looked plenty warm. "How are you, Eddie? I was surprised to hear from you again. Where's Alex?"

Alex? He felt a stab of annoyance. "I wouldn't know. We just had a band practice the other day, but I imagine he's working or playing. I called because I've always liked you and I enjoyed our lunch the other day. And from what you say, your boyfriend Rolf has taken leave of his senses and disappeared from view."

"Oh, that." She waved one hand dismissively and took a sip of her wine. "You still play in the band, then?"

He nodded. "Me and Ryan. Alex too. You've heard us, we're pretty good."

Her smile turned brilliant and he grinned back. So that's the way it was. If Alex wasn't going to be available, then she might be interested in him. That suited him just fine. It wasn't as if he was going to ask her to marry him. Just have a fling. Satisfy his urges. And apparently Rolf didn't enter into the equation any more.

He leaned forward and stroked the smooth skin of her arm. "How have you been? Do you still work out?" He gave her an appreciative look. "You must, because you look amazing. I always admired your dedication."

Trudy gave him a glowing smile, and he poured more wine into her glass.

~~***~~

CHAPTER FIFTEEN

A few hours later, Glory pulled up to the curb in front of her townhouse and turned off the engine. She'd had fun tonight. One of her assignments at the Conservatory was to teach a small class of five-year-olds on keyboard. Their little fingers were like silly putty, they were so flexible. And their ability to concentrate usually lasted a good four minutes at a stretch. She laughed. So much fun, and remarkably clever little people.

Grabbing her purse, she climbed out of the car. Better get moving, mornings came early these days.

As she rounded the back of the car, she noticed a familiar silver compact parked across the street. *Was Mum here?* She turned to look up the walkway, which was empty. Hurrying, she took the steps two at a time.

"Mum?" she called. She fumbled for her keys. *Was she waiting inside? If so, how did she get in?*

Alex's door opened opposite and he loomed in the entrance. "Glory? Oh, good. Your mother's here."

He stepped back to make room and Glory turned to walk into his suite, a feeling of déjà vu hanging heavily over her head like a shroud.

She'd only been out with Alex once. *How did Mum know to move this fast?* Her gaze took in the masculine-looking living room with dark leather couch and easy chair, a big screen television against the far wall with a set of speakers positioned either side. He definitely had a lot more living space than she did.

Mum sat in the centre of the couch holding a big orange coffee mug with a hammer and saw emblazoned on the side. She smiled at Glory. "Hi, baby. I was just having coffee, waiting for you to get here. Do you want to join us?" She shot a sultry look toward Alex, who gazed uncertainly at Glory.

"No, thank you." She turned to face him. "I'm going home."

"Hey, you're welcome to a coffee. I just made it…"

She cut him off. "No, thanks. Mum, are you coming?"

Jean pursed her mouth in a moue of disapproval. "So unneighbourly. Okay, I'm coming. Maybe next time, Alex." She patted his cheek on the way by, which made Glory's blood boil even faster, and followed her daughter onto the stoop.

Glory didn't slow down. She plunged her key into the lock and swung her door back on its hinges so hard it hit the wall with a crash. She marched in, threw her purse in the nearest chair and pried her shoes off. If

Mum wasn't behind her by now, she was going to slam the door in her face.

When she turned, her mother was standing in the doorway, her expression one of complete surprise. "What has gotten into you!" She stepped forward and placed her pocketbook on the table. "How can you be so rude to your neighbour?"

"Come, Mother. I'm sure you were sweet enough to Alex for both of us."

"Perhaps I was. Only because I know how intolerant you can be." She frowned, then smoothed the line between her brows with the carefully placed tip of her baby finger.

"What are you doing here?" Glory hissed. "What is the point of this?"

"The point? I met Alex at the club the other night, remember?"

How could she forget? Mum had come in with a friend, the two of them dolled up in tight jeans, low cut sweaters and buckets of makeup.

Glory had watched as her mother approached the young men standing around the bar until she found a willing dance partner. After a couple of numbers, he'd backed off, so she'd set out to find another. By that time the band was playing a waltz, and she'd had to witness Jean slow dancing with a tall lanky fellow whose eyes had gone wide when she reached around to put a hand on his butt.

No one else in the band seemed to notice. But that was before they found out Glory's mother was in the crowd.

At the set break, Mum came over to the band table and Glory somewhat reluctantly introduced her to the members. Eddie promptly found a chair and sat her next to him. There ensued a low-voiced conversation between the two of them that raised the hackles on Glory's neck. No, she couldn't hear what was said. She could only imagine, given her mother's need to find a man and Eddie's proclivities to come on to whichever woman was closest.

Now here she was, visiting Alex. *Would there be no peace in her life?*

Alex had already closed his door. Glory lowered her voice as she faced her mother hovering in the doorway. "Did you come to see Alex or me?"

"Why, you of course, darling." Mum moved into the suite and shut the door. "You weren't home so I knocked on his door to see if he knew where you were."

Glory blew out a breath. "You knew where I was. I've been teaching this same class all year. That's why you came, because you knew I'd be out."

Jean waved her hand in the air. "Don't be silly. I don't pay attention to all that. Some days you're home, some days you're out. What class is this?"

"Never mind." Glory pressed fingertips to her temples as a headache threatened to rage out of control. "What do you need, Mum? Because right now I have to go to bed. I work early."

"Oh, well then." Jean clutched her pocketbook in her hand. "I'll be off. Just dropped by to say what a good time we had at the club the other night. You've landed with quite a group – good looking guys, all of them. Congratulations."

Glory squinted at her mother. "Thanks. Kind of you to say so."

"Good." Mother looked around the room, taking in the unmade bed and dirty dishes on the small table. "I'll be off then."

She opened the door and trotted down the steps, her high heels clicking on the wet pavement.

~~***~~

CHAPTER SIXTEEN

Glory carefully closed the door and sank into the nearest chair. Her headache was increasing in volume by the second. The table was strewn with her earlier efforts at dinner – carrot blueberry muffins she'd made the day before, a pot of rooibos tea and a plate half-filled with cut vegetables. Maybe she was just thirsty. She reached for the cup and downed the last of the tea, which was stone cold now.

There was a light knock. "Glory?" That was Alex's deep rumble. She stared at the panel. *Did she have to have this conversation now?* She was too tired, too upset.

"Glory?" Another rap on the door.

Sighing, she reached from where she sat to turn the handle. "Alex? What is it?"

His head poked past the door. "Listen, I wanted to talk to you for a minute." He glanced around, no doubt taking in the details of her tiny flat, the jumbled suitcase on the floor and the fact she was alone. Then he pushed the door open and came in, swinging it shut behind him.

"I wanted to see what was going on." He paced across to pull the other chair out and sat across from her. "I saw your mother leave. Are you okay?"

She didn't know what to say. *Had Alex invited her mother over? How did Jean know Alex lived next door to her?* It wasn't hard to figure out. Eddie had been talking Jean's ear off at the club. "I'm fine."

He gave her a piercing glance and took her hand in his, prying the curled fingers open to caress her palm. "What happened just now? Did you have a fight with your mum?"

"Why?" She glared back at him.

"Well, that's what it sounded like. Were you mad she waited for you?" He pressed his lips together.

"No," she said. "Why would I be?"

"I don't know." He seemed to gauge her expression. "That's why I asked. Your mum was outside when I got home tonight. I recognized her from the club. I knocked on your door, but she said she'd already checked. You were at your music lessons."

Glory felt an arrow pierce her heart. *Mum had known she'd be out, even if she'd just denied it.*

Alex shrugged. "I didn't know how long you'd be. I suggested she call your cell, but she said you'd have it turned off during the lessons, and all she wanted was a cup of coffee. So I invited her in."

The arrow in her heart took another twist and the pain was astounding. Glory felt tears start in her eyes and she wiped her cheek with the dish towel from the table.

"Glory, why are you crying?" He leaned forward and tried to take her other hand, but she resisted.

"I'm not crying," she said, and sniffled. "I've got something in my eye."

He pulled back to watch her. "Okay." He paused, seemed to mull that over. "I don't usually invite women into my house. But she's your Mum. I couldn't ignore her."

Glory shook her head. "That's okay. I understand."

"Do you?" He glanced down for a moment. "I want to get to know you. I'd like to take you out, but I don't want any misunderstandings. I thought I did the right thing tonight. She's your mother, and I felt I should treat her with respect. So what went wrong?"

More tears welled up. He'd just said all the right things, and they touched her heart at the same tender place the arrow had pierced. *How did he know to do that? And was he even telling the truth?* It pained her that she'd become such an untrusting woman.

~~*~~

Glory stopped at Benjamin's Bagels to pick up her Saturday morning order. Three poppy seed bagels, three sesame seed. Dad liked those the best. She peeked in the bag, happy to see Ben had included her package of cream cheese, as well as a thick wad of smoked salmon and a few slices of onion.

She hopped back in her car and headed into James Bay. It was an old part of Victoria consisting of narrow cul-de-sacs and one way streets. Surrounded by water on three sides, the small peninsula was part of the downtown core, yet had its own distinct personality. Half the houses were old, built around the beginning of the last century when Victoria was just becoming established. Shoehorned in between were newer homes and townhouse complexes that made use of the huge lots.

Dad lived in a small townhouse right at the end of Michigan Street overlooking Fisherman's Wharf Park. The centre of town was no more than blocks away, but he especially liked spending time on the wharves, talking to the fishermen, buying their fresh catch or eating at the fish and chip dock.

He was quick to answer the door when she knocked, and relieved her of the parcels as he waved her inside. He was wearing his usual attire of khaki pants and flannel plaid shirt, grey wool work socks on his feet. He wrapped one arm around her shoulders and gave her a kiss on the cheek. "There you are, my girl," he said gruffly. "Haven't seen you in a few weeks. Must have been awful busy, that you didn't have time for your pa."

Glory laughed and hugged him back. "I only missed one Saturday. It's not like I've moved to a different city or something."

He smiled and the creases at the corners of his brown eyes deepened. "I see you brought my favourite. I've just put the kettle on."

"Oh, good. I'm famished."

Glory took a chair at the table where her father had already set out plates, cups and cutlery. A jar of capers held a place of honour in the centre. She grabbed the bagel slicer, cut one of each kind and popped them in the toaster. Then she sliced a poppy seed for herself.

As she spread cream cheese, her father brought the kettle to the table and poured hot water into their cups. The tea bags floated to the surface and she leaned forward to sniff the homey aroma of English Breakfast.

Dad took the seat across from her and tackled his bagels. "What have you been up to?" he asked as he carefully placed onion on a thick bed of cream cheese. "I know about the new band, *Hot to Trot.* Where are you playing and what kind of music?"

Glory was used to the 'third degree' as she used to accuse him of firing at her as a teenager. Now she filled him in on the players, the gig at *Rooster's,* and the trip north.

"A wedding dance?" He looked at her in amazement. "Well, I never. Have you ever been to one?"

"No, I don't think so. I've been to a few weddings, but nothing like this. It's being held in a community hall."

Her father laughed and took a big bite of bagel. "We had them on the prairies all the time. The community hall was usually the only place that was big enough for the whole village and surrounding farmers to gather."

"I remember you talking about that, Dad. But there can't be farmers way up there, can there? I'm not sure what they do for a living, but I guess I'll find out."

"Mmm, this is good. The salmon is first rate. Is this Benjamin's again?"

She grinned. "You know it is. Where else would I get it?"

"How is Ben? Haven't seen him in a while. Still holding his own with the baking?"

Glory nodded. "He lets the cooks do most of it. He spends more time in his little office. Comes out when the shop opens to catch the lunch crowd."

Dad looked pleased. "I'll have to go by there soon and say hello. My hours have been cut, I'm only working thirty hours a week these days."

Alarm filled her chest. "How come? Are they laying you off?"

"No, no. Nothing like that. I've asked for less time." He gazed at her sideways. "I'm a little tired and the school board bought all the schools new electric washer-polishers. It doesn't take as long to do the floors for the corridors and gym. The stairs are still an issue, but even that is easier." Dad had worked as a janitor for the local school board as long as she could remember.

She gave him a worried look. "Are you well? You'd tell me if you weren't, wouldn't you?"

Dad patted her hand. "Don't worry, angel. I'm fine. Just tired, and this is a welcome change. The best part is the kids, they're as cute as ever."

Glory smiled and told him about her last session with the five-year-olds in the keyboard class. But the story brought to mind her issues with Jean. Her expression must have given her away, because he pestered her until she told him about mother's visit.

Her father thought for a minute, then loaded up his second bagel, carefully arranging a stack of smoked salmon on top. "You listen to me, Glory. You know what your mother's like. This is not new information. If this young fellow, Alex, is worth his salt, you won't have a thing to worry about. He sounds like a good man." He took a big bite and looked thoughtful as he chewed vigorously, then swallowed. "And if Jean manages to turn him, then he isn't worth a moment of your time. You'll know. Trust your instincts, my girl. Meanwhile, I'll have him researched."

He grinned at Glory's whoop of laughter. "You don't think I can find out about him? I'm a whiz on the internet these days. I'll have him pinned in minutes. Or hours, depending on what I find."

They were both chuckling as they finished their tea. Glory's smile faded as she wondered exactly what he might find out about Alex. Maybe she didn't want to know.

~~***~~

CHAPTER SEVENTEEN

Alex made a hurried stop at the house Sunday night and found his mother and brother at home. Ryan was studying in his room, his ears covered with a huge set of headphones. Mum had an FM station playing softly—classical music. She sat in the easy chair in the living room, the reading lamp directed at the pages of her book.

"Hey, Mum." He walked across the carpet to plant a kiss on her cheek. "Whatcha reading?"

She held up the spine for him to see. "You know, murder mystery or romantic suspense. One or the other." She took a sip from the mug on the tiny table at her elbow. He was positive it held nothing stronger than black tea. Mum had always been solid that way – she didn't indulge.

"I've just come to get some things for the trip. We leave Wednesday."

She smiled. "I know. Ryan has me fully informed. I've prepared a package for you to take up for the newly weds. I'll get it now. And I have something for Mrs Cooper." She laid her book down and disappeared into her bedroom.

Alex carried on down the stairs to the basement. His old room was situated at the back of the house and still contained a lot of his stuff. His ski clothes would be there, and the snow boots he was looking for. He didn't want to be long. He was taking Glory out for dinner again.

He grinned. It had been a lot of work to get her to agree to go out with him. Driving her home Saturday after the gig at the club, he'd almost had to resort to begging. But he wasn't proud, just determined.

He grabbed his things and headed back up the stairs. "Ryan." Opening his brother's door, he waved to get his attention.

Ryan lifted one earphone off the side of his head.

"I've got all the equipment," Alex said. "Is there anything else that I need to take? Because my week is booked solid until I leave Wednesday morning."

Ryan nodded, shaking his bangs out of his eyes. "I think you've got it all. If there's anything else, I'll call you." He pointed at his textbook. "Got finals this week. Managed to get them all fitted in before I go."

"Okay. Good luck. I know you'll ace it." He shut the door and returned to the living room.

Mum had a bag with a couple of parcels and cards in it that she handed to him. "Come say goodbye before you leave," she cautioned. "Where are you off to in such a hurry tonight?"

He laughed. "I'm taking Glory out for dinner."

Mum beamed. "I like her. Be a good boy and maybe she'll stick around." She patted his shoulder and he wrapped an arm around her.

"Thanks, Mum."

~~*~~

The Saigon Palace was busy tonight. They'd managed to get a booth near the back of the small restaurant. Glory used her chopsticks to dig into the bottom of her bowl. More noodles, but there was another spring roll hiding there, too. She fished it out and popped it into her mouth.

Alex's mouth curled in a smile. "You like those, don't you?"

"Mmm hmm." She nodded, mouth still full.

"So do I." He speared one with his fork and dipped it in sauce. "I didn't realize this food was so tasty. I'll have to bring Mum here. I'm sure she's never tried it."

Glory's eyes widened. "Really? She's never eaten Vietnamese food?"

He laughed and patted her hand. "We're just a family of Neanderthals," he offered. "Roast beef, mashed potatoes and gravy."

She had to smile. "I didn't mean it like that."

"We do eat bagels, however. That should get me some marks for effort."

She laughed. "Maybe. Depends on where you get them. Because Benjamin's are the most authentic."

He shrugged. "I know the drill. I've instructed my family where they're to buy their bagels from now on. No quick trips to the grocery store. Those aren't real." His eyes crinkled at the corners as he grinned at her.

She smiled, then looked down at her bowl. He was more charming than she'd first imagined. It was amazing that his own personality was so different from the one she'd imagined during those first encounters with the band. Confusing, too, because it made him so attractive.

"Are you packed for the trip?" he asked.

"Not yet. I have to get a pair of boots. I'll do that Monday or Tuesday."

"Yeah, you'll need snow boots for sure. Bring a couple pairs of lined gloves or mittens. Don't forget a toque. Have you got a winter coat? Because I might have something…"

She brushed that away. "I've got my ski gear, so I'll be fine. Just need footwear."

"Okay." He took another bite. "Mum says to say hi."

"She does? That's nice." She warmed at the thought. Mrs Vecchio had been really welcoming when Alex dropped by the house with her the other night. His mother was friendly and had chatted while he'd gone off to get something from the basement. "Say hi back for me. I hope she won't be lonely while you and Ryan are out of town."

He shook his head. "Mum is one busy woman. She plays bridge and sings in a choir. She's on some committee for the church. And she has a ton of friends."

Glory just looked at him. "She'll probably still miss you guys while you're gone."

His cheeks darkened and he ducked his head. "Maybe, yeah."

~~*~~

Alex pulled the truck up to the curb and Glory watched him turn the key to shut off the engine. He laid his arm across the back of the seat till his fingers were close enough to grab a strand of hair. He played with it for a minute, his gaze focussed on his hand, as Glory held her breath. "I love your hair," he said. When he glanced up his blue eyes were dark in the dim light from the street lamp. "I like to watch it sway down your back when you're playing. It looks so smooth and silky."

She felt a thump in her chest. It excited and alarmed her in equal measure.

He leaned forward and that same hand cradled the back of her head as his other palm came up to rest against her cheek. Then his mouth closed over hers and her breath stopped. His lips were wide and firm, his breath sweet. She didn't move and had just begun to relax when he opened his mouth and his tongue brushed across her lips.

Wild thoughts flashed through her mind. *Were they dating after all?* They must be, if he was kissing her like this. She braced a hand against his chest for support and felt more than heard the groan that emanated from deep within.

"Alex?"

It was a while before he lifted his head. "What, baby?"

"Are we dating?"

He kissed her again for a long time. When he raised his head, her brain felt foggy.

"I sure hope so," he said.

~~***~~

CHAPTER EIGHTEEN

Glory climbed out of the van and reached to grab her carryon bag. "Thanks for the ride, Mrs Vecchio." She turned as Ryan slid the side door open and stepped out.

He walked around to the rear where his mother had already opened the doors, and pulled Glory's suitcase out, along with his pack. "Thanks, Mum." He leaned to give his mother a one-armed hug, then turned and marched toward the entry doors of the airport.

"Have fun," his mother called.

Glory slung her bag over one shoulder, waved to Mrs. Vecchio and ran after him, dragging her suitcase. He had a long-legged stride and she had to move quickly.

The airport was packed with what looked like a crowd of university students heading home for pre-Christmas celebrations. Ryan muscled his way into a check-in line and was soon stabbing buttons and printing luggage tags on the automated machine. She was glad he was there, she always found it a challenge to make those airport units work.

"Hurry," he said. "They're boarding soon."

Another fast walk down halls dodging throngs of people, and finally into security. Ryan passed his driver's licence ID to the guard. "Bad shoulder. I need to be cleared by hand," he said.

The guard nodded. "Come over here, sir, we'll use a wand and pat you down."

Glory was through the line and putting her shoes back on when Ryan reappeared, pack in hand. "Where'd you go?" she muttered. "I thought I lost you. You've got my boarding pass."

"Sorry." He dug in his shirt pocket and pulled them both out. "Here, take yours. Then you won't be worried."

"Why did they drag you off?" She kept her voice low as she glanced around.

"I've got a metal pin in my shoulder."

She looked horrified as he pointed to his left clavicle. "High school football. It always sets off the alarm in security."

"Huh." She walked beside him to the escalator and stepped onto the moving platform. "You Vecchios are pretty physical guys."

Ryan muffled a snort. "It's how we were raised. Dad could do anything. He was strong, fast, and very capable."

She smiled. "Well, I guess his sons take after him."

~~*~~

Glory settled into her seat and watched through the small window as the baggage handlers tossed luggage into the body of the plane. She saw her wheeled suitcase take to the air before it thudded heavily onto the conveyor belt. Good thing Dad's old case was already beat up.

Ryan seated himself beside her and proceeded to turn off all his gadgets as the plane pulled away from the loading gate and headed out onto the runway.

"Right on time," he said, checking his phone. "Alex sent me a text earlier. They stayed the night in Quesnel and were going to leave early this morning. They should be just in time to meet us at the Fort St John airport."

She grew warm. She already knew this. She'd had two texts from Alex last night saying they'd arrived in Quesnel, and showing her a shot of the hotel room with his grinning face. Then this morning, at five she got another one as they were just getting on the road.

"Are we all travelling in his truck?" she asked, tightening her seatbelt as the engines began to race for takeoff.

"No." He leaned in to talk near her ear over the noise. "There isn't room, and we'll need two vehicles for getting around up there. I'm renting a truck at the airport and we'll drive up together."

She hadn't known that. Which truck would she be riding in? Probably Ryan's, given the others all had their gear stowed in Alex's truck. Oh, well, it wasn't as if she and Alex were going together. It just felt like it, that's all.

She watched the land fall away as the plane headed out over the ocean and mountains loomed in the distance. Then they were sailing above land again and climbing as snowy peaks appeared beneath the plane. She looked down to deep ravines, distant highways and rivers gleaming far below in narrow valleys.

The farther north they went, the heavier the snow cover. Rivers looked frozen, ribbons of white meandered between rocky snow-covered mounds. Now and then a lake with cracked blue ice covering it appeared like a gem on the diamond encrusted surface.

"Dad used to take us camping up here every year."

Glory glanced at Ryan who was leaning to peer over her shoulder through the small window. "Up where?" She gazed down at the jumble of mountains, plains, lakes and streams.

"Often to Williams Lake. It's just a short drive from the island. And most years we'd make at least one trip back to Big Smokey. He knew everyone up there. Coop came down to Victoria to go to college because his father was a friend of Dad's." His eyes were snapping with excitement and there was the ghost of a grin on his face.

"Did your dad grow up there?"

Ryan shook his head, his shaggy bangs shifting out of his eyes. "No, but he worked in the north in his younger days, mostly logging. He and Mum got married in Big Smokey, and moved to Vancouver Island later."

"Huh," Glory gazed back out the window and Ryan picked up the flight magazine. He snagged drinks from the steward as he passed with the cart, handing one to her.

"Thanks." She set it on the tray in front of her. "Is Alex still dating Trudy?"

Ryan's head snapped up and he closed the magazine. "Nope. Hasn't for a long time." He levelled a gaze at her.

Glory shrugged. "She keeps turning up at the club."

"Yeah, not much he can do about that." He wrapped his hands around his drink. "Your Mr. Suspenders keeps showing up, too. Are you dating him?"

"What?" She gave him a confused look. "Who is Mr. Suspenders?"

"The guy who sits with your friends, he always wears…"

"Oh." She couldn't help a laugh. "You mean Greg. Yes, he does like to wear suspenders. They're in style, didn't you know?"

Ryan grinned back at her. "Are you dating him?"

"He's a good friend, Ryan. I've known him for years."

He got a determined look on his face. "How good a friend?"

She narrowed her eyes. "Are you asking on behalf of your brother?"

"Maybe." His cheeks had flushed a dull red.

Glory leaned to whisper in his ear. "He's gay, Ryan. He's just a friend."

"Oh." His eyes widened. "Okay, then." He snapped the magazine open to the middle section and stared at the page.

Glory sipped her drink and watched the scenery pass below, mulling over all the stuff she'd gleaned from her father. Dad had been right, he'd found out a great deal about Alex Vecchio from the internet. Most of the information had been about body building. There were pictures of him in competitions dating back to high school and since.

Dad had sent her the links, and when she clicked on some of the websites and began browsing through, she'd gotten hot just looking at the images of Alex, toned and tanned, oiled up to display the ropes of muscle in his arms and chest, across his belly and down his thighs.

He looked good in his shirt and jeans when they were playing in the band, but seeing him without them was a whole different experience.

~~***~~

CHAPTER NINETEEN

Alex arranged for Ryan's rental truck and waited with Eddie for the plane to arrive, while Pete wandered the airport. When they finally landed, he wanted to grab Glory up in his arms and hug her to him, but had to be content with watching as she joked around with the others, waiting at the conveyor belt for her luggage.

She wanted to drive, so he had to leave her with Ryan, as Alex was handling a Manx Construction truck.

They could let Glory drive while they were on the Alaska Highway, but she would have to give it over when they left the main road. The highway was paved, but even that was a nebulous claim. Long stretches of road were cracked and broken from heavy traffic and frost heaves, with deep potholes that could break a truck axle if hit at the wrong angle or speed. It was a rough road.

Sure enough, just before Wonowon, the pavement ran out and gravel replaced it for uneven stretches between concrete and asphalt patches. It was slow going, especially when big trucks flew by in the other direction. Alex stayed in the lead, and even though Pete was driving the other truck by this time, he led them onto the verge each time an oil drilling service truck approached. Those rigs took up a lot of room, and were too heavy to stop quickly.

The snow was piled high at the sides of the road, but the right of way was clear. By the time they reached the sign for Prespatou, sleet was bouncing off the windshield.

"It's going to be dark in an hour, and we haven't reached Pink Mountain yet," Alex said aloud.

Eddie, who'd been dozing beside him, straightened in his seat. "Does that mean something? I've never heard of Pink Mountain."

Alex gave a rusty laugh. "The turnoff to Big Smokey is north of there at Prophet River, and it's still a ways east after we take the side road. It's going to be pretty late when we finally get there."

Eddie glanced at the gas gauge. "How we doing for fuel?"

"I've got a few extra cans in the back. So does Ryan, and there's a gas station there. We're okay."

Three hours later, Alex slowed in front of the community hall in Big Smokey. There were a couple of trucks in the parking lot, and the lights were on inside and over the front stairs.

As he pulled up and turned off his engine, the front door of the hall opened and a couple of guys came down the few steps to the snow path.

Alex grinned and flung his door wide. "Coop!" He trotted across the frozen surface to grab his friend in a tight grip. "There you are. You silly bastard. Getting married in this weather, out in the back of beyond?"

Coop gave his hearty laugh and returned the hug. He was the same height as Alex, but slightly built, with deep-set eyes the colour of grey slate. "You remember Dad," he said and pulled an older man forward. Mr Cooper was built like Coop, but walked with a pronounced limp from a logging accident years ago.

"How you doing, son?" he said and clasped Alex's hand in a firm grip. "Glad you could make it. We're looking forward to getting this young man off our hands." There was much laughter and slapping of backs.

Alex turned to the others who were gathering behind him. "You remember Eddie? He was a year ahead of us in high school."

As they talked, Alex waved at the other truck where the doors were slamming open. "This is my brother Ryan, you know him. And Pete, Ryan's sidekick. He's in the band as well. And this is Glory."

Glory climbed slowly from the back door of the truck as Pete held it for her. Her hair was mussed as if she'd been sleeping, and it gleamed like dull gold in the light of the single bulb over the hall door. Her shoes crunched across the snow to Alex's side. Then she smiled.

The other men fell silent and Coop gave a slow grin, glancing at Alex. His chest swelled with pride. She was pretty, but her personality showed through so that it wasn't just looks that grabbed a man's attention. It was the enticing curve of her smile, those sparkling eyes, that stubborn chin that gave warning when she was digging in her heels over something.

Alex loved her, just as she was—exactly as she was. It caught him by surprise, so that he didn't even hear what was said as Coop and his father turned and led them into the hall.

Once he regained his sanity, he glanced around with the others. The room was set up for the wedding, a low stage in the back corner for the band, tables and chairs arranged for the meal. If it was anything like he remembered, there would be a giant potluck with dozens of dishes arriving from every home in the area.

Beside him, Glory yawned, and he turned to Coop. "Where are we staying, at your folks' place? It's been a long road, and everyone's tired."

Coop nodded and gave the woman beside him another quick glance before looking back at Alex, his lips curved in a grin. "Yep. I'll lead the way in my truck."

~~***~~

CHAPTER TWENTY

Glory rolled over in the single bed, and slowly opened her eyes. There was dull, opaque light coming through the window. She raised up on an elbow and looked around. This was Coop's sister's room. The girl, Trisha, had been sleeping when they finally arrived at the house last night, so Glory had washed up and undressed in the bathroom, then tiptoed in to climb into the twin bed.

Now the room was unoccupied. The space was small, with the two beds crammed in next to a wardrobe against one wall. There were posters between the windows and around the door – mostly of horses, although the ones of rock bands seemed newer. It looked like Trisha was growing up.

Glory grabbed her phone and saw it was well past nine. Whoops. There was supposed to be a band practice today, with the task of getting the sound equipment set up. She noted a text message from Mercedes on her cell that must have come in some time last night.

Have fun with the band, it read. *Don't do anything I wouldn't do.*

She laughed and tried to reply, but the message wouldn't send. No reception out here, it appeared.

Glory threw back the covers. Someone had kindly put her suitcase just inside the door, and she unzipped it looking for jeans and a sweater. Although it was warm in the room, she saw deep snow in the yard outside.

As she made her way down the hall, she heard the rumble of male voices coming from the kitchen area. So it wasn't that late. She made a quick bathroom stop and when she finally appeared in the kitchen doorway, the men were all gathered around the table, coffee mugs in hand.

The room was large and homey. There was a wooden table positioned near the window, with a cushioned window seat beneath. The leaves of the table were extended and chairs were set around the other sides over a homemade hooked rug spread on the linoleum floor. A big propane stove sat against the other wall with two ovens and a six-burner top. A coffee pot perked quietly over a small flame at one end.

Mrs. Cooper spotted her and waved to the one remaining chair, rising to fetch another cup from the cupboard. "Have a seat, Glory. We've got bacon and eggs here for you," she said as she poured from the stovetop pot. "The toast is in the oven."

Alex moved the chair closer to his side, giving her a grin. "Thought we might have to send up a delegation to rouse you from bed," he said. "We're doing the sound check shortly."

"I know, sorry." She eased onto the hard chair and wrapped her hands around the mug Mrs. Cooper placed before her. "I just woke up."

He scrutinized her face and reached to tuck a strand of hair behind her ear. "I can see that." His touch was tender on her skin. She glanced down in embarrassment and picked up her fork to tackle the huge platter of food in front of her. Scrambled eggs, ham, bacon and a stack of toast fought for space on the plate. A bowl of cut-up orange sections had been placed near her elbow along with an array of jam and honey pots.

"Wow, I don't think I can eat all this." She glanced her apology at Coop's mother, who beamed back at her.

"Do your best, honey. Gavin here will take care of the rest." She gestured at the giant dog lying on the mat by the back door, his furry muzzle resting on big paws. His coat was a mottled grey and he had a wild look about him, from the shape of the eyes to the ruff around his neck.

Glory glanced nervously at Mr. Cooper. "Is he a wolf?" she asked.

The man grinned. "No, at least only part wolf, mostly German Shepherd. He's a great dog for the north."

She finished her coffee and put the cup down beside her half-eaten plate of food. "I'm ready," she said.

The men rose to don their coats. Her high-heeled boots were resting on the mat near Gavin, and she hesitated to approach, taking her time shrugging into her ski jacket. Alex reached to hand her the footwear, a bemused look on his face.

"Did you bring snow boots as well?" he asked quizzically.

She sat to put them on, doing up the zipper. "These are lined," she said. "I just bought them. They're warm and the soles have a good grip."

"Okay." He didn't look convinced.

Mr. Cooper called the dog out of the way, and the animal rose and ambled over to nudge the man's knee, tail slowly wagging. "See you later," he called. "You have to be at the church by five-thirty, so keep that in mind."

Alex leaned to give the man a one-armed hug. "Don't worry, pops. We won't be late. Tell Coop everything is under control."

He winked at Mrs. Cooper and ushered Glory through the door, following the other band members into the light snowfall.

"We can take one truck," he offered. "By the time we unload the equipment, there'll be lots of room in the cab."

Glory shivered as she made her way down the steps and along the drive. Even with a ski jacket on, it was darned cold, and her lined gloves didn't seem to provide the protection for her hands she'd anticipated.

The truck was just warming up when they arrived at the community hall. It was a hassle getting the equipment in and set up on the platform. The place was stone cold. Someone had come in earlier to start a fire in the wood stove in the corner, but although the flames were blazing, the fire hadn't had much effect yet in warming the wide room.

They plugged in and began to tune up. Ryan walked around the hall checking the sound from several different angles and adjusting the amplifier and speakers. By the time they finished a quick practice, more snow was falling as they hustled across the slippery lot to the truck.

~~***~~

CHAPTER TWENTY ONE

The wedding was lovely. Glory sat with Ryan, Pete and Eddie in the second row of pews in the little log church. It was packed to the back wall, but they'd gotten there early enough to secure a seat. She spotted Mr and Mrs Cooper in the front row on the other side, with their daughter Trisha sandwiched between them.

The minister had driven in from Prespitou for the ceremony, his truck parked outside in the lot with all the other trucks. The groom and best man stood together before the altar in identical grey tuxedos. Alex looked magnificent, his broad shoulders and lean waist shown to advantage in the tailored suit.

There was music supplied by an ancient pump organ. Glory had taken a look at it before the ceremony started. The instrument had obviously seen hard use, the carpet on the foot pedals was worn through to the wooden panels beneath. The ivory keys were yellowed and chipped, but the tone was still good. The instrument was played by an elderly woman who kept losing her place as she glanced down the aisle, waiting for the bride and her father to appear. When the bridesmaid walked in, the woman started into the wedding march.

The bride was wearing a beautiful pale blue dress of lace that had been her mother's wedding dress, according to the whispered comments from some of the older people around them. Her bridesmaid had on a calf length sheath of darker blue, with a cowl neck.

It didn't take long to do the deed. Shortly after the start, the couple were seated to the side of the altar, signing the church's register. Alex stood behind Coop, his eyes combing the congregation. When his gaze lighted on her, Glory felt a jolt of connection. His eyes crinkled in the beginnings of a smile before his attention was pulled away to sign as witness to the event.

Service over, folks began to move off down the road toward the hall, while the bridal party stayed in the church for photos. Glory joined the rest of the band, shivering in the cold as they rushed to the truck. Ryan drove the short distance, and they entered the community building without Alex to find things already underway.

Long tables had been set up end to end as a dinner buffet, covered with a series of tablecloths in differing hues. Dishes of a huge variety, from appetizers to desserts, were being organized along it.

People continued to pour in. As they climbed to the stage, Glory turned on her keyboard and began to play softly. Pete chimed in with his fiddle and the music flowed steadily beneath the hum of conversation as the crowd helped themselves to the food and sat to eat together.

When the toasts began, the band had a chance to sit down for a few minutes. Many speeches and much laughter passed before the dance started.

Glory had the music to a dozen waltzes lined up as Alex danced with the bride, then the bride's mother, the groom's mother and the maid of honour. Slowly the pace picked up and when all the required dances were finished, he joined them on stage and the music changed. *Hot to Trot* fell into the routine they performed at *Rooster's* and the dance floor began to fill up with young couples.

Tables were moved out of the way and pushed against the wall, with chairs lined up in a row down the side. Glory watched as the men walked down the line of females, hand out asking for a dance.

Babies had been put down to sleep among the coats stacked on the set of bunk beds in the kitchen at the back. Young kids cavorted in groups between the dancers or raced in circles at the edges of the flowing crowd. It looked like disorganized chaos, yet still the dancers moved.

Glory was fascinated. This was a different experience for her, and the chance for them to perform just added to the excitement. They started getting requests for some older rock and roll favourites and the group dove eagerly into performing them.

Then the cowboy arrived, complete with blue jeans, boots and spurs. He wore a black cowboy hat with the sides curled up and a tight red plaid shirt clipped down the front of his chest. Over that was a long slicker, slit up the back for riding, that reached almost to the spurs on his boots. Even in this crowd, he made quite a stir.

The man stood at the door for a few minutes, attracting a lot of female attention as he surveyed the activity. Then he walked with purpose across the floor and held out his hand to the bridesmaid, who was standing talking to the bride. She flushed, took his hand and went onto the dance floor. By this time the band had progressed to country western music, and he moved smoothly into a two-step, holding the woman a decorous inch from his chest.

"Bridesmaid's boyfriend," Alex mouthed when she glanced at him. She laughed. *Was he reading her mind now?*

The look he gave her said maybe he was.

~~***~~

CHAPTER TWENTY TWO

Alex was glad the wedding was over. He'd been touched and eager to perform as best man for his buddy, Coop. But he would rather have been with Glory than standing by the side of the bridesmaid. He understood what was required of his role, and he'd followed Coop's lead in making sure he danced with his sister, Trisha, as well.

But how was he to dance with Glory? As long as the band was playing the music, he was stuck on stage as he watched the other men waltz with their girls.

Pete had put together a list of tunes and they followed along. Next up was a polka. This was a bit of a challenge, but at the same time he could improvise all he wanted. None of this music was on paper in front of him, it was all in Pete's head as he broke out into each new piece with his fiddle.

Glory was playing for all she was worth, and he was amazed at how quickly she adapted to the new music. The crowd shifted again, and more of the older folk began to dance to the two-step and schottische.

Then Coop gave him the signal and they brought the last song to a close. Coop's new bride climbed the steps to the stage and turned her back on the audience to throw her bouquet. A crowd of hopeful young women gathered below but her bridesmaid caught it nimbly, the cowboy smirking in satisfaction a couple of steps behind her.

Everyone clapped. Alex realized there'd probably be another wedding in the not too distant future. He glanced at Glory. Would they get to that stage? They'd hardly begun going out together. Things had been too busy, too hectic to take the relationship much further and he was chomping at the bit to get going. Nor had he ever thought of getting married, yet now the idea seemed to be just hovering on the horizon in front of him.

Coop and his bride left the hall amid catcalls and plenty of vocal advice from the single guys in the group, which, hopefully, they were unable to hear. The two planned to stay the night at Prespitou before carrying on to Vancouver for their honeymoon.

The dance didn't wind up until after midnight, with a final waltz involving nearly everyone in the place, young and old. Glory played her heart out and brought it to a lovely and soulful close.

Then the tear-down began as the band hauled their equipment to the side and packed it into cases to be picked up tomorrow.

Mr. and Mrs. Cooper had already left the hall by the time they crowded into the truck. "Everyone strapped in?" Alex asked. He started the engine and let it idle for a few minutes to warm up before easing into gear.

"Eddie, you still got that bottle of rum in your case at the house?"

There was a low rumble of laughter from the back seat of the club cab. "Sure do. Time for a nightcap."

The other men laughed, but Glory gave a big yawn. "Sorry guys, you're on your own."

Mrs. Cooper had retired by the time they arrived at the house. Mr. Cooper let them in and Glory went off to bed. Coop had set the men up in the basement with two beds and a couple of blow-up mattresses on the floor, and they'd been remarkably comfortable the night before.

Eddie pulled out his bottle. Alex found a few glasses and splashed some in each, handing it around. He wouldn't have minded some cola to go with it, but that wouldn't stop him from enjoying himself. "Here's to *Hot to Trot*," he said, drink in hand. "You've done well, Ryan. It's a great band, if I do say so myself."

Ryan grinned as they all took a sip. "Thanks. But really, it's all down to the musicians. You guys do pretty good."

Pete smirked. "That's all, just pretty good?"

"Yeah," Ryan gave a cheeky grin. "Darned good would involve a little more effort on your part. On the other hand, Glory does great."

Eddie laughed. "Did you see that cowboy?"

"Was he for real?" Pete added. "I've never seen an outfit like that. Do you think he rides horses for a living?"

Alex shook his head. "That was mostly for show. But it certainly got the women's attention."

Eddie nodded thoughtfully. "I might have to give something like that a try."

"You think Corrie would be impressed?"

Eddie gave Ryan a dirty look. "Corrie ain't the only woman in town, you know."

He shrugged and looked at Alex. "Mr. Suspenders is gay," he said.

"What?" Alex felt a kick in his chest. "That friend of Glory's? How do you know?"

"I asked her. He's just a friend."

As he pondered that information, Eddie gave him a close look. "You really finished with Trudy? I mean, for good?"

"Come on." Alex gazed at him in disbelief. "You can't be serious. I moved out damned near a year ago."

"Yeah, but you went back when she called."

Alex took another drink, feeling it burn down his gullet. Kind of the way that question was burning in his chest. "She's worn me out. If she wants to cry, she can call Rolf. I've blocked her number on my phone."

He saw Ryan's little nod as if confirming something he already knew. "What?" he demanded.

"Nothing." His brother gave him a smile. "I think Glory's interested in you."

He groaned. It wasn't like he wanted to discuss this with the whole band. That was good information, he just needed to know what it was based on. But he'd wait to ask. "We'll see," was all he said. "Better hit the hay, you guys have to leave early to catch your flight."

For himself, he didn't have an early flight to catch. He reached for the bottle of rum.

Yet as he undressed for bed, he gave Eddie a tap on the shoulder. "Just so you know," he said, "Rolf is a dangerous man."

~~***~~

CHAPTER TWENTY THREE

Alex slammed the door behind him, shaking off his jacket to produce a small blizzard of sleet and snow in icy pellets. He quickly scanned the Coopers' cozy living room and his gaze fastened on Glory, her long honey-coloured hair, light brown and straight as a yardstick hanging over one shoulder. His chest tightened and he cleared his throat, rubbing his hands together as he took in the sight of her.

She was chatting with Coop's little sister, and it looked like she'd cheered Trisha up. The girl was laughing at something she'd said, waving her hands in front of her face. Ryan had left very early in the morning with the other men, as they were all flying home out of Fort St John on a fairly tight schedule.

He caught Glory's eye. "Truck's packed," he said. "Guess we should get going. Weather's turning colder and the roads look pretty icy."

Glory nodded and stood. She walked to the kitchen door. "Thank you very much for everything, Mrs. Cooper. You've been so generous with your hospitality."

Coop's mum dried her hands on a dishtowel as she came through the doorway. "You're welcome, Glory. It was very nice to meet you, and without you the band wouldn't have been nearly as good." This last was said with a twinkle in her eye as she caught sight of Alex.

Glory glanced quickly as if to check his reaction. Not that he could blame her. He hadn't been very open to adding a female to the group at the beginning. Now... He grinned to himself. He didn't mind a bit.

Glory gave a tinkling laugh. "Well, Mrs. Cooper. We don't want to insult the rest of the band."

The woman chuckled and hugged her tight. "I mean it. The music was great, we had such a good time. The wedding was perfect." She turned to Alex. "Alex, it seems I've known you all your life."

"Darned near." He ducked his head and wrapped his arms around her. "Don't worry. I'm sure we'll see you again soon. Coop is bound to start churning out babies any time now, and there'll have to be some visiting done over all that."

Mrs. Cooper's face got a pretty blush on it. "Go on with you." She turned to the window, gesturing toward the driving sleet. "The weather's turning for sure, you want to get going and be in plenty of time for Glory's flight."

Alex felt a jolt in his middle. Glory's flight. He wasn't going with her, she was travelling on her own, although his brother should meet her at the airport in Victoria as he'd get in quite a bit ahead of her.

Glory found her ski jacket and zipped it up, wrapping a scarf around her throat. Trisha rushed over to hold her in a tight embrace and Glory hugged the girl back, whispering encouragement in her ear. Alex wanted a hug like that too.

He escorted her down the slippery steps and held the truck door, watching as she climbed nimbly up into the passenger seat. She looked good in those jeans. Lucky they weren't going to be walking outside anywhere in this weather though. They didn't look warm enough for that.

Slamming the door, he gave a final wave to Mrs. Cooper as she went inside, and walked around to climb in the driver's seat as the engine rumbled under the hood. In these temperatures, he didn't shut the truck off unless he was somewhere he could plug it in or put it in a shed.

He fastened his seatbelt as they bumped over the frozen ruts in the driveway and onto the narrow snow-covered gravel road, empty of traffic. It would be a few hours yet before they'd reach pavement.

Alex looked over at his passenger, taking in her pretty face and shining hair. Did her face really glow? It seemed like it. She was full of sunshine, goodwill and cheer. She warmed him up. Just looking at her made him hot. He unzipped his jacket.

Peering through the windshield at the blowing sleet, he knew he should be concentrating on getting them back to Fort St. John in one piece and on time for her flight home. Northern British Columbia had a reputation for unpredictable weather.

"Are you buckled up?" he said. "It's damned slippery out there."

"Yes," she said cheerily. "I'm ready, if you are."

He couldn't help but grin and looked at her again, just to check if her hair was as smooth and flowing as last time he'd gazed at it. He wanted his hands in that hair.

He put the thought out of his head and the truck into a higher gear, moving slowly forward through the frozen crust on the road. The tires gripped solidly and he pressed the accelerator. Soon they passed through the little village, with the 'Big Smokey' sign prominent on the community hall where they'd held the wedding dance. There was only one vehicle in the parking lot now, a beat-up looking pickup of indeterminate colour and vintage. Maybe it had just given up the ghost where it sat, or maybe the driver had too much to drink last night and couldn't drive home.

The Big Smokey general store was on the right, three or four vehicles parked around the front door and several positioned at the gas pumps. He checked the dial on the dash, they were fine. He'd filled up the tank this morning before returning to the house with all the band equipment packed into the back.

As they left the side road and turned onto the main right-of-way, he saw the little log church off to one side, the two-room schoolhouse off to the other. Not much more than that to Big Smokey. But the community was a hell of a lot bigger than the sum of its parts. They had shown that to a fault the night before at the party.

He glanced at Glory. "You're pretty quiet," he said.

She looked over at him, a little smile on her face "I'm a bit tired," she admitted. "But it was fun, wasn't it? It's a very different world up here than I'm used to."

He nodded and accelerated. "Yeah, they know how to throw a celebration, all right."

The road was clear but the sleet was heavier and coming at them sideways, starting to freeze to the window. He turned on the heater, aimed the warm air at the windshield, and dialed up the fan. Immediately it started to clear.

A deer darted across the road and he hit the brake, swerving to avoid hitting it. The truck slid, then the tires grabbed and straightened. They slid again on the curve and Alex reduced the speed, eventually pulling over to the side of the road.

"What's wrong? Can we still go?" Glory peered worriedly out the side window at the snow beginning to accumulate in the ditch.

"We're fine. But we'll have better traction when I lock the hubs. Be right back." He climbed down and rummaged in the toolbox bolted behind the driver's seat, coming up with a metal hub wrench. He shut the lid and, head down against the blowing snow, bent to turn the locks on the front wheel. Then he walked around to Glory's side and did the same.

He threw the wrench back into the toolbox with a thunk, gave his hair a shake to rid himself of ice particles clinging to him, and climbed back in. "That'll be better."

A minute later Glory looked back through the rear window to where they had left the main road, turning onto a side road that headed straight into the bush. "We didn't come this way, did we?"

"No," he glanced sideways at her, then quickly back to the track. "But Coop said this shortcut is used by everyone and should get us onto the Highway at Wonowon in about an hour instead of three, so we'll save time driving. And it's gravel, we won't have to worry about sliding around. We'll have good traction."

He turned the windshield wipers up, trying to see through the heavy snow blowing across the road in front of them. "Man, we should have left earlier."

"Sorry," she said. "Did I delay us? Maybe I shouldn't have had that shower."

He glanced over at her woebegone look. "No, honey. That didn't make any difference. Given it's a seven-hour drive to the airport, a half-hour either way doesn't matter. The forecast said heavy snow, and that's what we're about to get."

He watched her blink, then turn to gaze out the front. *Honey?* He'd never said that before. He'd better watch his mouth, he might embarrass himself at what popped out of it. He frowned through the clouded windshield at the disappearing highway. The snow was definitely getting worse.

Glory tightened her seatbelt, and he placed a comforting hand over hers. "Don't worry, we'll be fine. It'll just take a bit more time with this weather. You might have to catch a later flight, but that can be arranged when we get within phone service closer to the city."

The snow grew heavier by the minute. Soon it was almost impossible to see. He was reduced to a virtual crawl, peering through the flashing wipers at the invisible road ahead. "This doesn't look right to me," Alex muttered, his mouth tight and grip fierce on the wheel. "There're no tracks here, no one has come this way today." The snow was cloaking the countryside now, his tires cutting a six-inch track through the layer of white.

They passed a driveway, almost indiscernible from the other terrain, snow so deep the landscape had been flattened to the gaze. He peered ahead intently. "Maybe we should turn around. There's not a soul to be seen, no one to ask for directions."

"You ask directions?" Glory looked at him wide-eyed, a sparkle in her gaze. "A man who asks directions?"

He smiled and flashed a glance her way. "I can do a lot of things," he said, growing warm at the thought. Then he frowned back at the roadway. He couldn't see the ditches now, it looked like a blanket of white from the wall of trees on one side to the wall of trees on the other. He slowed even more.

"I'm going to turn around. This is crazy. Better to take the extra time on the main road and get to Wonowon safely." He stopped in the middle of the pristine field of white, gazing around them. Then he backed the truck up a few yards, turned the front wheels, put it in low gear and pulled forward cautiously. He stopped at what seemed to be a safe distance from the trees and turned the wheel the other way, sliding the gearshift into reverse. The truck backed slowly in a curve, then gave a little lurch as the back end sank. He jammed on the brakes, cranked the wheel again and pulled forward.

"Thank God for four-wheel drive," he muttered as the back end rose and the truck eased forward. He gave it a bit more gas just as a flurry of snow blew down the straightaway and engulfed the windshield.

As Alex hit the brakes, the front end of the truck simply dropped out from beneath them, landing with a resounding crunch as the rear flipped into the air. The band's equipment in the back banged and slammed together as it slid forward on the truck bed and the back wheels spun uselessly in the air above the road.

~~***~~

CHAPTER TWENTY FOUR

Alex unsnapped his seatbelt and slid forward, his foot hitting the brake pedal. Not that it made any difference. They certainly weren't going anywhere any time soon. He shot a worried glance at Glory. "You okay?"

She hung from her seatbelt, which looked as though it was cutting into her shoulder.

"Undo it, if you can."

She struggled with the buckle, unable to unhook it with her weight resting against the strap.

"I'll come around." Alex shut off the engine and cracked his door open, heaving it wide with his shoulder. The wind sent a gust of snow swirling into the cab. He leaped and landed thigh deep in the ditch. Gripping the frame of the truck, he pulled himself up onto the road and slammed his door shut, then forced his way through the deep snow around the vehicle.

It was an alarming sight. The nose of the pickup was buried deep in the ditch while the truck bed teetered high off the road, the back wheels still spinning. The black body of the vehicle stood out starkly. There was no way they were getting out of this mess without some serious help.

He squinted around. The light filtered through the fast falling snow, making the landscape appear totally flat. Distances were hard to judge. But he'd seen a driveway going through the trees a mile or two back there. They'd start with that, in the hopes they'd find a dwelling of some kind at the end of it.

Reaching down, he pried Glory's door open. She'd managed to get her seatbelt unfastened and braced herself awkwardly in the cab. She clutched her purse in one fist, absolute confusion in her eyes. "It's okay, Glory. We'll be okay. Give me your hand." He tugged her out the door and reached for her other arm as her feet scrabbled in the deep snow. A wave of panic rose in his throat. *If he didn't get Glory out of the storm, and soon, they were in serious trouble.*

He propped her upright against the side of the truck. "Where's your toque?" he asked insistently.

"In the back seat."

"I'll get it, and your mitts?"

"I'm not sure." She stifled a shiver, folding her arms tightly across her chest.

"Let me take a look." He dove into the cab, and found her gloves on the floor of the front seat.

Scrounging around, he pulled out a scarf and toque from the back.

Slamming the door shut, he pressed the remote lock, sliding the keys into his inside pocket. "Here you go." He tugged the knitted cap down on her head and handed her the gloves. He watched while she threaded them on her fingers.

"Now put this on." He placed the scarf around her neck.

Pulling his toque lower, he raised his hood and tied the cord at the neck. Then he grabbed her hand and started walking. There was no time to lose.

~~*~~

Walking back up the road was a lesson in perseverance. He wanted to keep hold of Glory's hand, but they were better off walking in one of the deep tracks left by the truck tires, so he ploughed ahead. Every now and then he glanced back to make sure she was still with him.

The wind was fierce, and the blowing snow was like needles stabbing the skin. The next time he turned around, Glory had fallen and was awkwardly trying to get back on her feet.

He lunged toward her, grabbing her jacket from the back and levering her upright. "Listen, hold onto me. It isn't far now, but I need to know you're coming. Grab the back of my parka."

Staggering forward, he felt the tug of her hands as she struggled in his wake. Then he saw the break in the trees. A driveway, leading into the bush. *They might just find a place to hole up. But if there was no house in there...* It was a risk they had to take.

He gazed along the road the way they'd come. No one had been down here today but him. And likely no one was coming. He tested the side of the road with his feet, but this wasn't a ditch, it was a track leading into the forest.

"Hang on, Glory. I think we're getting there."

It was tough going in the deep snow. The tire tracks had made it easier on the road, but here they were ploughing steadily forward through deep drifts. Some time later, the drive took a curve and he spotted the shadowy outline of a dwelling in the trees. "Okay, now we're onto something."

He turned to check and Glory chose that moment to lean against him, her head stuffed into his chest. "Don't stop now, we're almost there," he said. She didn't answer, but struggled to stand straight, shivering uncontrollably.

Alex seized her arms and pulled her upright. "Come on," he said, alarm flaring in his chest. "We have to keep moving." He leaned forward, shoving one shoulder into her midriff. She gusted out a breath as he hoisted her up, wrapping one arm around her legs. He stumbled forward in the swirling snow, his lungs labouring. They couldn't stop, it was too dangerous. Too cold.

The cabin slowly came into view. It was small, made of logs, the low-slope roof burdened with a bank of snow. No smoke came from the metal chimney. Nor were there any tracks around the door. An old rusted truck was abandoned partway into the trees, barely visible under its load of white.

Alex trudged to the door set into the small overhang. There was no lock, just a wooden latch. He flipped it up and leaned on the panel, which creaked open under his weight. He stepped inside, out of the swirling storm.

The entry was small. Several old tattered parkas hung on a row of nails against the wall, a pair of big boots reclining beneath. Junk filled most of the space around the walls. There was a window on one side letting in a bit of light, the snow piled high against the single pane of glass. A low stool stood near the door with a chamber pot on top. No plumbing in this house, obviously, not that he'd expected any. Facing them was a second door leading to the main cabin.

Alex dropped his arm and let Glory's limp body slide down his chest. Her feet hit the floor and she stumbled against him. "Wake up," he said. "Wake up. We're here."

She leaned heavily, the shivers shaking her body in a steady ripple of movement that sent answering currents of fear down his spine. He wrapped his arms around her. "Can you stand?"

"I think so," she said but didn't move.

"Come on." He pulled her forward through the second door. They walked into a large square room. The walls were log, the floor bare plywood, the ceiling low—

everything the colour of wood. A set of stairs against the back wall led upward to a loft of some kind.

There was a small jumble of furniture, a table with a bench and two chairs up against one wall. A set of shelves by the single large window. A wood cook stove against another wall, with a dry sink next to it. A barrel heater stood in the centre of the room with a wood box nearby, a few split logs flung into the bottom. A second barrel stood upright beside it, full of water. It was frozen solid.

~~***~~

CHAPTER TWENTY FIVE

Alex seated Glory in a chair and stood back. "Can you stay here for a minute? I need to start a fire, but it'll take a bit of time. I have to find more wood."

She nodded, her eyes unfocussed. He leaned forward and kissed her hard on the mouth. "Wait here," he said. "Rub your hands together to get them warm."

He found the wood pile just to the left of the doorway under a heavy covering of snow, with the chopping block beside it. A short-handled axe was embedded in the top of the stump. It didn't take long to split some kindling and carry in enough wood to get a fire going.

When he got back to the cabin, shaking the snow off his parka, Glory was pacing up and down in her high-heeled boots, rubbing her arms. Her face was pale and she shivered steadily. He hugged her tight and rubbed her back, then knelt in front of the barrel heater, taking a deep breath to calm his racing heart. "This won't take long," he assured her.

He found a sharp thin-bladed knife by the wood box and used it to create a pile of shavings that he placed in the ash on the floor of the heater. Then he piled on the kindling and a few of the smaller logs. Wooden matches were stored on a shelf above the table.

The shavings caught with the first flare and burned brightly. Carefully he loaded on the firewood, waiting as it caught before adding more. His fingers were stiff with cold and he rubbed them together, blowing on the tips to ease the discomfort.

He glanced at Glory as she paced unsteadily about the room, her shoulders shaking. She stopped to lean weakly on the table for support. He stood and pulled her toward the rocking chair, pushing her down. He wrapped a weathered-looking gray blanket around her shoulders. "Rock," he said, his mouth tight. "Keep rocking, don't stop. I have to know you're moving."

Before long, the fire was burning strongly. He looked around for a pot and filled it with snow, resting it on the square metal plate welded to the top of the barrel. Perhaps some hot water to warm them both. Rifling through the shelves he found half-used boxes of tea and a bag of coffee. The coffee pot on the heater was still partially full and starting to thaw. Examining the murky contents, he decided not to risk it and dumped the black liquid down the dry sink. He heard it splash and glanced beneath to find a bucket under the drain. Okay, now he understood how that particular system worked.

The fire was burning hotly now. It wouldn't be too long before the room began to heat, even though he'd observed the windows were single-pane and he could see through a few gaps between the logs that made up the walls. But someone lived here and stayed warm during the winter.

Alex went to the rocking chair and lifted Glory up. "Come here," he said. He sat down and pulled her onto his lap, wrapping the blanket around her as they cuddled. "It's going to be okay. It'll be warm in here soon."

He held her, rocking softly to the sound of the wind howling outside, and slowly they grew more comfortable. Her head fell against his shoulder and he realized she'd fallen asleep, even though a shudder still seized her now and then. He swallowed against the wave of protectiveness that rose from his belly. He shouldn't have taken that shortcut, forget what Coop had said. He should have just stayed on the main drag and taken the time to get to Wonowon the safest way possible.

Now the truck was useless, upended on its nose in the ditch, and they were marooned in the woods in a snowstorm with no phone service and no help available.

He tightened his arms around the woman on his lap. He'd do whatever it took to look after her and keep her safe. He listened to the fire crackle and made a mental list of chores to be done before the early darkness fell.

~~*~~

Ryan pulled into the truck rental stall at the Fort St John airport and shut the motor off. They'd been forced to make a run for it, and there hadn't been time to fill the gas tank. He knew he was going to pay through the nose for that with the rental company.

Pete and Eddie removed luggage from the back seat while he stopped in the small office located in the parking garage. He slapped the truck keys on the counter and took out his credit card, hoping there was enough room left on it for the extra charges. It was fun having a band, but it sure as hell didn't pay all the bills.

By the time he finished the transaction, they ran for their plane, dodging the throng as they made their way to the waiting area. Passing through security was a hassle of supreme proportions. Finally out of the lineup, Ryan grabbed his wallet and boarding pass, then searched for a chair to sit down and lace his boots. Behind him, he heard Eddie arguing with the security guard. He turned to shoot a warning look at the belligerent guy, catching Pete's glance of complete resignation.

"We're not going to make the flight," his friend mouthed. They both turned to look at the plane on the runway as a line of passengers walked out in the blowing snow and climbed the stairs into the body of the aircraft.

"Yes, we are. Eddie can look after himself." Ryan grabbed his carryon and took off, heading straight for the gate, Pete hard on his heels. When he looked back, to his surprise Eddie was right behind them, his duffel bag clutched firmly in his grip. They just made it. The staircase was being pulled away as Eddie stepped into the cabin. Before they found their seats, the doors were closing.

"Where's Glory?" Pete asked, leaning across Eddie's thick form. "Wasn't she supposed to be on the same flight?"

Ryan shrugged. "She was catching a later one. I'm sure they'll get here on time. Alex knows what he's doing."

Eddie grinned, his teeth gleaming beneath his bristling black moustache. "Alex took a bedroom stop, no doubt. He's hot for that chick."

Ryan frowned and gave him a heavy nudge in the ribs. "Alex doesn't take chances," he said. "If he gets caught in the storm, he'll do the safe thing and drive slow and careful."

Eddie laughed, giving Ryan an itch to lambaste him one in the nose. "He's finished with Trudy," he said, "and looking for another woman. I think he's found her."

Ryan glared and turned his head away. He couldn't argue with the first part of that statement, he just didn't like discussing his brother's love life with this clown, even if he was Alex's buddy.

~~***~~

CHAPTER TWENTY SIX

The cabin was warmer now, and steam started to rise from the pot on top of the heater. Alex added more snow. If they wanted to wash up or have a hot drink, they'd need water. The barrel of ice that sat on the floor beside the heater was starting to show signs of thawing, but it would be a while before there was any water from that source.

Glory subsided into the rocking chair again, looking comfortable rather than stressed. Her eyes drifted closed, and guilt swamped him. This was his fault, they shouldn't have turned off the main road.

"I'll head out to the truck and see what I can bring back before it's dark," he said. "What do you need from your suitcase? I won't be able to bring everything."

She sat up straighter in the chair. "I need my cosmetic bag," she said. Her cheeks turned rosy. "It's got my toothbrush and—some other stuff."

"I can get that. Don't go outside, okay? It's too dangerous. I won't be long."

Her expression turned to alarm and he quickly crossed the dusty floor toward her. "Seriously," he said. "Don't go outside. I'll definitely be back." He pressed his hand on her shoulder and watched her face, waiting for a response.

When she nodded, he tightened his mouth in determination and headed for the door. In the entrance, he grabbed his parka off a nail and shrugged it on. It was cold to the touch, and he made a mental note to take it into the inner room when he got back.

He pulled the door open and stepped outside. The snow was deeper, their tracks starting to fill in. The wind howled through the trees and swirled around his legs as he marched in the direction of the road, following the now faint trail they'd left on their way in. It was tough going, the snow reaching his knees and higher as he ploughed along.

By the time he got to the road, he was breathing hard. He walked on through the blizzard, until the truck became visible in the distance, nose down and nearly buried. No one had been through this way since they'd gone off the road.

He prayed they wouldn't be stranded for too long. The repercussions might be devastating. Manx Construction would be worried about him and about their vehicle, but that was almost the least of his worries. His mother would be fretting, not knowing where her oldest son was. She'd had a lot to deal with over the years, the worst of which had been when their father dropped dead of a heart attack while on a construction job. The shock had stunned them all. Yet she had soldiered on, keeping her sons on track in their mid and late teen years. That hadn't been easy.

He hoped Ryan kept a level head and reassured her that all would be fine. And what about Glory's family? They'd be worried sick, with no news of her whereabouts. Once the other band members arrived home, the hunt would be on when she didn't show.

He had a hell of a time getting a door open on the truck, scooping snow and pushing it out of the way. He climbed inside and scrambled around for their cases. Luckily they were on the back seat and not in the truck bed. It would have been an almost impossible task to get inside there and find them.

He undid the clips on Glory's bag and searched around, coming up with a large zippered case that looked like it held those mysterious items women always carried with them. He peeked inside but felt embarrassed examining her things. Grabbing a sweater for her and his shaving kit, he clambered back out.

Surprisingly the wind was dying down but the snow continued to fall in a dense curtain all around him. After tying an orange warning tag to the truck bumper, he headed back down the road.

When he got to the driveway turn off, he spied a set of prints in the snow superimposed over his own. They looked like impressions made by a very large dog, which seemed unlikely. Dogs didn't roam far from home in this type of weather, and these paw marks were remarkably far apart, indicating a long reach.

His gaze sharpened as he peered through the thick fall of snow. The tracks led straight down the drive toward the cabin. As he got closer, he saw movement ahead of him and stopped where he stood as his gut clenched. A tall, mottled grey shape paced sinuously past the front door of the cabin and turned toward the woodpile. A thick ruff around its neck and nose to the ground, the wolf moved with purpose as it explored their tracks in the snow.

Alex froze. *What should he do now? Was he in danger? Was the animal hungry enough to consider him dinner?* He waited, anxious, as the wolf changed direction and patrolled back toward the front door. Glory had better not choose that moment to open the door and look out, because who knew what her reaction would be, or what would happen then.

He moved forward a dozen feet, heart hammering in his chest, as the wolf raised its head and stared directly at him. They both remained immobile. Then the wolf turned and trotted noiselessly behind the woodpile and into the woods.

Alex ploughed his way steadily toward the cabin door through the heavy snowfall, keeping an eye on the spot where the wolf had disappeared. The light was dull as night approached, and he needed to get inside.

Lungs labouring, he reached the door and stepped through, slamming it behind him and throwing the latch. He paused to catch his breath and allow his heart rate to slow.

Better not tell Glory about that encounter. She was already nervous as hell about their precarious situation.

~~***~~

CHAPTER TWENTY SEVEN

The wind had died but the snow continued to fall. They had canned beans for dinner, warmed on top of the barrel heater in a saucepan. Alex made tea, although the water hadn't reached a boil so it was warm but weak and a bit flavourless. He lit the coal oil lamp on the table, thanking his lucky stars that the base was full of fuel. The glass chimney was smoky and streaked from Glory's attempt at cleaning it. It still gave enough light to navigate around the room.

"Who do you think lives here, Alex?" Glory carefully forked three beans into her mouth and washed them down with a mouthful of tepid tea.

He grinned to himself. Beans were obviously not at the top of her list of favourites. "A guy named William," he said, pointing to a stack of mail on the shelf beside him. "William Heverton. He doesn't get much mail. No bills for a phone, for electricity or water. No credit cards, it looks like. I suppose he pays property taxes somewhere, although I'm not sure where."

She shrugged and stared at the beans.

"But someone writes to him." Alex ate his last mouthful and scraped the plate with his fork.

"I wonder what he'd think if he knew we were here in his house." Her eyes were luminous in the flickering light.

He smiled at her melancholy expression. "I think he'd be fine with that. At least we're warm and safe and if he came home right now, I'd be thankful. We'd have some help to get the truck out of the ditch."

Her lower lip trembled. "How will we ever get home?"

"We'll be fine, Glory." He patted her hand where it rested on the tabletop. "There are other driveways on this road. If worse comes to worst, I'll walk back to the main road and flag someone down. Don't worry. We just have to wait out the storm."

The large wood box was filled to the brim, and he'd hauled in more logs, stacking them in the small entry. He wouldn't be wandering around outside in the dark looking for firewood, not with a timber wolf in the area.

He'd found a lantern in the entry and brought it in. Two lamps gave better light, dim though it was. He rose and took the lantern to the stairs. "Wait here," he said. "I'm going to have a look up above."

He found a small upper room, with a window at each end looking out into the dark night. The ceiling was low above his head. He could stand in the centre of the room, but the roof sloped off on each side. There was a steel frame bed, with an old thin coil-sprung mattress on it, and an ancient dresser. It was warm up here, the heat from below had chased away the chill.

He stared at the mattress. He'd be sharing the bed with Glory. That was exactly what he'd been driving toward ever since he met her. He just had never imagined doing it in a place like this, or under these circumstances. The springs creaked loudly when he pushed his fist into the mattress, and the smell of smoke rose from the bedding. Even so, it was better than sleeping on the thin plywood floor. One leg of the bed had already punched a hole through, and a small piece of wood had been nailed into place as a patch to hold it up.

It didn't matter. It was warm up here. This is where they'd sleep.

Pulling open the dresser drawers, he found unmatched socks, shirts, and old but clean long woollen underwear. He left the lantern hanging from a nail in a log above his head and returned downstairs. Glory was gingerly washing their plates in a shallow pan of water in the sink. Her fingers were bright red and tender from exposure to the frost in her thin gloves, but she held a ragged dishcloth, gently rubbing it across the dishes.

"Here, I'll do that." He took the cloth from her hand.

She glanced at him sideways. "I can help," she said. "You've done everything so far."

He suppressed a smile. "Listen, sit down and take off your boots and socks. We'll hang our clothes above the heater so they'll be dry in the morning."

"I'm not taking everything off!" She looked astounded, then glanced at her feet uncertainly.

"Yeah, your feet are wet. There's some stuff upstairs, see what you can find to wear to bed." His neck got hot at the thought and he concentrated on drying the plates and cutlery, placing them back on the shelf against the wall.

While she was gone, he wandered the room, listening to her muffled footsteps above his head and trying not to imagine what she was doing. He pried off his boots and set them on a chair near the fire, putting hers next to them. Those high-heeled boots were pretty cute, and yes, they were lined, but they sure weren't warm enough for northern weather.

There was a bookcase by the stairs loaded with old hardcovers popular from years ago. He found *Robinson Crusoe, Gone with the Wind, Arabian Nights*, and numerous Zane Grey novels. There was *King Solomon's Mines*, and a well-worn copy of *The Last of the Mohicans*. At least he'd read that one as a youngster, but the others were unfamiliar.

Glory crept down the stairs and he watched as she slowly came into view. He couldn't help his smile. She wore an ancient long-sleeved tee shirt that reached her thighs, a pair of boxer shorts sagging from her hips, and mismatched wool work socks on her feet, all pulled out of the dresser drawers upstairs. Her clothes were slung over her arm.

"That works," he said. "Don't come down. Just give me your clothes and I'll hang them on the line. You crawl into bed and I'll be right up."

She shot a startled look his way and hesitantly handed over her clothes.

"You don't have to worry, Glory," he said, his mouth tight. "You're safe with me. I told you that from the start."

"I know." She gave a small smile and held the railing with her tender fingers as she retreated back upstairs.

He took a deep breath. He meant every word. She was safe with him, no matter how high the toll on his self-restraint. He turned determinedly toward the line above the heater and hung her garments one by one. When he got to the flimsy panties and lacy bra, his heart hitched a beat and his fingers lingered long on the delicate fabric.

~~***~~

CHAPTER TWENTY EIGHT

E ddie waited until the plane had slowed to a stop on the runway in the Victoria airport and the seatbelt sign turned off. He thumbed his cell phone on and checked for messages. Nothing from work. He'd call them as soon as they were let off this frigging aircraft.

He turned his head as Ryan stood to retrieve his bag from the upper rack. Alex was a good guy, but his little brother was picky as hell. All about get to the band practice on time, memorize the sheet music he copied for them, stop playing when he hit the last drumbeat. Control, control.

He'd bet a good lay that the kid never had any fun.

Dragging his duffel from under the seat in front of him, he unsnapped his belt. Time to boogey. Mrs. Vecchio was picking them up and she'd drop him at his car on the edge of town. And if he didn't have a shift on the delivery truck tonight, he'd be making another very interesting call to Trudy.

Alex said he was finished with her. Eddie had checked right after the wedding dance when they were drinking his rum in the Coopers' basement. So there would be no misunderstandings between them. He didn't usually step on a friend's toes when it came to women, but in this case there were no toes to step on. Alex said so.

Corrie wasn't coming back any time soon. She'd made that perfectly clear. That didn't mean she'd never come back. They'd been through this before. If he got out of line even a little bit, she'd get her knickers in a knot. And this time her knickers seemed to be tangled right up. It looked like she was determined to make him suffer big time before she forgave his transgressions.

Didn't mean he couldn't have any fun while he waited for their reconciliation. And Trudy must be ready by now to step up to the next level.

~~*~~

Alex filled the barrel heater with more wood and turned down the damper. He hung his clothes on the line, which left him standing in his underwear. That became a bit of a disadvantage. The thought of Glory in bed upstairs had started a reaction that was hard to hide in his semi-naked state. He blew out the lamp on the table. The light from the lantern above spilled down the stairs and illuminated his way up.

Glory had climbed into bed and lay staring at the timbers above her head. When the top step creaked under his weight, her head jerked around. "There's only one pillow," she said. She wrinkled her nose. "It smells of smoke."

"Yeah, everything in here smells of smoke. I guess that's what happens when your heat comes from a wood burning stove." He moved across the sagging floor and pulled a couple of dresser drawers open. "We can make something that will work for now." He found a tee shirt and stuffed some clothes inside it, tying the bottom closed.

Then his hand fell on an old pair of underwear and he pulled them out. He needed something dry to wear and doubted Glory would be thrilled if he slept commando. Taking the lantern down from the overhead nail, he brought it across to the bedside.

"Shove over," he said, setting it on the stool beside the bed. "I'll need to get up in the night to feed the fire so I'll sleep on this side."

She scrambled across the mattress. "Do I take the pillow?" she asked hesitantly.

He glanced at her in amusement. "Sure, unless you want to arm wrestle for it."

She gave a strangled laugh.

"Take the pillow," he said. "I'll use this," and he slapped the stuffed tee shirt onto the head of the bed. He bent to blow the lantern out, then shucked his boxers in the dark, hanging them on the rung of the stool. He pulled on the dry pair of briefs and climbed in. The mattress sagged alarmingly under his weight and she promptly rolled against his side, lighting a fire in his belly as her curvaceous body rested against him.

"Oops." She struggled over but was obviously hanging on tight with her fingertips to the edge of the ancient mattress to keep from tumbling into him again.

He lay on his back and looped his arm under her. "Try this, Glory. It's more comfortable and we need to keep warm anyway." She rolled to his side, her head landing gently on his shoulder as if it was always meant to reside there. She placed her hand hesitantly against his chest and he sighed with longing at the sensation of her pressed against him. She was edgy, he could feel it in her tense muscles. "Relax," he said. He kissed the side of her head and lay back. "Go to sleep. We're both tired. How are your hands?"

There was silence for a minute. "They're sore," she whispered.

He fumbled under the blanket till he caught her hand in a tender grip, carefully smoothing the fingers against his chest. "Yeah, the cold is hell on fingers. They'll feel better in the morning."

Her body slowly relaxed and she sagged on his shoulder. The comfort was immense. Yes, he wanted more. Always more, his body urging him to act. But it wasn't the time, and she trusted him. That would have to be enough for tonight.

Now, if only he could sleep.

~~***~~

CHAPTER TWENTY NINE

Alex got up in the night to stoke the fire. By early morning, the wind had picked up again and he heard it howling through the trees around the cabin. That must mean the calm of yesterday, leaving the silence of the falling snow, was just the eye of the storm. Now it was back in full force. Likely the wolf was holed up somewhere as well, not roaming the forest in this weather.

Something flapped on the roof above his head. He hoped the shingles weren't trying to peel off. He wasn't sure how he'd repair a low-slope roof in these weather conditions. He hadn't noticed much in the way of tools and equipment lying around the cabin. Will Heverton either kept such items in his truck, or he didn't bother with repairs as a rule.

Although the cabin was basically sound, there were signs of neglect all around him. The gaps between the logs should have been filled during the summer months when the weather allowed it. He knew of several contractors who built with logs, and the caulking they used was different but the goal was the same—make sure the walls were weather-tight. He knew some up here in the north used a hay and mud compound to fill the gaps. Didn't cost anything, but worked quite well.

It was dim in the room, the heavy clouds and swirl of falling snow blocking out any light. He turned his head on the make-shift pillow. Glory slept on her side facing the wall, her back curved toward him and her rounded butt pressed against his side. Something lurched in his chest. This was killing him. Sleeping with her but not *sleeping* with her was a magnitude of stress he hadn't anticipated. How long were they going to be stuck here?

He carefully tugged his arm from beneath her pillow and slid his legs over the side of the mattress, planting his feet on the flimsy floor. The springs in the bedframe squeaked under his weight but she didn't stir. This had been a real trial for her. He figured the fear of what was happening had at least equalled the physical discomfort of cold and slogging through the deep snow.

He sloughed off the old boxers and put his own on, then headed toward the stairs. He'd tend the heater and get dressed downstairs. They were running low on firewood. Good thing Will Heverton had taken care of that part of the household chores at least.

~~*~~

Ryan drove his truck down the highway, heading for the turnoff to the Victoria airport. Glory was supposed to have called from up north to tell him she was on the flight, and he hadn't received anything from her. No message, no phone call. But she could have been caught in the same frantic race to board that he and the guys had when they'd finally arrived at the Fort St John airport.

He'd checked online. Her flight was on schedule, so he may as well show up and give her a lift home. He plugged his phone into the outlet on the dash and hit his speed dial for Alex. If his brother had gotten her there on time, he should be well within range of a cell phone tower right now. The call went immediately to voice mail.

That could mean all kinds of things. Perhaps his battery was dead and he'd forgotten to plug it in. Maybe he wasn't even aware of it yet, hadn't tried to use it since getting within distance of cell service.

The weather had been pretty rugged by the time they flew home from up there, and he'd heard it had ramped up even more after that. Some flights had been grounded. It would be interesting to hear Glory's story of what had happened.

He pulled into the parking lot and grabbed a ticket for the dash thinking this wouldn't take too long. Slamming out of the truck, he trotted into the Arrivals lounge and found a seat near the walkway where the passengers would soon appear.

He took a deep breath and tried to relax. It was almost Christmas, and he'd been too busy to pay attention. Josie would be expecting something from him, and he and Alex always coordinated on a nice present for Mum. He'd better get his thinking cap on, because there were only a few shopping days left before the big day.

He watched the electronic information board. The plane from Fort St John had just landed. The passengers would soon be arriving in the reception area. He stood when the first people walked through the doorway and took a position just outside the rope so Glory would see him as soon as she came by.

He waited. The number of people ebbed and flowed, and then trickled off to nothing. Still she didn't show. Maybe she'd stopped in the washroom. He'd had to do that on occasion, especially if he had too much to drink during the flight. When she got here, he'd keep that supposition to himself.

It became apparent there was no one else coming and he walked over to the guard on the other side of the roped off entrance. "I'm waiting for someone off the flight from Fort St John. Are there any more passengers?"

The fellow cupped his speaker and droned into it. There was a squawk from his ear piece and he shook his head. "No, sir," he said. "That flight's disembarked. The next one coming through is from Edmonton."

Ryan glanced behind him toward the luggage conveyor belt. Had she gotten by without him seeing her? He legged it down the hallway. Most people were gone now, but a few still waited, scrutinising the few pieces of luggage as they swept by. No Glory.

That was odd. He stepped outside and tried her cell. No answer. Still no answer from Alex. He called Pete, but he hadn't heard from either of them. When he phoned Eddie, it went to voicemail, so he left a message. Then he caught Mum at home.

"What do you mean. Why wouldn't she be on the flight?" Mum sounded worried.

Ryan muttered to himself. "I just wanted to know if she'd called the house, or if you've heard from Alex."

"No, to both of those." There was a pause. "You did say the weather was getting nasty. It's probably just the usual problem. Her flight didn't go because the weather was too bad."

"Yeah," Ryan gave a mental shrug. The flight *had* gone. She just wasn't on it, which probably meant they didn't get there in time to catch the plane. But no point in arguing with Mum. It would just raise concerns he didn't have any answers for.

"Probably," he muttered and rang off. Back at the information counter, he checked on the next flights. One from Fort St John would be in early tomorrow, and the next at noon. Well, he'd just have to make the trip back out here. Meanwhile, Alex better call.

~~***~~

CHAPTER THIRTY

Glory waited motionless in the bed until Alex had gone down the stairs before she rolled over and gazed around the room to the sound of snow pellets hitting the window. She'd woken to the comfort and warmth of his body pressed against her side, his arm beneath her head. The feeling was so reassuring in the midst of this turmoil and confusion.

At home, she would already be up and heading out to work. Ben would wonder where she was and why she hadn't called, or if she was sick. She always phoned in, although she seldom took a day off. And Dad would want to know how the trip went and why she didn't answer her phone.

She wiped a tear from her cheek and hunkered down under the covers. They smelled of stale sweat and wood smoke. The guy who lived here likely didn't launder his bedding very often. After all, where would he wash it? There certainly was no washing machine, although there was a wash tub hanging on the wall in the entrance.

She heard Alex tossing firewood into the heater downstairs. Who ever heard of a barrel heater? Yet, that's exactly what it was. A forty-five gallon drum laid on its side, with legs of bent metal bars welded to the underside. The bung hole became the damper. Someone had welded a round piece of metal to pull over it, opening and closing the air supply.

A square door had been cut out of the metal above the bung hole, and hinges installed. That's where Alex shovelled in the endless supply of firewood, some of the pieces so big they were simply tree trunks cut into lengths. A stove pipe had been cut and soldered onto the top at the far end, leading straight up through two floors to the roof.

It gave off a tremendous heat when fired up. The flat metal plate soldered to the top allowed them to heat food or melt snow over it. Right now she was hankering for breakfast. She just didn't know what it might consist of. Not beans, she prayed.

When she arrived downstairs, Alex had already gone outside, his parka missing from the back of the chair where his boots had also rested. It gave her the chance to get her clothes from the line above the heater and put them on where it was warm. She had her shirt buttoned and one leg in her jeans when he blew through the door on a swirl of snow with a huge armload of firewood.

"Yikes," she squeaked and backed hastily out of his way, trying to hop her other leg into the pants.

He grinned and dumped the wood in the box against the wall. "Sorry, lady. Did I interrupt something?"

She giggled and batted at his arm. "Very funny. Turn your back."

"Why? You're not indecent, far from it. I know what indecent looks like."

She stared at the smirk on his face but had to laugh at his silly remarks. She managed to pull her jeans up, snapping them closed. "You're impertinent," she said, sounding like a schoolmarm. "What's for breakfast?"

"Good question." He dumped his parka on the chair and put his arms around her shoulders. "How did you sleep? How are the fingers this morning?"

She rested her head on that thick shoulder and his arms tightened. "I slept fine," she murmured. She felt him press a kiss to the side of her head. It excited and confused her in equal measure. Pulling back, she held her hands out. "My fingers are on the mend." They were still tender and had remained bright red. "That colour will fade, right?" She gazed at him uncertainly. "I don't want my hands to look like that when I'm working with my students. They'll wonder what's wrong with me."

He bent his head to place a tender kiss on her fingers and smiled into her eyes. "I think they'll be fine. Maybe rub some lotion into them." He pointed at a bottle on the table. "Sit there while I figure out breakfast."

She slid onto the bench and reached for the bottle of lotion in the centre of the table. It smelled of honey and felt incredibly soothing on her skin. She scrutinized the shelves beside her. "I can't figure out what this guy eats," she said. "There are cans of beans and beef stew, and that's about it."

Alex had opened the door and spoke from the entry. "There's stuff out here as well." He appeared with a sack of oatmeal. "My guess is this is breakfast."

"Oh, good. I can eat that. Although…" She glanced around the room as if looking for a fridge. "No milk?"

"Nope, no milk. But there is brown sugar. We'll manage."

"I can do that," Glory said. She grabbed the pot from the top of the heater and found warm water filling it halfway. "Is that enough water, do you think?"

Alex peeked in and grinned. "Looks good to me."

"Okay." She squared her shoulders. "Where's the salt?"

"Yeah, I've been wondering that too."

They combed the shelves, pawing through an assortment of junk residing above the table. Glory found a box of salt on the proover over the cook stove. "That makes sense," she said, pouring some into her hand and dumping it into the pot of water. "He probably does most of his cooking on that stove instead of the heater."

Alex measured it with his gaze.

"I just don't see getting both of them going," she added. "We won't be here that long, surely. When can we leave, do you think?

Her worry must have been apparent because he took the bag of oatmeal from her hand and patted her shoulder. "Not long, Glory. This storm has to blow out pretty soon. This is the second day, so we've got to be nearing the end. Then we can get something done."

"Okay." She stirred the water as he poured oatmeal. "That's enough," she said as he kept pouring.

He looked doubtfully into the pot. "I'm pretty hungry."

She giggled. "Yes, of course. Sorry. I'm not used to feeding someone with…" She glanced at his heavy shoulders and back to his face. "Better add a bit more."

He shrugged. "I have a good appetite," he said.

"You mean two cans of beans won't keep you going?"

She smirked and he swatted her behind. "Very funny, you had some of those beans."

"Not many," she muttered and he gave a low laugh.

~~***~~

CHAPTER THIRTY ONE

Eddie glanced at the display of his cell, and answered on the second ring. "Ryan, what's up?" He pulled to the side of the street in Oak Bay in front of a small two-story stucco house built on a large lot. He'd been here many times, delivering mail order parcels to the pretty widow who lived here.

Ryan sounded flustered. "Have you heard from Alex?"

He pulled the phone from his ear and gazed at it in amazement before putting it back to the side of his head. "Why would I have heard from Alex?"

"I don't know, I'm just checking. Have you heard?"

"No, I haven't." Eddie tried to hide the irritation in his voice. "I don't expect to hear from him. He comes home, he goes to work..."

He heard a rude noise through the speaker. "Listen, Eddie. He didn't come home. He hasn't shown up and Glory didn't catch her plane last night. She wasn't on the flights I met today, either. They've disappeared."

Irritation was replaced with alarm bells ringing in his head. "Come on, nobody just disappears. I told you he was going to do a bedroom stop with that girl. Anyone could see it in his body language."

But he didn't really believe that. Alex would drive Glory to the airport and head home. He'd show up at work when he said he would. He was that kind of guy. "Did you check with Glory's family? Maybe someone knows something." Eddie didn't believe that either, but he was reaching for a logical explanation. "Call me back if you hear anything, and I'll do the same."

He pressed the button and put his cell phone down. He had other things to attend to. Glancing at the front door of the house, he pulled his log book out and found the parcel number. Rummaging in the back, he grabbed the package and climbed down from the delivery truck. The door of the house opened before he even got there, as he knew it would. This woman was hot and she was anxious.

Dressed in tight black pants and high heels, her bright blue sweater had a wide neck that allowed it to hang off one shoulder, showing deep cleavage and a lack of any type of bra, unless it was strapless, which he doubted. If he was a betting man, he'd place all his chips on her wearing nothing under that sweater.

"Mrs. Walters?" he said. "I have a parcel for you. I just need you to sign here." He held out the electronic recorder and waited for her to take it from his hand.

She gazed up at him with limpid sky-blue eyes that exactly matched the sweater. Were they contacts, or was she just very adept at finding the right colour in her clothes? "Wouldn't you like to come in for something to drink?" She chuckled. "I feel like I know you, you've brought so many parcels to my door."

Eddie gave a slow smile and rubbed the edge of his moustache with the tip of his finger. "Well, I guess I have time. I've got a few more deliveries tonight but it isn't that late." And he stepped through the door, closing it behind him.

He intended to call on Trudy tonight after finishing his shift, but there was no reason why he couldn't spend a few minutes warming up Mrs. Walters. Who knew what could happen? There was no getting around it, Eddie was one lucky sucker.

~~*~~

They spent the day poking around the log cabin to the whine of the wind howling through the trees and around the eaves. Glory found an accordion on the lower shelf of the bookcase and pulled it out, along with a mouth organ that had been shoved in a corner.

"Do you know this book?" Alex asked, picking his childhood favourite from the shelf.

She examined the cover. *The Last of the Mohicans*, by James Fennimore Cooper, had the figure of a woodsman emblazoned on the front. He was leaping high, moccasins on his feet, long hair and loincloth equally airborne.

"No." She glanced at him curiously. "Have you read it?"

"Yeah, when I was a kid. Listen to this." He flipped open the cover and turned to Chapter One.

It was a feature peculiar to the colonial wars of North America, that the toils and dangers of the wilderness were to be encountered before the adverse hosts could meet. A wide and apparently an impervious boundary of forests severed the possessions of the hostile provinces of England and France.

She laughed. "Sounds so familiar, doesn't it? Just look around us at the wide boundary of forests."

He grinned and nodded.

"Read some more," she said and settled at the table. So Alex read the first chapter, then the second.

When he stopped, she sighed and gazed at him. "It's a romance in wilderness form," she said.

He narrowed his eyes as he held her gaze. "A romance, eh? That sounds interesting."

Flustered, she quickly stood from the bench. "I've decided what we'll have for dinner. I gather we aren't going anywhere today." She looked a question at him.

His shoulders came up in a shrug. "I can't see it. It's too dangerous to go wandering out there in this weather. I'm hopeful tomorrow I can walk down the road and find some help."

"That's what I think, too," she said. "I can make pancakes, there's flour and baking powder. And I found a can of pineapple. How does that sound?"

"Pretty good." His lips curved in a grin. "Let's add a can or two of beef stew. I need a bit more than pancakes."

"I know. Can I cook them on that heater?"

Alex nodded and rose. "It's plenty hot. You mix the batter, I'll bring in the wood for the night. It'll be dark soon.

When dinner was cleared away, Glory washed dishes and Alex reached for the accordion. He began to pump the bellows, his fingers meandering up and down the ivory and black keys until he settled on a tune. He began to sing softly.

Glory turned in surprise. "I know that song. My father sang it when I was little. *I was dancing with my darling to the Tennessee Waltz, when an old friend I happened to see. I introduced him to my loved one and while they were dancing, my friend stole my sweetheart from me.*"

Her mouth turned down. "I always thought it was such a sad song. But Dad liked it."

Setting the accordion aside, Alex reached for her hand and pulled her onto his knee. "Come here," he said. "It's just an old song, there are plenty like it. Why so sad?"

She pushed her lips out in a pout and leaned on his massive shoulder. The man was a muscled machine. "No reason."

"Come on, there must be a reason." He rubbed a hand up her back and held her against his thick chest.

"My mother, mostly," she said. "Dad is a really nice man, but Mother is something else."

He remained silent, his fingers conducting a two-step on the back of her neck.

"Mother made a move on my boyfriend," she muttered. "I don't trust her now."

He let out a breath that she hadn't been aware he was holding. "I wondered what that was about," he said. "You were pretty angry when she came to my place and I gave her a cup of coffee."

Glory glanced away. She felt awkward, acting like a kid where her mother was concerned. "Sorry," she offered. "It caught me off guard and I got my ire up."

"Yes, your ire. Please don't point it at me. Do you still see this boyfriend?"

She turned in surprise to catch his lips curled at the corners in a grin. She opened her mouth to say something foolish and he kissed her, one hand on the back of her head to urge her down to his mouth. It was magnetic, as if he had flipped a switch and was now pulling at her with his strong attraction.

But she wasn't into men right now. She had made that decision. A decision that seemed to fly out the window when he placed his mouth on hers. She parted her lips and invited him in.

~~***~~

CHAPTER THIRTY TWO

Frustrated, Ryan got back in his pickup and fired the engine. Again, no Glory on the last flight of the day from the north. The airport parking lot was jammed with vehicles and it was slow getting back on the highway.

He couldn't keep driving out here in the hopes she'd turn up. It was past time to take further action. Pulling to the side of the road, he grabbed his cell phone and called the local police detachment. After being put on hold twice, he finally got through to the constable on duty.

No, his brother hadn't disappeared in Victoria. No, not even on the island. He explained several times what had happened. There had been no help from the cell phone company as to where Alex or his phone were located. The Coopers said he and Glory had departed as planned the morning after the wedding.

Ryan left all the details he had, promised to call into the detachment office to sign the form, then made a second phone call. He caught Mrs. Cooper at home and asked her to call the RCMP, because Alex and Glory had disappeared.

Firing the truck again, Ryan headed home. Time to fill his mother in on the situation. He'd been hedging since Glory didn't show the first time, which of course meant they didn't know where Alex was either. But he couldn't hide it from her any longer.

~~*~~

Glory woke to bright sunlight glowing through the upstairs window. The wind had stopped. She turned her head, but to her disappointment the bed was empty on the other side. She'd been anxious and excited when she climbed into bed last night. Alex was a very attractive man. She was drawn to him in a way she hadn't felt before.

She'd begun shuddering with cold again and it had taken a lot to calm down and relax into the warmth of the blankets. But she must have fallen asleep before he got there, because she didn't remember him coming upstairs and crawling in.

The heater door banged downstairs, and she heard the sound of firewood being hurled into the belly of the beast. Alex was looking after things.

They'd survived the night and it looked like the storm was over. Maybe they'd get home today. The thought eased some of the tension in her belly. This had been a very scary adventure, yet Alex had taken care of her. She grew hot at the thought. Sleeping beside him had been wonderful. His body was warm and hard, muscles rippling under the skin all over, but especially on his shoulders and chest.

She rolled to her side. Her hands weren't as sore now. Perhaps they were on the mend. She'd never known cold like that, it pierced a body to the marrow and froze all the extremities. Ploughing through the snow behind Alex, her scarf had been wrapped across her lower face to cover her nose and mouth, and she'd pulled the toque down over her forehead. But still she shivered, and the shaking didn't stop. Now she felt luxuriously warm and comfortable.

She remembered turning in the middle of the night to find Alex gone from the bed. The lantern light was on below and she heard the fire being stoked. Then the light went out and his tread sounded on the stairs. She'd rolled away as he slid into bed behind her. His cool body cuddled against hers, so that his knees pressed against the backs of her legs. Soon they were both warm and his arm was wrapped firmly around her, one hand cradling her breast. She'd slept.

Now she heard footsteps and Alex poked his head through the opening of the stairwell. When he saw she was awake, he grinned and took the last steps. "The storm's passed."

"I guessed, can't hear the wind." She smiled at him. "How long have you been up?" Excitedly, she took in his bare chest and borrowed baggy undershorts with a sweeping glance.

"I just woke. I was stoking the fire." He sat on the edge of the mattress, which dipped under his weight as the springs creaked. "How are you this morning?"

"I'm fine." She gazed into his dark blue eyes and felt something stir in her mid-section. It had been so reassuring to sleep beside him. Well, on top of him, really, because he was heavier, so the mattress sagged under him and she just tumbled in his direction all night.

"You look fine," he murmured. He moved closer. "You look wonderful." One hand brushed her hair off her forehead and tucked it behind her ear. Then he leaned in and laid his mouth over hers. His lips were hot and firm, his lashes swept her cheek as his eyes closed. Excitement curled in her breast and then his hand was there against the old tee shirt she wore, caressing and fanning her nipple beneath the thin cloth. She opened her mouth for air and his tongue invaded.

"Oh, my, Glory," he said against her throat. "You kiss like an angel." Then his mouth was back on hers.

Sometime later, he lifted his head and it took a moment for her eyes to open. His were dark and mesmerizing. "I want you. I want to make love to you."

She gazed into his eyes for what seemed an endless moment as excitement churned inside, then she ran a palm across his bristled cheek. "Yes," she whispered. "I want that, too."

There followed a slow shifting of bodies and hands, his leg over hers, his mouth on her skin. She clung to his shoulders, feeling the mass of muscle and sinew beneath her fingers. He lifted her effortlessly across the mattress to make room as he settled beside her. His hands were everywhere, soothing and coaxing as her breath came faster.

He was breathing heavily as well, she wasn't the only one affected. When she clasped her fingers through his hair, he reared up and nailed her to the mattress with a kiss that staggered her. His hand snaked under the old shirt and his mouth soon followed, latching onto a nipple. She arched her back in response. "Alex. Oh, heavens."

His mouth came back to hers as he pushed the sagging boxers down over her hips. He managed to get his own underwear off, then settled between her legs, holding himself off with one hand braced against the mattress. He gazed into her eyes as the blankets tumbled to the floor.

Then the bed shuddered under her. There was the sound of something snapping and breaking. Alex lifted his head in alarm. The bed shifted, then tilted sideways as one leg of the bedframe seemed to drop out from under them. Glory slid across the mattress toward the floor, his knee the only thing holding her in place.

~~***~~

CHAPTER THIRTY THREE

Alex struggled with his next breath and placed one foot on the floor, bracing to keep Glory from falling. Then he grabbed the edge of the mattress and heaved. It slipped jerkily off the old springs onto the floor and she landed on her back, Alex balanced precariously above her. He braced his arms either side of her head. "Are you okay?" he whispered.

She nodded wordlessly, her stomach still flipped upside down by the sudden flight from the bed frame to the plywood beneath her.

"Me too," he said, and knelt between her legs on the mattress. "Couldn't be better." He continued to woo her with his hands and his mouth and soon she felt his urgency pressing against her entrance. His hand moved down to guide his advance and she held her breath. But he slid smoothly in, pausing as he filled her. The connection between them was instant, and at the same time, overwhelming. Confusion clogged her chest, yet euphoria hovered in her belly and lower.

"Glory." His breath was coming in bellows deep in his chest. "Are you all right? Does it feel…"

"It feels perfect." She pressed her mouth against his bicep and bit down, trying to contain her emotions. He jerked to attention and began a smooth advance and retreat, leading her along, drawing her along, until she couldn't bear the tension any more and groaned aloud as she came.

~~*~~

Alex was drained. Every ounce of energy had been expended and he sagged on the lumpy mattress, Glory's head resting on his shoulder and her hair spread across his chest. The strands seemed alive, caressing his skin. He ran his other hand down her back and over her buttocks. Her skin glowed, her body rounded and womanly.

"We could do that again," he said, a smile in his voice.

"Maybe in a few minutes," she said. He felt rather than heard her laugh. She beamed up at him and his heart expanded in his chest. It was painful and he flinched under the pressure. Was he having a heart attack, like his father? He didn't think so. But he'd felt this before, the night he first kissed her in the truck outside her townhouse. A heart event of a different kind.

He laid his lips over hers and began a leisurely kiss that expanded and grew until his chest was tight and his heart was working hard to catch up to his breathing. He caressed her breasts, then worked his way down to place his mouth where his hand had been.

He thought he heard a noise from the road. He raised his head only to be distracted by the sight of the dark blond curls between her thighs. His fingers found their way there, threading through to the secret place damp and slippery from their lovemaking. He felt himself getting hard.

The noise was louder and he sat up to listen. Yes, that was an engine, and it was closer. Damn, this might be their best chance.

"There's someone out there," he said. He leapt to his feet and jumped over Glory to grab his shorts and pull them on. Dashing by the window he glanced out but couldn't see anything in the bright sunlight. The sound increased in volume.

Running down the stairs, he grabbed his jeans and pulled them on over his erection with difficulty. He had to tend to business now. He pulled on socks and boots and bent to tie the laces as the noise loomed closer. Glory's head appeared at the top of the stairs. She was stark naked.

He stopped and stared, then belatedly met her gaze as heat climbed his cheeks. "I can hear an engine," he said. "Some one's out there. Maybe get dressed."

Her hand automatically rose to cover her breasts, her face and neck showing the abuse of his three-day beard. He grinned and flung a shirt on, then his parka and dashed for the door.

The sun on the snow was blinding. He squinted against the glare as his fingers fumbled with the buttons on his shirt. Sure enough, something moved between the trees along the drive. A truck slowly appeared, a plow attached to the front throwing up a huge spume of snow into the woods. Someone was clearing the drive on this old cabin?

Alex stared in astonishment.

The truck pulled a wide arc, ploughing a circle in the drive, then drew to a stop. The driver climbed out, leaving the engine running. He was a big man wearing old padded pants and a weathered black parka, rubber boots reaching his knees. He pulled a torn glove off one hand and ran his hand through thinning grey hair.

"Hi, there," he said.

Alex nodded. "Hi, yourself. I have to say, I'm glad to see you."

The fellow grinned, showing a couple of missing teeth on the bottom. "I figured you would be."

"You did?"

"Yup." The guy turned to glance back down the driveway. "Saw the truck in the ditch." He waved his arm in the general direction of the road. "I knew Will went to town to visit his sister over Christmas. Then I saw the smoke from the chimney so figured someone was in here. Name's Jim, Jim Flegg."

He shook the man's hand. "Alex Vecchio," he said. "This cabin saved our lives. I got going down the wrong road and tried to turn around. Couldn't even see the ditches."

"Yeah." The fellow shrugged. "Snow blind," he said. "Can't tell one place from another in that light. Want some help getting the truck out?"

Alex laughed. "Sure do. Just let me tell my girlfriend."

Jim looked with interest toward the cabin door. "Girlfriend, eh? Lucky you. Don't think this place has seen any action since it was built. Will is going to be downright jealous when he hears."

Alex smiled to himself as he walked back to the door of the cabin. This had worked out better than he could possibly have hoped. He was very grateful this fellow had arrived in time to help them escape the snow. And equally grateful he hadn't arrived any earlier than he did.

~~***~~

CHAPTER THIRTY FOUR

As the Manx Construction pickup was eased out of the ditch and hauled onto the road, the band equipment in the back crashed and banged together as it tumbled about in the bed of the truck. Alex cringed, hoping the damage wouldn't be too bad. Glory's keyboard was in a case, as were the guitars and violin. Hopefully Ryan's drums didn't get spiked by something.

The engine wouldn't turn over and, to his alarm, the battery sounded weak. "It's the cold," Jim Flegg volunteered. "Let's get it off the road and up the drive to Will's place. We can warm it up from there."

Alex didn't know how they would warm it up at a place with no electricity or operational equipment, but Jim had all kinds of ideas. He took a snow shovel with a broad metal blade from the back of his truck and carefully loaded it with glowing coals from the barrel heater, then carried it outside. He shoved it along the snowy ground until it was positioned right beneath the engine, then threw a tarp over the hood. "Give it a few minutes," he said. "It's too cold to start now, but it'll be good in a bit."

He trundled back into the cabin and made himself at home on the bench, introducing himself to Glory. "Got any coffee?" he asked companionably.

Glory blushed prettily and promptly put the pot on to heat. She bustled around gathering their things together while Alex went upstairs. He gazed at the old mattress lying on the floor as the heat of memory rose in his chest. Seizing a corner, he heaved it back onto the bed frame, brushing his hand over the bottom sheet. He hoped they hadn't left any telltale marks on the sheets because there were no clean linens to replace them.

Then he looked at the hole in the floor where one leg of the bedframe still hung through the thin plywood. Jim Flegg was right downstairs and he didn't want to have to explain what had happened.

"Need some help up there?" Flegg called. "I've got some tools in the back of my truck."

Alex came down the stairs and met the man's curious gaze. "That's good," he said, "because I don't and there doesn't seem to be anything around here to use for repairs." Alex was red in the face by the time a patch had been applied on the thin plywood floor, to Jim's accompanying remarks about how that bed had probably never seen so much activity.

The coffee was ready and Jim settled in to enjoy a cup. "New around here?" he asked.

Glory choked back a laugh. "You can say that again."

He gave her a good-natured grin. "Little alarming at first, eh? Well, you did fine, and Will is just gonna be glad you found a safe place to wait out the storm."

Alex glanced at the mound of mail on the shelf. "I'd like to leave him something for the food we used and all."

Jim waved that off. "He don't need it."

But before they trooped out to the trucks, Alex slid some money into one of the envelopes, added his business card with a 'thank you' written on the back and put it on the table under a coffee mug. He closed the damper on the heater, and threw the latch on both doors.

Jim pulled his pickup alongside the Manx Construction vehicle and shook out a set of jumper cables. The truck started almost right away, but Jim didn't seem surprised. He just nodded. "Batteries don't work when it's too cold," he said.

He drew the snow shovel out and emptied the remaining coals on the ground before putting it back in his truck. Alex thanked him heartily and tried to press some money into his fist, but Jim laughed and shook his hand instead.

They were on their way home. Looking back in the rear-view mirrow, Alex saw the snow piled high against the walls of the cabin, smoke still leisurely curling from the metal stovepipe. The deep path from the front door to the woodpile was well trampled from the many trips he'd made fetching firewood, and the drive was cleared with drifts of snow ploughed into the trees on either side. There was no sign of the wolf or the trail he had trod around the yard.

The place had served them well, in more ways than one. He glanced at Glory, wishing they'd had just a little more time before Jim Flegg appeared. He dragged his attention back to the road.

~~*~~

The main highway out of Big Smokey had been ploughed, and it was fairly easy going all the way to Prophet River, with little traffic. This was the route they should have taken to begin with. Alex stopped at the gas station to top up the tank and found some packaged sandwiches to take with them on the next section of the drive to Prespatou.

Glory disappeared into the bathroom and was gone a long time, not that there was a lineup. He didn't see another female the whole time they were in that small community. When she reappeared, her hair had been done, barrettes clipped on to hold it back, and she wore makeup. He liked how she looked, but found he didn't need that stuff. She was beautiful without the extra help.

Back on the road, he plugged in his cell phone, hoping for some reception.

"Nothing yet?" Glory asked.

"Nope. The guy at the gas station said it would be closer to Wonowon before we can make a call."

She sighed, and he reached to take her hand in his as he turned onto the road and headed south. The sun was blinding on the snow and he had to let her hand go to pull the visor down and fumble for his sunglasses. "Don't worry, Glory. It won't be long now. You'll be able to phone your Dad and let him know you're okay."

"And Ben. I'd hate to lose my job because of this."

"He'd be a fool to let you go," he said and caught the surprised glance she shot in his direction. "Well, he would. None of this is your fault, and you received permission for the days you took. I'm sure he's smart enough to understand."

She laughed lightly. "Ben's a good guy. I'll be all right. What about you?"

"I'm okay. The Manx brothers are very businesslike but they value their people. They know I'd be there if I could. Besides, Jim steps in on the job if there's a problem so he's probably taken over as foreman of the worksite until they hear from me." He didn't mention that it was his mother he was most worried about. No point in looking like a wimp. Or would she see it that way? He glanced at her sitting so straight against the black leather seat, her purse on her knees and sunglasses settled on her pert little nose. He looked back at the road. She wasn't overly fond of her own mother.

As if reading his thoughts, she said, "Your mum must be worried."

He nodded self-consciously. "I'm sure of it. I just hope Ryan's been reasonable and didn't get her all alarmed."

"Ryan's a good guy," she said, touching his arm. "He'll do the right thing."

A conflict of emotions hit him square in the chest. Pride in his younger brother, that she should recognize his strong qualities. And jealousy that she complimented Ryan and not him. He felt like a juvenile, yet the thought stayed tangled in his mind.

Then she leaned her head against his shoulder. "Your folks must have been pretty special people to raise two sons like you and Ryan. You looked after me, Alex, even when we were lost in the forest. I can hardly believe we survived, but you didn't seem concerned about it. You just did what you thought had to be done to keep us warm and dry."

His throat tightened so all the words got lodged in his gullet. He cleared his throat carefully. "Just did what I could, Glory. It was my fault we were in that situation in the first place. I'm sorry about that. I know you were frightened."

She nodded. "A little. I admit it. But not for long." She rubbed her head against his arm and he nearly drove off the road. His chest was so constricted he was having trouble breathing. She was like a magnet, and he was fast being drawn into her force field.

~~***~~

CHAPTER THIRTY FIVE

Twenty miles out of Prespatou, Alex looked at the flashing lights in his rear-view mirror in astonishment and began searching for a place to pull off the narrow road. Then the cop hit the siren a couple of times, and he stopped on the verge, although it was barely wide enough for traffic to pass—if traffic were to show up, which hadn't happened yet.

"Man, what is his hurry?" he muttered. "It's not as if I can out-run him on this road." He put the truck in park and powered down the window, reaching in his back pocket for his wallet. By the time the cop arrived at the window, Alex had his driver's licence in hand.

"Some ID please," the cop said, frost clinging to his hair and eyelashes as he stood in the crusty snow.

"Right here." Alex handed it over.

The cop read it carefully, then looked up. "Can I see the registration for the truck please?"

Alex reared back. "For the truck? Sure, but it's not my truck." He reached past Glory and opened the glove box, pulling out some papers. "Here you go. It belongs to my employer, Manx Construction."

The cop took the documents and went back to his vehicle. He climbed inside and seemed occupied with his dashboard equipment.

"What's he doing?" Glory asked, cranking her neck to look behind.

"I don't know. I wasn't speeding, so I can't figure out—" He glanced in the rear-view mirror. "He's working on his laptop. Don't know what he thinks he's going to find."

Alex rolled the window up to keep them warm and they waited tensely as the engine idled. Finally the police officer climbed out and headed back to Alex's window.

"It's this way," the cop said conversationally. "There's been a watch put out for you and your truck."

"On what grounds?" Alex demanded. "I haven't done anything."

"No, no. More of a safety watch. No one knew where you were and you didn't show up home when expected. So we've been keeping an eye out in case you were in trouble and needed help."

"Ahhh." Alex nodded his head and glanced at Glory. "Our families must have called the cops. Well," he turned back to the window. "That's a good thing. We're fine, by the way. The truck is okay, we're okay. Does this mean you'll be letting our folks know you found us? Because we can't get any cell phone service right now—"

The officer laughed and nodded. "No service till just outside Wonowon. But yes, I'll be sending out word that you've been found and are in one piece." He turned to Glory. "You're Glory Stephens, I take it. Can I see some ID?"

Glory dug in her purse for her licence and Alex turned to clarify. "You'll call my family?" he asked again.

"Yes, right away. I already checked the wanted information for Ms. Stephens picture, but with the ID…"

Glory handed her licence over and the cop studied it carefully before passing it back. "Well, then, the best possible outcome. What happened that you fell off the radar?

Alex gave the ghost of a laugh. "We had an accident near Big Smokey. The truck ended up in the ditch and we didn't get it out until the storm had passed."

The cop nodded. "Yeah, that was some storm. Obviously, you found a place to wait it out. That's good news. I'll let you go and send in my report. Drive carefully."

Alex rolled the window up and sat for a minute in relief. He gusted out a breath.

Glory rubbed his back. "I know. A big weight lifted. Everyone will hear that we're okay, even before we can get cell service. We can relax now."

He leaned across and pressed a kiss to her mouth, then kissed her again. He caressed the side of her face, thinking her eyes were like mirrors, reflecting back his excitement at just being with her. "The next thing is to put you on a plane. When we get to Fort St John, you'll be on the next flight south."

~~*~~

"Mum, did you hear?" Ryan darted through the back door of their home. He felt like life was a lot brighter than it had been just hours before. The uncertainty of whether Alex was coming back had been almost unbearable. Is that what his older brother had felt when their father died? That now it was all up to him? Because Ryan had felt the weight of the family rested on him, the responsibility for everything, and he hadn't been ready for it. Now it was gone, replaced by sheer relief.

He found his mother stirring a pot on the stove. "Oh, wow. Is that hamburger soup?" He leaned over to sniff the aroma.

"Did I hear what?" She batted him out of the way and scraped a cutting board full of finely chopped celery into the broth. "And yes, it's hamburger soup."

He ginned, then tugged his phone out of his pocket. "About Alex. Did you hear about Alex?"

Her expression transformed to uncertainty. "Alex?" she said. "What about him?"

"The cops phoned. They said—" Ryan stopped talking as the house phone sounded.

Mrs. Vecchio's cheeks went white as she darted to the counter and grabbed the handset. "Hello?" Her voice was querulous.

"Mum, it's okay." Ryan laid a hand on her shoulder as he whispered encouragement in her ear. "It's good news."

"Mrs. Vecchio?" A formal voice came from the speaker. "This is the Oak Bay police calling. Is this Mrs. Vecchio?"

"Yes." Her voice had faded. "Yes, it's me."

"We have news about your son and his friend. They've been found and were spoken to by a member of the RCMP on the highway near Prophet River in northern BC. They were both fine, and are heading south. Alex Vecchio expects to be home tomorrow, as he is driving the whole way. Just thought you'd want to know."

She seemed lost for words, so after a moment Ryan plucked the phone from her hand. "Hi," he said, "this is Ryan Vecchio. My mum is a bit overwhelmed by the news. But just to clarify, Alex is driving down and expects to get here tomorrow, right? And Glory is flying in tonight."

The officer paused and cleared his throat. "Just checking my notes. Yes, that sounds right. They were out of cell phone service apparently, but should be able to contact you directly once they get closer to a place called Wonowon."

"Yes, that's what I heard. Thanks a lot, I'll tell Mum." Ryan hung up the phone and turned to watch his mother. She'd seated herself at the table and was staring into space, unmoving.

"Mum? You okay?"

She didn't stir for a moment. Then as she shifted on the seat, a tear spilled over one eyelid and rolled down her cheek. "Yes, I'm fine."

"You don't look fine." He sat down and pulled his chair close to hers. Putting an arm around her shoulders, he leaned into her. "It's okay, Mum. They're safe. Alex is coming home. You know what he's like. He's as reliable as anyone I know."

She sniffed and nodded. "I know. You both are, both my wonderful sons. Holy moly!" She leaped to her feet at the sound of liquid sizzling on the stovetop. "The soup!"

~~***~~

CHAPTER THIRTY SIX

Eddie parked one block over and spent the next ten minutes walking up and down the sidewalk. Trudy had said to arrive at ten o'clock. No earlier. He wasn't going to blow this encounter. He was wound up enough to explode if he didn't get a chance at this woman, and soon. He'd been waiting and talking and encouraging—by now he had nothing left in the tank for seduction. It was action all the way. Tonight was the night. On the other hand, he couldn't arrive before ten o'clock.

Nor did it seem wise to park his car right outside her house. From what he understood, Alex had no interest in her any more. As for Rolf, he didn't know the man personally but he'd heard enough about him to know he might be a loose cannon where Trudy was concerned. On the other hand, if Trudy said Rolf was gone, well he'd go with that.

He checked his watch again and turned around to head back up the street. As he approached her house, he noted the lights were on over the front door and in the living room but the outside of the place was looking a bit rundown. Maybe Rolf wasn't a yard-work kind of guy. He knew when Alex lived here, the lawn was mowed, the bushes cut back. But not now. It could be just one more welcome sign that Rolf was long gone.

He walked up the front step and stopped at the door, pressing his thumb on the button. The *dingdong* sounded loudly in the hall. He waited but didn't hear anything from within.

He pressed the button again. Finally he heard the sound of footsteps coming toward the entry, then the door opened. Trudy stood there, an enticing smile on her face. She wore a short silky housecoat tied loosely around her waist and gaping at the neckline. His mouth fell open.

"Eddie! I hoped it was you. Come on in." *Who did she think was going to be standing there? Dressed like that, it had better be him at the door.* As she stepped back, he noticed her feet were bare, the toenails painted a dark red. She waved him through and leaned past him to close the door. He caught a whiff of some strong perfume, a spicy and floral combination that caused the hair on the back of his neck to stir in some kind of animal reaction.

This was going to be fun, he was positive. Not that he'd ever had any doubt. But Trudy was difficult to predict, and Alex always said she was changeable. Happy and cooperative one minute, resentful and vengeful the next. This looked very much like the former.

"This way." She led him to the kitchen at the back of the house. "Would you like a drink?" Her gaze was little-girl innocent and slightly wistful.

"Love one," Eddie said. He grinned and felt his moustache twitch. He could play games as well as anyone. "Can we drink it in bed?"

At first she looked shocked, and he wondered if he'd made a misstep. But then her expression turned mischievous. "What a good idea. You carry the wine, I'll get the glasses."

Trudy led him up the stairs to the second floor, hips swaying enticingly under the silky housecoat, and through the first doorway. It was a large bedroom, the bed at least a king size. *Well why not?* Trudy was tall and Eddie took up a lot of room himself. The perfect setup to play.

"Put the wine bucket there." She pointed to the nightstand and set down two wine glasses. "You can pour."

"No problem." He pulled the cork, poured what turned out to be a nice chardonnay into both glasses and handed one to her. "Here you go, gorgeous." Her face turned rosy and she smiled as she took a sip.

"I'll just put my jacket over here." Eddie crossed the room and hung his jacket on the back of the chair, toeing his shoes off. He undid the top buttons of his shirt with one hand as he crawled across the bed toward her, watching for her reaction. Her smile inched up a notch, and he grinned and buried his face in her cleavage.

"I knew it," he mumbled. "You smell like a garden, a beautiful garden."

She sighed and, setting her wine glass down, fell back against the pillows. "Eddie, you are such a guy."

"A guy? Is that good?" He didn't wait for a reply, using a finger to part the lapels of her housecoat. One breast came into view, the nipple distended. He wondered if she'd had surgery. This was one large breast, heavy and tight under the skin. *Who cared?* Not him.

He latched on, supporting himself with one hand while struggling to undo the rest of the buttons on his shirt with the other.

"Let me help," she said. "I can do that." Her fingers flicked his belt open and began on the zipper of his pants.

Eddie paused to catch his breath as the zipper slid down, his erection straining against the thin barrier of his underwear. Her hand reached inside to catch the elastic and pull it out of the way as he popped free.

"Can I come back tomorrow night?" he muttered.

She laughed and lowered her head. "You sure can."

~~*~~

Alex pulled the truck into line for drop-off at the air terminal in Fort St John, and shut off the engine. He climbed out and reached Glory's door in time to open it for her as she descended to the sidewalk. His mouth was tight. "I'll get your bag," he said.

"Thank you." *What was wrong?* She watched him open the back door and drag her suitcase out, setting it on the ground near her boot. She reached for it, but he grabbed the handle and extended it so she could wheel it behind her.

"I hate to leave you like this," he said. "I should stay and make sure you get your flight. Make sure everything is okay. They booked you in, but things can change."

"Oh, Alex." She kissed his cheek in relief at his words, and he turned his head to catch her mouth with his. The kiss turned intense and she thought she might have fallen if not for the support of his strong arms. She lowered her forehead to press it against his deep chest.

"I'll be all right," she murmured, relishing the feel of his body against hers. "And you need to get going. It's still a long way home."

"I know," he muttered into her hair. "I just hate to go. I'll call you and leave a message when I find a hotel. Not sure where I'll stop, but far enough south that I'm home tomorrow night, that's for sure."

He lifted her chin and gave her another searing kiss. "I'll see you just as soon as I can."

She smiled tremulously. "I'll be fine. Drive safely please." It felt new and different to be talking to him as if they were in a relationship. Nothing had been said to that effect, yet she was pretty sure this was a commitment kind of guy. He didn't act like he'd have a quick fling and then walk away.

She felt his gaze resting on her back as she trundled into the terminal. The doors swished shut behind her and she stalled to look back as he climbed into the cab and started the engine. She'd see him tomorrow night hopefully.

Shuffling through security, she found a seat in the waiting lounge. With more than half an hour until boarding, she pulled a novel from her suitcase and flipped it open to the book mark.

An older woman sat down beside her. "Going to Victoria?" she asked.

Glory smiled. "I hope so, since that's where this whole crowd is headed."

The woman laughed. "And leaving your special guy behind. That must be tough."

She gave the woman a quizzical look. "How do you mean?"

"I saw how he kissed you goodbye." She gave her a meaningful glance. "Can't be easy to leave *that* to travel south."

"Oh," Glory didn't know what to say. "I hope we didn't embarrass you," she finally offered.

"Nope. It was a treat, I just want to congratulate you, don't often see stuff that hot."

Her cheeks warm, Glory looked back at her book, hoping they'd make the boarding call soon.

~~***~~

CHAPTER THIRTY SEVEN

When Glory got off the plane in Victoria, both Dad and Ryan Vecchio were waiting for her. She ran into her father's arms and wrapped him tight in a hug.

"There you are, my girl," he muttered into her hair. "There you are." She was crying by the time he let her go.

She turned to Ryan.

"How are you?" he said. He opened his arms so she hugged him too, laughing along with her tears. "I'm sorry you drove all the way out here. I couldn't get any messages out during the flight to warn you my dad was meeting me. Have you two met? This is Howard Stephens. Dad, meet Ryan Vecchio." The men shook hands.

"It's okay." Ryan's shaggy bangs fell over his eyes and he shook them away. "I knew your dad was going to be here. I just wanted to know what happened, and how Alex is."

"Oh, of course. Why don't we—" Glory pointed down the concourse to the restaurants. Soon they had picked up her suitcase and were seated in a booth together. "Just tea," Glory said to the waiter, "any kind of herbal tea. You should see the stuff we drank up there, thick black coffee."

The two men leaned in to hear more and Glory ended up telling the whole story—about taking a different road, sliding into the ditch in the storm and finding a cabin to hole up in. "I think we were just lucky to find that place."

Her father nodded emphatically. "That's for sure."

"Although," she hastened to add, "we had passed other driveways before we stopped to turn around. So if we didn't find that one, we would have kept going to the next place."

Ryan raised his brows but glanced at her father and said nothing. Finally he asked, "How was Alex when he left you at the terminal?"

Her cheeks grew warm and she took a sip of tea to give herself time to get composed. "He was fine," she said. "He had all the band equipment with him, and we stopped to check. Nothing seemed to be damaged from being jostled in the bed of the truck. We were worried about the drums."

Ryan waved that way. "How were the roads?"

"The roads were clear the last fifty miles into Fort St John. I imagine they'll be good the rest of the way down. But I haven't seen a weather report so I'm not sure."

Her father shifted in his seat. "It looks good from what I've seen. Some rain in the Fraser Valley, but nothing more than that."

Ryan leaned back. "You guys were lucky."

She nodded. "We were. But Alex knew what he was doing. He kept us safe." Her jaw was tight and she had trouble meeting his brother's gaze. This relationship, if that's what it was, was so new, she was uncomfortable talking about it. So she did her best to talk around it, not sure how successful it was.

"I have to say," she added, "I'm very glad to be home. I'm also pretty tired." She stifled a yawn. "And I guess I'm working tomorrow morning. I haven't gotten hold of Ben, but I think I'd better show up at five-thirty. He's probably been doing my shift and will be pretty relieved to see me."

Ryan nodded and slapped his hand on the table. "Yes, I have work tomorrow too. We'd best get going."

"Thanks for everything, Ryan." Glory leaned to give him a one-armed hug. "Say hi to your mum, and tell her Alex was just fine when I last saw him."

Ryan broke into a big smile. "I will, thanks."

Dad grabbed her suitcase and led her out to his truck in the parking lot. "In you get, we're going home."

Glory was asleep before they approached the outskirts of the city, and Howard woke her when he pulled up in front of the townhouse. "Here you go," he said. He turned the engine off. "Got your keys?"

Glory fumbled in her purse as Dad pulled her suitcase out of the back seat and wheeled it onto the sidewalk. He grabbed the handle and carried it to her door. "What about food? You got something in there to eat?" He shoved a bag at her with his other hand. "Just got a few things to tide you over till you can tend to details."

She teared up again and had to give him another big hug before she got her door unlocked. Dad carried everything in and put the sack on her small table. "Have a look around, love. See if you need anything else."

"I'm fine Dad. Just tired. I'll be okay now."

She locked the door behind him and collapsed on the unmade bed. Shuffling her clothes off and onto the floor, she pulled up the covers. The last thing she remembered was fumbling to set an alarm before she turned out the light.

~~*~~

Alex drove until his vision blurred and the alarm in his head urged him to get off the road. He'd passed Prince George an hour ago, and saw the signs for the town of Quesnel approaching.

He pulled into the first motel he spotted with a decent sign. Yes, they had a room. No food, though. He registered, then backed out of his parking spot and found a fast food joint, taking care of supper in fifteen minutes. Then he was locked in his room.

It was a decent size, with all the amenities most basic rooms provided. After a quick shower, he climbed into bed, the news on as he sent texts to Glory, then Ryan and Jim Manx.

When he woke in the middle of the night, the television was still on, and he reached to shut it off.

~~*~~

Benjamin gave her an incredulous look when Glory appeared in the doorway of his shop that morning. It was five-thirty and as usual, he had just unlocked the door. Tom hovered behind his shoulder, waiting to get into the kitchen.

"Where have you been? Your father called yesterday to say you'd been detained, but he was unsure when you'd be back."

Tom gave her a smirk. "Took a holiday without letting us know, huh?"

Glory swatted his thick arm. "I did not. You'll be amazed when I tell you about my adventures."

"Well, let's get the batter mixed and the water on before we hear that story," said Ben. "It sounds like it'll be a long one."

"How did you manage without me?" she asked.

Tom snorted. "We hardly noticed you were gone." Then he gave her a sly smile. "Ben filled in, and he's damned tired of it, from what I hear. So it's very good that you're finally back. Hand me that pan."

Ben mixed the yeast and sugar into lukewarm water and set it to rise, then supervised as she filled the pot of water to boil.

"You think I've forgotten how to do this, right?" she muttered.

"No, just admiring your skill," he replied. He pulled the coffee pot from the counter in the front of the shop and set it to perk. "We're going to need coffee for this story, I can tell." He winked at her. "Now tell us what happened, and don't leave anything out."

Tom guffawed but grabbed a stool and pulled it up to the counter. "This started with a wedding dance, didn't it?"

~~***~~

CHAPTER THIRTY EIGHT

Alex heard his phone alarm calling through a dense fog. When he finally pried his eyes open, he saw it was six o'clock. Time to get moving.

By the time he was on the highway south, he'd texted Glory and had calls from Mum, Ryan and the Manx brothers. Luckily he had a handsfree link for his cell in the truck. Jim Manx didn't seem upset, just relieved to hear his voice and to know he'd be back on the job tomorrow. "We're moving ahead pretty fast," he added, "so you'll be surprised at the progress. And the building inspector from hell has been more cooperative than you would believe." Alex laughed as they hung up.

The call from Mum hadn't been quite as lighthearted and he'd had to pull over on the shoulder of the road at one point because his vision blurred. He wouldn't admit he'd been crying, but he definitely had tears in his eyes. Mum sounded good when she rang off, looking forward to seeing him when he got home.

The Fraser Highway was a twisting road, narrow in parts, with a lot of tunnels through the mountains and heavy truck traffic going north. He was tired by the time he arrived in the lower mainland, heading determinedly for the last ferry to the island.

He caught it by the skin of his teeth, the second to last vehicle to load on the ferry deck. He was a man on a mission, because although he would see his family first, he was also going to see Glory tonight if it was at all possible.

He climbed the stairs two at a time, bought himself a quick supper in the cafeteria, and was back in his truck within twenty minutes. He set his alarm and put the seat back for a nap. If he was lucky and got to see Glory, he didn't want to be totally exhausted.

~~*~~

Glory woke in the darkness to a light tapping at her door. She turned her head and sat up, her pulse pounding in her throat. Alex had sent her numerous texts and they'd talked briefly as he waited to board the ferry. He'd promised to come to her door if it wasn't too late. She glanced at the clock. Twelve-thirty, and she had to be up in four and a half hours. It definitely wasn't too late.

She slid from the bed and tiptoed to the door just as another soft knock sounded on the other side. "Alex?" she called.

"Open the door, Glory," he said.

A thrill went down her spine. Was she overdressed? She glanced down at the sheer nightie she'd pulled from the back of her dresser drawer. No, definitely not overdressed. She slid the bolt and opened the door.

Alex stood on the other side, one leg cocked, his jacket slung over his shoulder. He glanced at her, then down the length of her nightie.

"Oh, baby," he said. "You shouldn't have. But I'm sure glad you did." He stepped through the opening and shot the bolt behind him. "I just need a kiss."

When he moved closer, she felt the cold air pouring off his clothing. Taking his jacket, she threw it over a chair. Then she put her hands on his shoulders and stood on tiptoe. "I need a kiss too," she said, and placed her mouth over his. He fell into the embrace, his arms wrapping tightly around her, his feet parting as he pulled her into the vee of his strong legs.

"Glory, I want you. I know you work tomorrow—"

She put a finger to his lips. "Stay an hour," she said. "I get up at five."

He groaned. "An hour isn't nearly enough. But I can work with that." He stripped his shirt over his head and tossed it on top of his coat. "I'm an organized man, I can work with an hour."

She giggled at the grin on his face. "Don't overstay your welcome," she cautioned, her gaze fleeing to the bed.

"Don't worry, I'll leave whenever you say. But if I can persuade you—"

She climbed under the covers. He shucked his pants and followed. "Move over, honey." He lifted the quilt and peered under at her bare legs. "Oh, man."

He slid in beside her and wrapped one arm around her waist. "You don't know how often I thought of this, driving down that highway. The road seemed to go on and on, I couldn't wait to get here."

She sighed against his shoulder. "Did you see your mum?"

He paused, his gaze returning to her face. "Yeah, I did. She was relieved, to say the least. Ryan was there, and he's been looking after things."

"I know, he met me at the airport. Wanted to know how you were, so he could report back to your mother."

"Okay." He laid his mouth against her throat as one hand rose to cup her breast under the nightie. She caught her breath. He was like a live wire, the electricity instantaneous when he touched her.

"Alex."

"Hmmm." He tugged the nightie up and his mouth fastened on her nipple. She lost her words, consumed by emotion as his hands explored her tender places, his mouth causing her temperature to rise higher and higher.

When he lifted himself over and settled between her legs, she had nothing left to say. Gazing into his dark blue eyes, she absorbed his heavy invasion and felt no resistance, just a welcoming heat, a relief that he was here and then excitement mounting... mounting... until it overwhelmed her whole body. He moved faster and she couldn't hold back, but instead let go and freed everything she was.

Later, Glory stirred against his side, and felt his hand smooth down her back and over her buttocks. She glanced at the clock. "You have to go," she said. "I have to get ready for work soon."

"Yeah, sorry." He kissed the top of her head, tightened his arm for a moment, then released her. "Can I see you tomorrow?"

She laughed. "Yes, but call me because I'm so muddled I don't have a clue what I have on tomorrow. I'll have to look at my calendar. I have a music class at some point, if they haven't fired me."

He slid from the bed and pulled his jeans on. Gathering the rest of his clothes in one arm, he dug his door key out of the jacket pocket. "Okay. I work tomorrow too. I'll call."

She laid her head back on the pillow as the door clicked shut, immediately falling into a deep sleep.

~~***~~

CHAPTER THIRTY NINE

Trudy rolled over and Eddie slid across the bed toward her. "Don't go away, baby. You know there's more fun where that came from."

She laughed and pushed her feet over the side of the mattress. "I have to use the bathroom. You just lay back and save your energy. You're going to need it."

Eddie's full blown laughter followed as she made her way to the door. "Don't get dressed on my account," he murmured, and she felt the weight of his gaze on her bare skin. She glanced over her shoulder.

He lay spread-eagled and naked, his hands cupping his balls as he gave her an appreciative look. His moustache bristled. "I'm not going anywhere," he said. "Don't take too long."

Entering the bathroom, she closed the door and leaned back on the panel. The man was a machine. He never seemed to need a break.

She peed and washed her hands at the sink, staring at her reflection. What she needed was a shower, but then Eddie would want to join her. Perhaps she'd just sponge herself off and they could have a nap before engaging in any more activity. She filled the basin with warm water and added a wash cloth. As she applied soap, she heard a noise from the hallway. Probably Eddie going downstairs for another beer. He seemed to have many appetites, and they were all unbridled.

She rinsed the cloth and smoothed it across her breast, pausing on the bitemark there. Damn him, Eddie had gotten a little out of control. She'd deal with that later.

There was another thump from the hallway and then Eddie yelled. Trudy stepped hastily out of the bathroom. A tall dark shape loomed in the doorway to the bedroom. Then it moved closer and she recognized Rolf, his erect muscular silhouette and dark brown leather jacket. He was tall, taller then Eddie, and his hair was slicked back in his trademark style, short at the sides and greased on top. But it was his ferocious expression that caused her to freeze in the doorway.

"Rolf! What are you doing here?" she stuttered. "I took back your key."

He smirked. "As if I didn't know how to have another one made?"

She moved closer, holding the washcloth against her breast to hide the bite mark. "Why are you here? You had a competition in Seattle tonight."

He frowned. "They tossed me out, and it's all your fault."

"My fault?"

His enraged gaze swung to Eddie, who had jumped to his feet on the other side of the bed and was quickly donning his underwear.

"Don't bother," Rolf said, his voice cold as ice. "You're not going to need it." He strode across the room, seizing Eddie by the throat with both hands.

Eddie struck out blindly, thrashing with his fists, his legs caught in the briefs he'd been putting on.

"Rolf, stop it," Trudy screamed, racing toward them. "Let him go!"

Rolf threw a back-handed slam that caught her in the chest and sent her sprawling. Then he chopped down heavily on the side of Eddie's neck. The blow sent him to the floor, lying motionless on his stomach. Rolf leaned forward and set his hands on both sides of Eddie's head, grabbed hold and twisted sharply sideways.

Trudy knew he was dead before she even managed to crawl across the floor to check. But she never got there. Rolf wrapped his hands around her arm and tossed her awkwardly onto the bed. Her arm throbbed but she was too terrified to respond.

"If you're going to entertain someone, then entertain me," he said in a steely voice, peeling his jacket off. He unsnapped his pants and tugged the zipper down. "Come on Trudy. Nothing to say? I told you I'd be back. Your job was to be patient and wait for me. Now you'll pay."

~~*~~

Ryan was at work when he got the call from Jim Manx. "Sorry to bother you, Ryan, but I'm looking for your brother Alex."

Ryan's heart gave a heavy thump. That was odd. He'd just seen him last night right after he got off the ferry, and Alex had been on his way home. Well, probably not straight home. Ryan wasn't totally blind to the tension and attraction between his brother and Glory Stephens. He'd likely stopped at her place last night.

"I haven't spoken to Alex this morning," he said. "But I saw him last night, so he definitely arrived back in town. It was a long drive, and he may have just slept in. I'll call around, Mr. Manx, and get back to you."

He waited a few minutes for his co-worker to come back from a break, then left the cell phone booth to walk down the mall and make his calls. No answer from Alex, but he hadn't expected one. Manx had probably already called his cell. Next, he called Glory, but no answer there either. She was likely busy, didn't she work at a bagel shop? He wracked his brain and found Benjamin's Bagels online, quickly dialling the number.

No one answered. He checked his watch. They might not open till lunch time. He dialled again. A stranger's voice answered. "Benjamin's Bagels."

"Yes, sir. I'm trying to contact Glory Stephens. It's an emergency."

"Glory?" There was a pause. "Just a minute."

Ryan waited, watching the early shoppers parade by where he sat on one of the benches in the mall walkway. Then he heard Glory's voice.

"Hello? This is Glory."

"Hi, Glory. It's Ryan. Sorry to bother you at work, but you didn't answer your cell. I'm looking for Alex."

"Ryan?" She paused. "I haven't seen Alex today."

"But did you see him last night? I don't mean to pry, but he didn't turn up for work this morning."

"Oh, my goodness," she gasped, then her voice was muffled as if her fingers covered her mouth. "I saw him last night." There was silence for a moment, and she sounded acutely uncomfortable as she continued. "He went back to his place about four-thirty. Has something happened to him? I'll bet he slept in, he was really tired. Maybe he's sick—" Her voice rose higher. "Do you have a key? He might need help."

Ryan's heart was thumping heavily. "I don't have a key, but I'm going to go over there right now. If his truck's there, then he's likely at home."

"Ryan, phone me! I'll turn my cell on. Call me and let me know. Please." She sounded out of breath, her voice thin.

"Don't worry. I'll call." Ryan phoned Alex again as he walked rapidly back to his booth, but still no answer. He just had to give his co-worker some notice, and then he was gone.

Ryan pulled up in front of the townhouse complex and felt his whole body relax. The truck Alex drove was parked on the street. The hood was cold to the touch. He was likely sleeping after that huge solo drive south. It would have been hard enough to make that journey with another driver to spell him off, but hell to do it on his own.

He parked behind the black Manx Construction pickup and jogged across the street to the townhouse entrance. He knocked sharply on the door, imagining Alex rolling over with a grimace to face the fact that he'd failed to show at work when he should have.

There was no answer. He knocked again, and waited impatiently. "Alex," he called. "Open the door." His knuckles rapped loudly on the panel, but there was no sound within.

He turned slowly, scanning the area. *How was he going to get inside?* Maybe Glory was right, and his brother was hurt. He might need medical attention. There was no one around, no one from the townhouse complex who would have some answers for him. He thumbed Glory's cell number again.

"How do you get hold of your landlord?" he said. "The truck is here but Alex isn't answering the door." He heard her gasp of dismay, but then the sound of tapping on her phone and she gave him a number.

It was a property management company that answered. Ryan wasn't getting any cooperation at first, but after demanding to speak to the manager and explaining there could be someone inside in a serious medical emergency, he finally got the help he was looking for. An agent would meet him onsite within twenty minutes. He spent most of that time trying to peer in the windows or hammering on the door.

His temper was right on the edge by the time a van slowed in front of the complex and pulled into a parking spot a few doors up. A middle-aged woman climbed out, shouldered a carry bag, and stepped onto the sidewalk. Ryan went to meet her.

"Mrs. Harris?" At her nod, he led the way to the townhouse steps. "Right here. Sorry, here's my driver's licence. I'm Ryan Vecchio and Alex is my brother. He was expected at work this morning but didn't show."

Pointing across the street, he added, "His truck is here, and he's not answering his cell phone."

"Hi, Mr Vecchio." She tucked a strand of bleached blond hair behind her ear. Setting her case on the step, she unsnapped the flap, showing a display of keys. She began to examine the tags, one by one. Ryan shifted from one foot to the other as Mrs. Harris carefully leafed through until she came to the right key. Smiling triumphantly, she pulled it out of the shallow pocket and flipped the flap closed on the case. "Here it is. You'll have to let me go in first, we have our own protocol."

He stepped back. "Of course."

Mrs. Harris knocked on the door, then rapped loudly with the key. She waited as Ryan mentally throttled her. Finally, she set the key in the lock and turned it. The door swung open. Ryan whipped past her and into the suite, as she hastily walked behind.

"I'm to go in first," she said loudly, but he was already down the hall and through the bedroom door.

~~***~~

CHAPTER FORTY

The empty bed was unmade, the pillow with an impression of someone's head still pressed into the centre. Otherwise the place was fairly orderly. The suitcase Alex had taken north was sitting unzipped on a chair by the closet, most of the clothes still folded inside.

Ryan looked around the room. His brother's cell phone was on the nightstand by the bed, and he picked it up. There were six unanswered phone calls all from this morning, three from Manx Construction, two from him and one from Glory.

Heart pounding, he peeked into the bathroom and checked behind the shower curtain before looking in the kitchen, almost afraid of what he might find. No one there. The living room was forlorn looking, with the big leather couch and television stark against the otherwise empty space. He heard Mrs. Harris coming down the hall, checking the rooms.

Just then the cell phone in his hand rang, and he recognized Glory's number.

"He's not here," he said into the speaker. "Glory, I just got in, but he's not here. Did he say anything that might tell you what he'd be doing this morning?"

She stuttered and he imagined her embarrassment, but thankfully it didn't stop her from cooperating. "He was going to work this morning. He said he'd get a few hours' sleep, and then in to the work site. His boss had told him how fast they were progressing and he was anxious to see it for himself."

"Yeah, that sounds like him," Ryan muttered. "Was he sick? Did he have a cold or something?"

"No, he wasn't sick." There was a long pause and Ryan tried not to imagine how well Alex had been last night.

He let out a resigned breath. "I don't know what to do. Should I call the cops?"

"Oh, Ryan. What will they do? I mean…" Glory sounded desperate over the phone. "Will they think there's something really wrong with him, if you call them again? Could he get a reputation for trouble or something?"

"I don't know." He thought for a moment. "Alex has a friend in the local detachment. Maybe I'll try him first. I didn't think to contact him when you guys disappeared up north, but now he might be our best bet."

~~*~~

Trudy sobbed into her pillow on the bed in the spare room. Her nose was stuffed and she could hardly catch a breath. She was alone at last.

The police were finally gone. The body was gone. The forensics guys had left and the street was empty of all the official vehicles that had been blocking her driveway.

It had taken hours from the time she called the police until the whole process was finished. She was exhausted. She'd promised to go in to the police station and give a formal statement later this afternoon, as soon as she got herself under control. But what did control look like in these circumstances?

Her life was a shambles. When she couldn't get Alex to come back, she'd lost it. Alex had always come back. She might have hysterics now and then, but they were good together, really good. Yet when he'd called it quits for the final time, he must have meant it. How could he turn his back on her after all they had shared over the years?

She'd changed direction then and focussed on Rolf. He was a body builder, in terrific shape, and took the work much more seriously than Alex. He entered competitions, held titles and stood tall in the world of competition. Things had been good for a while, but Rolf was a different kind of guy. She wasn't allowed to have hysterics when she was with him, he'd laid down the ground rules for everything she did. That is, until even he left. Everyone left her. The tears came heavily, and she rolled to her side in agony.

So why did Rolf come back? Why did he have to arrive at the very moment she was having a little fun with Eddie?

She wiped her face on the sheet and flipped onto her back. She couldn't lay in that bed in the master bedroom. Probably never again. The whole night had been dreadful. She ached from Rolf's attacks, her body in agony from the abuse.

She had to pull herself together. Sighing, she staggered down the hall to the bathroom and took off her robe. Turning on the water, she stepped into the shower, feeling the warm water pelt her tender skin. She wanted to appear heart broken when she got to the police station, and she was. She'd known Eddie for years as Alex's buddy, and now he was dead. But she also had to appear sober and completely believable. It was understandable that she'd been a mess when the cops arrived at the house. Eddie was still lying dead on the floor. She'd been panic-stricken.

But now her job was to pull herself together. Because she had lied to the police when they arrived at her home. And she needed to sell that lie one more time when they took her formal statement.

~~***~~

CHAPTER FORTY ONE

Glory hung her baking uniform on a hook and slipped on a cardigan, then shrugged into her jacket. Tom lifted his head as he gave the counters a last wipe with a cloth. "Where're you heading so fast, Glory? You just got back in town." His smile was friendly, but his eyes watchful.

"Gotta get home," she muttered. "Life is going to hell in a handbasket."

"What's going on?" He washed his hands at the sink and dried them on the towel tucked into his belt, before piling all the linens in the basket by the laundry door. "You've been jumpy as a bed bug all morning. Can I help?"

"Oh, Tom. You're the greatest, really you are. I don't think anyone can help. It's just… complicated."

"What, you don't think I'm smart enough to figure it out?" His mouth turned down in a mock frown.

"No, you know it's not that. It's… well, my boyfriend got home last night…"

His mouth turned in the other direction, his smile beaming. "You've got a boyfriend? That's great. I thought you'd given up on men, else I would have asked you out," he teased.

She laughed self-consciously. "I did give up on men, but this guy's different. He got under my radar, I guess."

"Ah, Glory." Tom wrapped a beefy arm around her shoulder. "I'm glad for you, really. So what seems to be the problem?"

She leaned against his comforting bulk. "He got home last night and didn't show at work this morning. No one knows where he is."

"Okay, that's odd. Where do you think he's gone?"

She shrugged. "I don't know. His brother doesn't know. He's a steady kind of guy, and he told me he was going to work this morning."

"Probably had one too many, and couldn't get out of bed." Tom's expression was comical in his efforts not to laugh.

Glory felt tears gather in her eyes and blinked to keep them at bay. "He isn't at his apartment. His truck's there, but he's gone."

"Oh, oh. That's not good." He gave her a concerned look. "What are you going to do?"

"His brother knows a cop, so he's going to call him. Perhaps he can help."

Glory walked through the back door into the alley and pulled out her cell phone, punching in Alex's number, but as expected there was no reply. When she tried Ryan, he answered on the second ring.

"Have you heard from him?" he demanded.

Glory shook her head, knowing he couldn't see it. "No, nothing. I just wondered if you…"

"No. Can't find hide nor hair of him. I've put in a call to the Saanich police, Detective Scott Burrows. He knows Alex, so might be willing to make inquiries. I don't know what else to do." His voice echoed his despair.

"It's just so odd, Ryan. I don't know what to think." The tears were fast advancing and her voice broke.

"Calm down. He'll turn up." Ryan didn't sound convinced but he was trying. "Burrows isn't in until tomorrow, so if Alex doesn't show up today, we can talk to the Detective and see what he says."

"Okay." She clicked off and turned back to find Tom hovering at her shoulder.

"Glory," he said. "I'll help anyway I can. Do you have any clue about where he might be.?"

"No, nothing." She sighed and gave him a hug. "I'll let you know if there's anything you can do. Thanks Tom."

She got home in time for a quick lunch—smoked salmon on a bagel—and change of clothes before she headed off to the Conservatory. She had two classes with seven and eight year olds, but was totally wiped when they were finished. The kids were great, and very pleased to see her back after she missed their last class. But the situation with Alex was dragging at her.

Back at her suite, she knocked at his door in the faint hope that he was back, but there was still no answer.

~~*~~

Alex rolled over at the sound of his doorbell. Who would be outside at this time of the morning? Must be Ryan, so that meant there was trouble. Was Mum okay? He pulled on some briefs and staggered down the hall. Man, he was tired. Spending most of the night with Glory had worn him down to the nubs. He didn't have much left in the tank for this or even work in about an hour. Damn.

He tugged the door open and was immediately slammed up against the doorframe by two guys in uniform. What the fuck? His elbow hit the light switch and he gaped at the cops holding him pinned to the wall.

"What are you doing?" he gasped in outrage. "What the hell is going on?"

"Quiet," one ordered while the other fumbled to get a set of handcuffs off his belt. "Just hold still. If you cooperate, it'll go better for you."

Alex shifted his weight and lunged, sending the second cop flying. "Cooperate with what? I don't know what the hell you're doing, but I don't deserve this!"

He was immediately grabbed in a chokehold. "Alexander Vecchio, you're under arrest on suspicion of murder. Cuff him, Max."

Alex stopped struggling, more from shock than anything. He eventually found some clothes and...

Alex slowly woke and looked around the jail cell. Eddie was dead, and he was locked up like an animal in a cage. How had things gone so wrong? And why was he the one under suspicion? He'd been out of town.

The bunk above his head squeaked as his cellmate shifted and rolled over. He wasn't sleeping either. No one slept in this place. It had been a nightmare from the moment he'd been dragged in here. The sounds of so many men corralled in such a small space, the smells of unwashed bodies and poor sanitation, the sight of a line of dejected men who'd given up on life. It was a recipe for disaster, and he didn't know the solution.

~~***~~

CHAPTER FORTY TWO

Ryan's cell phone call the next day pulled Glory out of a work trance that she'd fallen into about half-way through her shift. Roll the dough out, cut the bagels, drop each one in the boiling water until they bobbed back to the surface, fish them out with a sieve and arrange them on a baking sheet. When the pan was full, sprinkle them with sesame seeds, poppy seeds, chopped dried onion, put them in the oven and set the timer. Roll the dough out—

She had barely slept last night. Worry kept her awake, and she missed Alex bone-deep. It seemed unreal that they had only been together a short time. But he was a big reassuring presence. He took up a lot of space, and she found great delight in him. Now there was no comfort.

"Ryan?" she answered. "Did you find him?"

"I found something," he said. "I think you should come over to the house right now. Can you do that?"

"What?" She glanced around manically, taking in the dough yet to be processed, the flat pans waiting for the ovens, the timer ticking off the seconds on the batches already baking. "I can't leave now."

Tom lifted his head from the task of digging dough out of the mixer. "What is it, Glory? Do you need to leave?" He surveyed the counters. "I can manage the rest of this. You go if you have to. Let me know what happens."

"Are you sure?" She looked anxiously at him. "Okay, I think it will."

She turned her attention back to the phone at her ear as she ran for her coat. "I'll be there in fifteen minutes."

~~*~~

Mrs Vecchio was seated in the living room. She leaped to her feet when Ryan walked through the door. "Is there any news?" Her face fell at his doleful expression and he felt like a failure for not sorting this out already.

"Glory's coming over," he said, "and Detective Burrows will be here shortly. He's promised to tell us everything he knows."

"Oh, God." She fell back in her chair. "What does that mean? I don't think I can take any more…"

"It's okay, Mum. It's okay. Let me get you some tea." He hurried to the kitchen and put the kettle on, wishing this would all just go away. Why would Alex take off and not even tell someone where he was going? It didn't make any sense, especially since he'd just gotten back from the road trip from hell. Although Ryan had gotten the impression things had gone quite well for his brother, at least where Glory was concerned.

He poured hot water into the cup just as the doorbell rang. That would probably be Glory. When he got back to the living room, his mother had already opened the door. There was a cop standing on the top step.

"Mrs. Vecchio?"

Ryan watched Mum take a step backward as the officer entered. "Hi," he said, sticking out his hand. "I'm Detective Scott Burrrows. I've met you before, Mrs. Vecchio, when Alex and I were in high school together."

"Yes," she said faintly, but she didn't shake hands. "I remember."

"Come in," Ryan said at her shoulder. "I just put the kettle on, you want coffee?"

"Uh, sounds good."

Ryan showed him to a chair in the living room. "I'll just be minute."

By the time he returned with the cups, Glory had arrived. She looked as pale as Mum, and just as hesitant in dealing with a police officer.

Burrows introduced himself to Glory and took a sip of coffee before setting his cup on the corner of the coffee table. "Ryan, it was good you called me. I've done a search and found your brother. The situation is a little bit tricky. Alex is being held in jail pending a bail hearing, which should happen tomorrow morning."

Mum slapped one hand to her mouth and her tea splashed over the lip of the cup, burning her fingers. Shakily, she placed it on the end table and shook the scalding liquid off. "What do you mean?" Her expression was horrified.

Glory hadn't said a word. She was staring at the officer with dismay. "Why is he in jail?" she said.

Ryan spoke over everyone. "What is he charged with?"

Burrows looked from one face to the other. "It's unclear at the moment what the charge will be. But to be honest, it involves the death of Eddie Marker. We don't know if his death was an accident or intentional. The investigation is in progress."

Ryan felt a thud in his gut that nearly doubled him over. The shrieks of dismay from the women sounded far away. *Eddie was dead?* He glanced at Glory, who looked like she might faint. He grabbed her shoulder and gave her a shake.

Mum cried as the tears poured down her face. "No," she moaned. "No, that can't be true. It can't."

Glory got up and staggered across to lean in and wrap an arm around Mum's shoulder. "How can Eddie be dead?" she said faintly. "How did he die?"

Burrows gave her a close look. "I'm sorry I can't say more. The investigation is in early stages." He pressed his lips together. "Sorry it's been such a shock. I thought you might know about Eddie."

"How would we know?" Ryan bit out. "Has it been in the paper? I haven't seen anything. Damn!" He stalked to the door and back. "I don't understand this. What does Alex have to do with it, anyway? He just got back to town. When did this take place?"

Burrows shook his head. "Sorry, can't say more than that. Ryan, do you want to step outside for a minute? I just have a few questions."

Ryan gave him a hard look. "Sure." He turned to the women. "I'll be right back."

Out on the front step, the officer pulled a notebook from his pocket. "I wanted to ask what you know about the relationship between Alex and Eddie. Were they competitive, did they go after the same women? How did they get along?"

Ryan moved backward away from the cop. "I don't have anything to say. I don't have a clue what's happened, or how Alex is involved. So until I find out more, I have nothing further to add. Thanks for letting us know what's going on, at least. How do we find out when his bail hearing is set?"

Burrows nodded. "I can understand your position, Ryan. You think you're protecting your brother, but the more information we have, the better we can put the picture into focus, you know? It would be helpful to get your perspective."

Ryan shook his head. "Not today. What about bail? When is the hearing? And can I get in to see him?"

~~*~~

Glory was too stunned by the news to pull herself together. She sat beside Mrs. Vecchio, holding her hand

227

and rocking on the couch cushion. How did Eddie die? And what did Alex have to do with it?

As the shock wore off, her teeth began to chatter. Confusion reigned in her mind. *How well did she really know Alex? They'd been close, but only for the last few days. So what did that mean? Had she totally misjudged him?*

The thought raised a whole other area of confusion, causing her head to ache from the pressure. The Vecchio's seemed to be nice people, but she was new to Ryan's band and new to this relationship with Alex. She was frightened, as if she'd taken a huge leap into the unknown without first checking the terrain. *That wasn't like her. She was finished with men.*

Ryan closed the door as the police officer left. She pinned him with her gaze. "When did Eddie die?" she asked.

Ryan shook his head. "I don't know, and I don't know how to find out."

Mrs. Vecchio gasped back a sob.

"I think Alex needs a lawyer," Glory said. "And if he has a lawyer, we should be able to get some information such as when and how Eddie died. Do you know anyone?"

Ryan glanced at his mother and Mrs Vecchio seemed to pull herself together. "Uncle Albert will know what to do."

~~***~~

CHAPTER FORTY THREE

Alex paced his cell one more time, then flopped down on the bunk bed and stretched out, linking his hands behind his head. The waiting was killing him, and it had only just begun. Why did it take so long to see a lawyer? But the system ran slow, and he didn't personally know any legal counsel who took criminal cases. The one phone call allowed had gone straight to the answering service for Legal Aid, and they weren't working Sundays. There was no court to listen to his bail hearing that day, anyway, so it didn't make much difference.

The guy in the next cell hammered on the bars with his fists and shouted for the guards. When they didn't immediately appear, his shouts turned to loud obscenities, and Alex closed his eyes. He was holed up right next to the inmate from hell.

At least he'd finally heard from a lawyer, who'd promised to come attend at the jail tomorrow morning. The hope was to get a bail hearing in the next day or two, so he'd be released. After all, what evidence could they possibly have against him? Eddie had been hale and hearty when they parted ways in Big Smokey and Alex hadn't been anywhere near him since he'd returned to town.

He squeezed his hands together as the loss burned in his chest. Eddie was a bit of an actor but he'd been a good friend. And now he was dead. How he died and why, Alex had yet to find out. But it was a real loss. The band Ryan put together had become a big part of his life, and that had just been ripped to shreds, as well.

His nerves were shot. The idea that the police could charge him with murder was defeating in itself. They must have some information or they wouldn't have gotten this far with the case. But what could they possibly have to link him to the death? And where did it come from? He almost worried he might have done something in his sleep to deserve this, and now he couldn't remember anything about it.

The tension in his chest wound tighter. He dropped to the floor and began to do push-ups, slow and controlled. Because if he lost it in this place, how would he ever put himself back together?

~~*~~

The next morning Glory got a call from Ryan and although she was at work, her phone was on. Things were too tense to leave any slight opportunity to chance. Alex had a bail hearing this afternoon, Ryan had informed her. Glory found a spot in the parkade and left her Mini.

She grabbed her bag and walked out of the underground parking onto the sidewalk. The courthouse was on the next block, and she didn't want to be late. Hurrying up the street, she crossed at the light and approached the huge staircase at the front of the building. It wound up two floors, entering on the second level. Inside, she paused and looked around. People stood in groups talking quietly, or sat on benches along the wall, looking as nervous as she felt. Where were they supposed to go?

Hesitantly she approached the information booth and stood in line. Just then Mrs. Vecchio walked past, her younger son leading the way. "Ryan. Thank God. Do you know where we should be?"

They turned at her words, and Mrs. Vecchio gave a faint smile. "Glory, I'm glad you're here. Alex will be cheered by your presence, I'm sure."

Glory flushed under the older woman's gaze, but she wasn't so sure. Her relationship with Alex, if it could be called that, was so new to be almost non-existent. *Did Alex think of her as his girlfriend?* She didn't even know.

"This way," Ryan said. "He's in courtroom C, down the hall."

When they arrived, court was already in session, and they quietly tiptoed to a bench near the back and took a seat. There were two bail hearings before Alex Vecchio was called, and the Sheriff escorted him into the dock. Glory could hardly see him for the sudden tears. He looked pale and thinner than just a few days ago. His hands were cuffed in front of him, and he shuffled in leg shackles to the bench where the Sheriff pointed.

She heard Mrs. Vecchio sobbing beside her but couldn't look away. Alex was studying the crowd in the seats, his eyes roving back and forth until he spied the little group, then his gaze riveted on Glory. When she met his gaze, he stared with such a look of despair, she could hardly bear it. Then he looked away, his jaw bulging and shoulders tight.

The judge hit the gavel with his hammer and brought the court to order. Two lawyers in black gowns approached the bench and spoke at length, while Glory and the others waited tensely. She barely heard the words, the back and forth of whether bail should be granted on the charge of first degree murder caused her hearing to falter and she didn't take in what was said after that.

Then suddenly it was over, and everyone stood. As the judge left the room, the Sheriff urged Alex to his feet and led him out the rear door.

She leaned in to speak low. "What happened?"

"Not sure," Ryan muttered. "I'm going to grab the lawyer." Mrs. Vecchio seemed frozen to the bench and Glory put a hand on her arm. "Don't worry, it'll be okay," she murmured, not sure at all if that was true.

She glanced toward the door where everyone was departing the room, and froze. That was Trudy, the ex-girlfriend. She was sure of it. *So what was she doing here? Did she have some other action happening, or was she involved in this murder inquiry? After all, it had apparently happened at her place.*

Ryan returned. "Okay, let's go. Alex got bail, and they'll let him go tomorrow morning. We've got a meeting with the lawyer tonight."

Glory barely heard. She moved along the corridor with the crowd, but Trudy was hard to miss. She was taller than a lot of the men, and moved with confidence through the throng. Glory followed as she got to the front entrance and started down the grand staircase outside. At the sidewalk, she paused and Glory moved faster. "Excuse me," she said. "I've met you before."

Trudy turned, and her expression grew frosty. "I'm sure we haven't," she said, and headed down the street.

Glory caught up and fell into step beside her. "But I know who you are," she said. "You're Alex Vecchio's ex-girlfriend. What were you doing in the courthouse? Surely you have no interest in his bail hearing."

"Of course I do," the woman replied loftily. "Alex is a dangerous man, and I wanted to know if he would be kept in jail."

Glory's mouth fell open. "Are you afraid of him?" she asked.

"Afraid?" Trudy stopped in the middle of the sidewalk and gave her a pitying look. "You have no idea what he's capable of. You're a babe in arms where men like Alex are concerned. Watch your step. If they ever let him out, you could be in extreme danger."

As Trudy strode off, Glory stood still as, confusion and sorrow battled in her mind. *Was Alex dangerous?* She was positive that wasn't true. He'd treated her with nothing but respect, assuring her that she was safe with him, no matter what. And she had been safe. They hadn't done anything that she hadn't wanted to. In fact, he'd held back until she was more than ready for the next level of intimacy.

~~***~~

CHAPTER FORTY FOUR

Ryan called her that evening. "Just thought I'd let you know what was said at the lawyer's office."

Glory stopped pacing her small apartment and sat at the table, pad of paper at the ready. "Go ahead, Ryan. What did you learn?"

She heard him take a deep breath. "Eddie died the night Alex got back to the island," he said. "He died at Trudy's house. Apparently, Alex is supposed to have gone to Trudy's on the way home and found Eddie there. They said he flew into a rage and attacked him. Eddie's neck was broken." Ryan's voice had grown quieter as he talked, and Glory was sure he was crying.

She was crying too. *How could this be possible? It seemed such an outrageous claim.* "What time did he go over there?" she asked. "Because he was here most of the night..." *How could Alex kill his friend, unless he went over there after he left her bed?* That idea was devastating.

Yet his truck had been in front of his townhouse when she left for work the next morning.

"It can't be true," she said into the phone.

"I know," Ryan spoke low. "I don't believe it either. I thought he'd stopped going over there."

Glory's breath caught in her throat. She had thought that too. *Were they both wrong about Alex?* "But, Ryan, what time did he leave your mum's place that night?"

His voice faltered. "Uh, I'm not sure. He caught the last ferry, which gets in at ten-forty."

"Yes," she interrupted, "and he got to your place just after eleven."

"Yeah, that's right."

"Well, he didn't stay there very long, because he arrived at my townhouse at twelve-thirty." Glory hugged herself to try and stop the shaking and wiped a hand down her cheek. "I remember looking at the clock. I'd been expecting him, because he'd sent me text messages, so I knew where he was."

Ryan sighed. "I don't know what time he left. I guess he had thirty or forty minutes to get to her house and then over to yours. Is that possible? Doesn't seem right, does it?" There was a pause. "I don't understand it. We'll have to wait and see. The lawyer said they have an eyewitness who saw Alex there and witnessed the murder." His voice shook slightly. "Hold onto some hope, Glory. I know he's innocent. We just don't have any evidence to prove it yet."

Glory hung up and stared at the page in front of her. Alex got off the ferry at ten-forty. She made a mark on the page. He drove to his mother's house and got there about eleven-fifteen. She wrote another number. He visited there for a while, and arrived at her townhouse at twelve-thirty. She added a question mark. She'd talk to Mrs. Vecchio when they'd all calmed down. Maybe she remembered what time Alex left the house.

He'd be out on bail tomorrow. Her heart leaped in her chest. She wouldn't be home, she'd already missed too many days of work to take another one off. But she'd see him tomorrow sometime. The shaking started again.

Glory began to get ready for bed, knowing it would be hard to sleep. Maybe she'd call Dad. He had a clear mind, and talking things out with him always calmed her down.

~~*~~

Alex climbed out of the Sheriff's van and walked along the downtown street. He was finally free from jail. The conditions for his release had been alarmingly encompassing. He couldn't leave town, although he'd been given permission to go back to work, so was able to go out to the job sites as needed. He had to be at home by eight each night and stay there until six in the morning. The police would periodically check on him to make sure he was abiding by the rules.

And his mother had put up half a million dollars to secure his bail. *How did she do that?* He was ashamed to learn she'd pledged the family home against his release. If he stepped out of line on the conditions, she could lose the house.

The turmoil in his chest was staggering. The embarrassment and shame of being held in a cell along with all the other inmates had been extremely tough to deal with. He never wanted to be in that position again, yet he very well might be if he didn't find a way to beat the charges against him. But to know his mother had pledged the house felt so belittling, he could barely go there in his mind.

He'd thought to get a cab home but now he needed the walk. He took a deep breath of the fresh air and then another. Thank God, he was free. It had been awful, frustrating, exhausting. He was enraged and shamed by turn. *What did Glory think? Why would she even be interested in him after this? Did she think he'd killed someone, murdered his friend?* He put his head down and walked faster up the street, avoiding eye contact.

Was his job still waiting for him? He didn't know, but he somehow doubted it. He'd worked years for his trades ticket, and more years to secure a foreman's job. Now he didn't know if Manx Construction would even want him back. His needed a workout badly, to level out the emotions and get stabilized. His life was in shambles.

~~***~~

CHAPTER FORTY FIVE

When Trudy answered the door, Rolf stood casually on the step waiting for her. At least he hadn't just walked in. Her heart gave a hard thump. "I don't think you should come in," she said. "It won't look good with the police statement and everything."

He stuck his foot in the gap so she couldn't close the panel. "It doesn't have to look good," he growled. "Let me in."

She hesitated a moment too long. He placed his hand flat on the door and gave it a solid push. Trudy staggered back with the force of it and he moved inside, closing it behind him.

"Now, tell me what happened with the police," he demanded. "What did you say in your statement?"

Trudy tried to control her breathing as she moved back a few paces and watched Rolf seat himself comfortably in the middle of her couch. "It went fine," she said, praying her voice didn't shake. She took a deep breath to steady herself. "I told them Alex arrived and flew into a jealous rage."

"What time did you say he came?"

She stuttered for a moment. "I said eleven o'clock at first, but then they told me he was at his mum's at that time, so I said it was probably twelve-thirty. I said I was too shaken to notice the exact time."

Rolf nodded. "And did you say why it took so long to call the cops?"

She nodded, watching him closely. "I said I must have fainted. Because when I came to, Eddie was dead and Alex was just leaving."

"See, that's why you have to learn to take instructions, Trudy." He rose and moved slowly toward her, forcing her to step back a pace. "If you fainted and woke up to see Alex leaving, you didn't see him kill Eddie. You're a bad girl, and now you have to be punished for it."

"No, Rolf. Please, I just need to get ready for my training session. I don't have time for..."

"For what?" he teased visciously. "A roll in the hay? A wild romp? A quick fuck?" He seized her arm, digging his fingers into the flesh, and led her toward the stairs. "Let's see which one we can imitate, shall we?"

The pressure on her arm was painful and she had to move with him to keep from being yanked unceremoniously up the steps. "I don't want to right now, Rolf," she protested.

She tried to dig in her heels, but he jerked her forward. "Don't play with me," he gritted. "This won't take long, believe me."

She realized that what had seemed a good solution at first, using her story as a way to appease Rolf and protect herself, had now turned into some kind of life sentence for her, under Rolf's total control.

~~*~~

Glory had just left work at Benjamin's Bagels when a cop car pulled up behind her red Mini where it was parked on a side street. A police officer got out and headed off down the sidewalk toward the police station at the far end of the block. She recognized him instantly. "Mr. Burrows," she called. "Detective Burrows?" She couldn't remember what his rank was, but at least she'd gotten the name right.

He stopped and turned. "Yes, what can I do for you?"

"You're the one investigating the murder of Eddie Marker?"

He gazed at her for a long moment as recognition dawned. "You're Alex Vecchio's friend. We met the other day at the family home."

Glory nodded. "I just had some questions."

"Well, fire away. I'm not the one investigating the case, by the way. I just met with the family because I've known Alex for years."

"Oh." She glanced uncomfortably at her shoes, the worn runners that she always wore to work in the kitchens. "I wondered, who else was there at the scene that night, who might have committed the murder? Because Alex didn't do it."

He pursed his lips a moment, then waved down the block. "Do you want to come talk to me? I'm willing to listen."

Glory followed him into the building and up a flight of stairs to a small cubby where he took off his coat and hung it on a hook. He settled behind the desk and shuffled some papers, soon coming up with a folder that he opened on the desk blotter. "Let's see. What did you want to know? According to the witness statement, Trudy Newman and Eddie Marker were the only ones there. They were in the bedroom, having sexual intercourse." He glanced at her face for a second, then back to the page. "The doorbell rang and she ignored it, but whoever was there was persistent, and she finally went downstairs to answer it."

He sat back, giving her a level gaze. "It was Alex. He had recognized Eddie's car out front."

Glory returned his gaze, her stomach churning. Alex had gone to see Trudy a few times after they broke up. He'd said she called and insisted he come. And Ryan told her he'd stopped going. "What time was this supposed to happen?"

He looked back at the sheet. "First the witness said eleven and then changed it to twelve-thirty."

"And who was the witness?"

He shook his head. "That's confidential at the moment."

"Right." Glory took a breath. "Well, if there were only two people there, and Eddie is dead, even an idiot would think the witness statement came from Trudy."

A small smile appeared on his lips for a second. He nodded. "Possibly," he said.

Glory continued. "Alex was driving from the ferry to his mother's at eleven o'clock. He got there about quarter after. And he got to my place at twelve-thirty. I looked at the clock when the doorbell rang."

"Okay." He dragged out the word as he tugged on his lower lip. "There might have been enough time between leaving the Vecchio's place and getting to yours, right?"

"I doubt it," she said. "If you're not investigating this, who is? I need to talk to them."

He gave her a considering look. "Leave it with me," he said. "Is there anything else?"

"I need to know what time Eddie died." Her voice shook. It was so horrendous to think about him being killed, yet she didn't have time to dwell on it because Alex's future was at stake.

He flipped some pages. "Don't know yet, still waiting for the complete autopsy." He glanced at her. "What's his alibi? Because apparently he told the arresting officer that he left his family's home and went straight to his townhouse to bed. Alone. Therefore, no alibi."

Glory shrugged as her heart lurched. That was a bad move on his part, but he was probably trying to be a gentleman and protect her, uncertain if she'd be offended when he used her as his defence. "He left my place at four-thirty. I needed to get to work at five-thirty, so he went home, right next door. He had his underwear on, the rest of his clothes under his arm and his door key in his hand."

Burrows gave a small smile. "He didn't say that when questioned. Why wouldn't he mention that?"

"I don't know." She straightened her shoulders. "But that's what happened."

The officer stood and stuck out his hand. "They'll want you to come in and give a statement to that effect."

"Of course, I can do that."

"I promise I'll follow up on this," he said. "And I'll let you know when the autopsy is filed. We should know time of death at that point."

"Thank you."

"Glory," he said, "did Eddie and Alex get along? Were they competitive with each other, especially over women?"

She cocked her head. "Like Ryan told you the other day, I don't have anything to say about that. I joined the band a few months ago, and didn't know Eddie very well, anyway."

"The band?" He looked back at the folder and returned to his chair. "Tell me about the band."

~~***~~

CHAPTER FORTY SIX

When Glory got home, Alex's truck was gone from the spot where it had been parked in front of the townhouse complex. She unlocked her door with shaky fingers and gathered her music supplies. She had her group of preschoolers this afternoon, and she hadn't seen them since her return to town. It always lifted her spirits to teach this class.

She let out a breath, feeling the tension slowly unwind in her stomach. Was Detective Burrows on their side or not? It had been hard to tell, so she'd been nervous talking to him. But these charges weren't right, and it was dangerous to just leave it in the hands of the police. She had to do what she could to rectify the situation.

There was a light knock on her door and she stood breathless, staring at the panel for a moment before reaching to open it. Alex stood outside wearing a leather jacket and work boots, his body tense and fists clenched.

She put down her papers and moved toward him as he stepped forward. His arms wrapped fiercely around her. "I didn't do it, Glory," he muttered. "I'm innocent."

"I know," she wailed into his chest, her voice muffled against his jacket. She inhaled his smell and realized how reassuring it was to have him here. She'd missed him terribly, and as the fear subsided, indignation set in. "It's outrageous. I don't know what evidence they have, but they've got it all wrong."

She pulled him through the doorway. "I met with Detective Burrows this afternoon. You told them you went right home to bed from your mother's place."

His face and neck turned red. "Glory, I wasn't going to embarrass you and I didn't think they needed to know where I spent the rest of the night. That was before I knew what I'd been accused of doing." He shuddered and she pushed him into one of her two chairs, seating herself on his knee as his hands cradled her.

"I have to leave in two minutes," she said as she leaned in to his kiss.

"Oh, Glory. I didn't know if you'd even want to see me." She saw the glint of moisture in his eyes as he ran a hand through her hair. "I just... I'm shamed and humiliated." His voice was gruff, his mouth hot and demanding on hers.

"Don't be, please." She gazed into his eyes. "It's all wrong and I hope we can fix it. But don't feel that way. You haven't done anything. I told Detective Burrows you were with me."

He let out a sigh, then buried his face in the curve of her neck and took a deep breath. "God, I've missed you. It felt like…" He gave a choked laugh. "Well, it seemed like a very long time."

"I have to go," she said. "I'm very sorry for the loss of your friend."

"Ah." His chest expanded. "He was a good friend. Eddie was a little flakey, as you might have noticed, but he was always there for me." He dropped his arms and planted a quick kiss on her mouth. "I'll be home when you get back. Knock on my door."

She flushed and knew he saw it.

A little smile curled his lips. "I'll wait," he said.

~~*~~

In the hospital, Burrows poked his head into the forensics lab doorway downstairs in the basement, and looked around the crowded room. "Who's working on the Marker murder?"

"I am." A fellow who looked about twelve years old, popped his curly head up from a computer screen and lifted his hand to wave. "Working on it right now, in fact."

Burrows crossed the room, took a seat beside the guy's desk and showed his badge. "What have you got so far?"

"Well, Marker died from a broken neck. I'd say someone grabbed his head and yanked or twisted it sideways." He demonstrated the motion with his hands.

"You'd have to be pretty strong to accomplish it because Marker was a big boy, but I understand the accused is a body-builder."

Burrows nodded. "Ex-body builder, but still. I think he's got the muscle to get this job done."

"Okay," the kid glanced at his screen. "We didn't find much in the way of DNA from the accused anywhere on the premises, which would appear to be a problem. I mean, there were some old traces that might feasibly be linked but nothing that would put him there in the last eight months, I would estimate."

"Okay." Burrows frowned. *The girlfriend might have been telling the truth about Alex spending the night with her.* "As I understand it," he said, "Vecchio was her boyfriend before. I know they were together in high school. They broke up and he moved out last January."

"Yeah, that makes sense. This stuff is old. So we don't have anything that places him in the room any time in recent weeks. What we do have is DNA from at least two other males that we haven't been able to identify. Recent stuff, in the last day or two as well as a bit older."

"Okay. Anything to say one of them might be our killer? "

"Not yet, we're still processing the samples off the body, but if they were there in the last day or two, that certainly would bring them into the picture, wouldn't it?"

"Hmm." Burrows thought that over. "What about time of death? Have we got that yet?"

"Still working on it," the kid said cheerfully. "Should know soon."

Burrows left. *Must be time to talk to Trudy Newman's current boyfriend.* The investigative team might have gone there already but there was nothing in the file to indicate what they'd found.

~~***~~

CHAPTER FORTY SEVEN

When Glory returned home, Ryan's truck was just drawing away from the curb and heading off down the street. There were two silhouettes inside the cab, so perhaps the family had had a meeting together. That would be good. They needed each other right now.

She parked across the street and gathered her music portfolio. The lesson at the Conservatory of Music had gone well. None of her students had had a meltdown as sometimes happened at the tender age of five. As she came up the stairs, Alex opened his door and stepped out. His smile was tender. "I thought you'd get home about now. Have you eaten? Because I have some take-out if you'd like to join me."

Glory walked through the doorway. "No, I haven't eaten, thanks. I'd love to join you." She laid her portfolio on the side table by the couch as he took her coat.

"It's not Saigon Palace," he said, a slight smile on his mouth. "But it's a lot better than prison food."

"Oh, Alex." She turned in his arms and he hugged her tight, her coat jammed awkwardly between them. "I'm so sorry."

"Don't worry," he murmured into her hair. "I'm getting over it. I just don't want to go back there." It was a long time before he let her go.

The dining table was already set for two, a large bag seeping delicious aromas sitting on the kitchen counter. "It arrived just as Ryan and Mum were leaving, so it's still hot," he said. "I'll get some serving spoons."

"How is your mother?"

Alex spoke from the kitchen. "She's doing better, according to Ryan. It's been a stressful time."

It was Chinese food, she discovered, as the first lids came off. There was silence for a few minutes as they served themselves and passed the containers back and forth.

Alex stopped with the fork halfway to his mouth, then put it down on the plate in front of him. "Glory, I haven't been over to see Trudy since shortly after you moved in here," he said. His gaze pierced her to the heart. "That last time, I'd gone there because she was screaming at me over the phone to come and fix things. And when I got back home, I saw you were just leaving for work. I was beat, and I felt stupid."

She put her hand on his muscular arm as he continued. "I couldn't fix what was wrong. She'd taken up with a mean, demanding guy, and it broke her, you know? She was the only one who could fix that. I blocked her number on my phone so she couldn't call me any more. I haven't been near her since."

"Except for the night at *Rooster's* when she kissed you," Glory said, her voice small.

He gave her a disbelieving look. "I did everything I could to avoid her at the club. I wasn't interested any more, and we'd been through for a long time. I was trying to move on." He took another bite. "And I'd seen you."

"You didn't like me at first," she said.

"It wasn't that. I liked you all right." His cheeks turned red. "I thought you were sleeping with the guy who'd rented the townhouse next to me. I was jealous. I didn't know you were the tenant."

Glory gazed into his dark blue eyes, seeing the desperation and something else, a kind of hope and caring that she'd come to rely on.

Finally he glanced back at his plate. "Eat your dinner," he said gruffly. "And don't look at me like that. I'm teetering on the edge here."

She blushed and glanced down. *What did he mean by that?*

"Eddie was a fool," he muttered. "He wanted his wife back, but did he act like it? Corrie was his first love. If he'd kept that in mind, he'd still be with her. But he couldn't wait."

"Did he cheat on her?" Glory speared a piece of broccoli.

"Yeah." Alex took another bite. "She caught him at it a few times, and each time they'd have a big fight. But she always took him back. He never thought their separation would be permanent."

"And now he's dead and she's all alone. That's so sad," she said.

"I knew he was going after Trudy." Alex leaned back in his chair and cradled a cup of coffee in his hand. "Up north, he asked me outright if I still had any interest in her. I couldn't believe the question. He'd heard me sound off often enough about the way she harassed me. But then I realized he was signalling his own interest. I wasn't surprised to learn he was at her house a couple of days after he got home."

"How did you feel about that?" Glory had to ask but was almost afraid of the answer.

Alex gave her a piercing look. "I told him I didn't care, and I don't. Glory, you have to believe me. I was just sorry he wasn't going to get back with Corrie. He loved her, he just couldn't rein in his ego."

Glory sighed and pushed her plate away.

"Had enough?" he said. "I'll have to pay more attention. It doesn't take much to feed you, so maybe I ordered too much." He took her hand in his. "I can't take you out for dinner, Glory. Not unless we get home really early. I've got a curfew from eight at night till six in the morning, it's part of the conditions of bail."

"Oh, Alex. What else? Are you allowed to work?"

"Yeah, I'll begin tomorrow. I got Jim Manx on the phone earlier and he's ready for me to start back on the job. I didn't know…" He cleared his throat and turned his head to gaze out the window. "I didn't know if they'd want me back. When the newspaper covered the bail hearing, they mentioned Manx Construction. Why would they do that? I figured my job was toast." He shrugged. "They're good guys. Jim just said, we'll wait and see."

"Alex," she said. "I work early tomorrow, have to be there at five-thirty."

"Okay." His expression was gloomy. "I understand."

"Shall we go to bed?"

She watched his eyes light up. "Oh, man." He pressed his lips together in a tight line, the dimples digging deep in his cheeks. "I wasn't sure…"

She tightened her hold on his hand as his fingers curled around hers. He got to his feet with a measured pace. "Come with me, baby. We have some catching up to do."

~~***~~

CHAPTER FORTY EIGHT

A lex led her down the hall to his bedroom, and pressed her down on top of the quilt. "Just lie here with me for a moment," he said. "I need to hold you."

He stretched out on his back and tugged her close against his side, then turned his head to press a kiss to her temple. He kissed her forehead, then her cheek. Man, he'd missed her. It had eaten at him, the whole time he was inside. 'Inside' is what the inmates called it, not very colourful but definitely descriptive. That's how he'd felt, even though there were windows and an outside yard to pace around for a designated few minutes every day.

He never wanted to be in there again, and at the thought his heart stuttered in his chest. What were his chances? The lawyers weren't as hopeful as he'd thought they might be. Given he hadn't gone over to see Trudy, hadn't touched Eddie, had just gone home, it was alarming how much evidence they seemed to have against him. Could he go down for a murder he didn't commit? He knew it had happened before to other men who were innocent.

Glory placed her hand on his cheek, and rubbed softly and he caught fire. He pressed kisses to her lips until she opened her mouth. Then he plunged inside. Every night as he went to sleep, he had relived that morning in the log cabin, making love to Glory. Yes, the circumstances had been tough, and the bed had broken through the floor beneath them in the middle of it. They'd had a tumultuous first time together, but he wouldn't change it for anything.

His fingers worked on the buttons of her blouse as he moved his mouth down the side of her throat. He heard her breath catch— his was coming fast already. He moved the sides of her blouse apart and stared down at her. Lovely, lovely woman. Unsnapping the clasp between her breasts, he lifted the bra cups away and she was naked to his gaze. Suddenly he was too hot, had too many clothes on. He needed to feel her against his bare skin.

One swift tug, and his shirt sailed toward the floor. Then he was pressed against her, his mouth back on hers. The comfort was intense, the excitement amazing. He lifted up to unsnap his pants and shuck them off along with his underwear.

He was feeling better already. It was like something the doctor prescribed to eliminate the negative feelings he'd been suffering ever since the police banged on his door early that morning. Why him? Because he was known to be acquainted with both Trudy and Eddie? Or because someone said it was him? He didn't know but he meant to find out.

Glory ran her hands down his back and he kicked into high gear, totally focussed on the action at hand. He hoped he didn't move too fast, she'd been a bit hesitant at first and he was in full flight. Her skin was like silk beneath his fingers. He ran his hands down her curved back and around her buttocks, then removed her clothes entirely. He pressed his face to her belly, laying kisses on the smooth flesh as he inched lower.

Her scent was calling to him, crying out for attention. He placed his mouth at the apex of her thighs and licked delicately into the secret folds. She was delicious and he almost came. There was something magical, hypnotic about her, an attraction that tugged him forward at breakneck speed even as her guarded look told him to go slow. A tug of war.

He licked again and she moaned low in her throat. Yes, that's how he felt too. Just like that. His chest moved faster, and he saw her breasts tremble with her rapid breathing. "You're perfect, Glory," he said. "Just perfect. I can't hold back now. Are you ready? Because I'm more than…"

Her fingers threaded through his hair pinning his face to her spread thighs. "Do it again," she whispered.

He did it again and again, and many other intimate attentions before he finally raised himself above her. She lay boneless, her eyes glazed over, panting softly. He pressed his way in, slowly, slowly, until he couldn't go any further. Then he pulled out and pressed in again. She held her breath a moment, then sighed long and low.

She was slick and tight around him. As her knees came up to encase his hips, it was all he could manage to hold back. "Now, baby," he said, pushing his way in. "Now, baby."

She levered her hips and pressed hard against him, and he felt her inner muscles grab and squeeze. She turned her head to the side and groaned as she came. A moment later, and he was there too, pressing hard and fast and holding himself there, right there, as he came.

He collapsed beside her on the bed, rolling her toward him and holding her close, cradling her in his arms.

~~***~~

CHAPTER FORTY NINE

Glory had an appointment at the lawyer's office after work to give a statement. She knew the topic was about timing—the arrival and departure of Alex from her house the night Eddie died. Pulling up in front of the building, she saw Trudy Newman step through the front door of the Crown counsel offices onto the sidewalk. Trudy adjusted the strap of her satchel over one shoulder and did up a button on her coat, then headed down the street toward Government. Glory pulled in quickly and parked, grabbing her purse from the seat beside her.

"Trudy," she called. "I need to talk to you."

The woman looked back but kept on walking. "Go away," she said. "I don't want to see you. Quit harassing me."

"I think you do." Glory sped up, walking quickly past several people who'd stopped to gawk at them. Must be tourists. "I have something to tell you, and it's very important that you hear it. For your own security."

Trudy stopped and stared at her, a sneer on her mouth. "Are you threatening me? Because I've been threatened by bigger and better opponents than you."

Glory shook her head. "No, not a threat. It's something you'll want to know. Two things, actually."

The woman braced her hands on her hips as her jacket gaped open. "You don't say," she said in a sarcastic tone. "Well, tell away. I'm all ears."

"The first thing is, you told the police your boyfriend Rolf was at a body building competition in Vancouver the day Eddie died. But the police have since found out that he wasn't there. He was kicked out of the event, told to leave. Something about a violent display of temper." Glory hoped it wasn't noticeable that her voice was shaking. This woman was intimidating, and she was glad they were standing in the middle of the sidewalk. If Trudy decided to backhand her or something, there would be witnesses.

Trudy's expression darkened. "How do you know this?"

"It doesn't matter how I know. I just do." She kept her face as expressionless as possible. "So his alibi is gone. That's fact one."

Trudy narrowed her eyes. "And fact number two?"

"Just this." Glory moved closer. She didn't want to blurt this business out to the general population. "Did you just give your witness statement to the Crown counsel? I saw you leaving their offices."

Trudy gave an imperious shake of her head. "Yes, of course. I understand you're next in line."

She leaned closer. "Did you sign the statement?"

Trudy eyed her carefully. "They're typing it as we speak. I'm getting a bite of lunch and going back to sign."

"Ah." Glory felt like she was getting somewhere now. "And did you stick to your story about Alex being there at twelve-thirty?"

"What business is it of yours?" Trudy glared and stepped forward in an effort to intimidate her. "Get out of my face with your questions."

"The thing is, Trudy, Alex was at my place at twelve-thirty. And he was there until nearly five o'clock."

Trudy glowered at her.

She ignored that and plunged on. "And the police now say that Eddie died between two and three in the morning. You can see the problem. Your lies will get you charged with fraud or giving false statements, while Alex goes free. You need to reconsider."

Trudy stared. Her hands tightened into fists in a futile gesture. "How do you know all this?" she hissed.

"It doesn't matter how I know." Glory kept an eye on her, wondering if she was going to get knocked about with those strong arms. "I've been talking to one of the detectives. If you don't change your story, you'll be in trouble with the police." She watched as Trudy seemed to shrink in front of her, until she looked like a balloon figure with most of the air leaked out. "I think maybe you loved Alex at one time, but now you just like to use him. And this time, it's gotten you into trouble."

Trudy staggered to a lamppost at the edge of the curb and leaned against it. Her hands clutched convulsively at her satchel as the tears welled up and rolled down her cheeks.

"Your tears have no effect on me," Glory said. "Save them for the cops, because I don't care. You get in there and tell the truth or you'll be in jail yourself."

Trudy gasped for air as curious onlookers slowed to gaze in their direction. "If I change my story, Rolf will kill me. He's already killed Eddie and he'll kill me, too."

Glory tightened her lips. "Then your best protection is to tell the truth. Rolf can't hurt you if he's spending his days in jail for murder," she bit out.

Trudy glanced at her in despair and looked away. "Easy for you to say. You don't know what he's like."

"No, I don't hang around with guys like that. But if I did, I'd be sure to keep the police on my side, because sooner or later I'd need them."

~~***~~

CHAPTER FIFTY

Alex drove his truck down the muddy road and stopped on the verge to survey the construction site below. It seemed as if he'd been away for months, instead of just a couple of weeks. A great deal had happened during that time, and he felt like a different man in some ways. The intervening time had been exhilarating and demeaning, exciting and frightening by turns.

Manx Construction had obviously made some progress since he was last here. The foundations had all been framed when he left for the north. The pour must have happened right after. Since then the framing boards had been removed, and a new pour of concrete done for the basement floors. Each unit stepped up the side of the hill from the one before it.

Framing for walls had begun on the first few units. The one closest to the road had two floors outlined, and roof trusses were stacked to the side to be hoisted onto the upper cross beams. He spotted Jim

Manx further down the hill, working with Stuart, the carpenter's helper, to lay the boards for the third unit.

Alex got out of his truck, feeling awkward about the mess he'd left behind in the progress of the project. It was one thing to get stuck somewhere and not be able to get to work for a day or two. Things happened, and every one had to learn to cope. But to get arrested and thrown in jail was hard to digest.

He climbed down the bank, mud collecting in the treads of his work boots. "Jim," he said when he got within hailing distance, "Stuart."

The men stopped working and turned to greet him. Stuart broke into a wide grin. "Man, have we missed you," he said. "We've been working our fucking asses off."

Alex felt a smile begin to form as he shook Stuart's hand, then glanced at Jim. He nodded. "Glad to have you here, Alex. We need you, and I'm too old and too busy to be doing this work along with everything else I've got on the go. Welcome back."

"Thanks." Some of the tension in his shoulders eased. "I'm sorry about what was said in the paper referring to Manx Construction," he muttered. "Don't know why they had to put where I worked in there."

Jim waved the comment away. "Like Henny says, any advertising is good advertising. We might even get some more work from that."

"Yeah," Alex muttered, "maybe a contract to build a new jail."

Jim stopped smiling. "I'm sorry, Alex, sorry for what you've been through. And I know it's not over yet. You just let us know when you have appointments and appearances that you can't miss and we'll go from there. We can work around it, do whatever it takes."

"Okay, let's get going." Jim pointed to a pile of lumber. "I'm going to leave you to it with Stuart here. We're just getting started on framing the walls. We might have a second team coming in later in the week to help move this along, so we'll need you to find a partner for Stuart while you supervise. We'll talk later at the office."

Jim climbed the bank as Stuart handed Alex a board and they bent to nail it in place.

~~*~~

The next day, Trudy walked back into the downtown building and found the lawyer's offices on the third floor. She asked to see Mr. Rollins. "He's busy at the moment," the receptionist said officiously.

"It's about the Alex Vecchio case," Trudy whispered, leaning across the desk so the other people in the waiting room wouldn't be able to hear. "It's new information that he'll want to know about."

"And what is your name?" The tone was imperious.

"Trudy Newman, I was at the Crown counsel offices giving a deposition yesterday, but now I need to see Mr. Rollins."

"Well." The receptionist didn't roll her eyes, but it was a near thing. "Just have a seat and I'll let him know you're here. It might be quite a wait." She bustled through the door and disappeared. Some minutes later, she returned, the colour high in her cheeks. "This way please."

Trudy followed her down the narrow hallway, cubicles sandwiched in on both sides with people working at computer screens under the fluorescent lights. The receptionist opened the door to a small boardroom and pointed to a chair. "Wait here," she said, and stalked off.

Trudy waited. Her nerves were shot, and her hands shook. Glory was right about how the evidence looked, and it was time she faced her predicament. She never should have lied, but Rolf could be very persuasive. She was frightened of him.

She straightened in the chair, hoping her heart would slow down. It wouldn't impress the lawyer if she looked spooked while giving a statement. She pressed her palms together to steady them, then jumped when the door opened behind her.

"Sorry." Mr. Rollins was a short, dumpy man, but dressed impeccably in a three piece suit, the vest gaping around the buttons at the belly line. His flushed complexion spoke of high blood pressure or too many martinis at lunch, or both. He extended his hand. "What can I do for you? They already took your statement at the Crown offices apparently. It was very damning for my client, Ms. Newman. If you have anything to add that implicates him further, you should take it to the Crown."

"That's the thing, Mr. Rollins. I want to change my statement."

He nodded. "Well, you should take it up with the Crown. You realize that as you remember or change more details, you begin to look weaker as a witness."

Tears welled in her eyes, and she gazed blankly at her hands clasped tightly in her lap. "I want to retract my statement," she said. "Alex didn't kill Eddie. I should know, I was there."

Rollins blew out a gust of air, and subsided into a chair. "I see. So Alex Vecchio is innocent, you're saying."

"Yes." Her voice had dropped to a hoarse whisper, there was no air left in her lungs. *Was this the right move?* It was dangerous, but then everything seemed dangerous right now. She needed to neutralize Rolf and have him convicted of the murder before she was the next person lying on her bedroom floor with her neck broken.

Rollins jumped to his feet. "Don't go anywhere. I'll be right back."

Within minutes two people entered the room and began setting up a recorder. Someone took her photo, then Rollins was back with a pad of paper and a couple of pens in his hand. He sat across from her as the camera was propped up on the boardroom table.

"Now, Ms. Newman," he began. "You told me you want to retract your statement in the Alex Vecchio case, is that true? Please look into the lens of the camera as you give your statement."

~~***~~

CHAPTER FIFTY ONE

Glory climbed into her little car and started the engine. She was tired today after her shift at the bagel bakery. Spending the night with Alex had been exhilarating, although she didn't get much sleep. Her body was a bit sore, pleasantly so, but work had come early again this morning. She put the car in gear and eased into the traffic.

A block down, she turned north and was just passing the lawyer's offices when Trudy Newman stepped onto the street. She slowed, watching the way she sauntered along the sidewalk. No wonder Alex had been attracted to her. The toned body, long legs and hip roll when she walked all added up to a very sexy and engaging package. Her heart stuttered a little before taking up its normal beat. She would never look like that. She wasn't tall, her legs weren't long, and her hip roll was probably much less noticeable.

Glory pulled into a parking spot at the side of the street and let the engine idle. *Should she talk to her again about changing her statement, or would it be overkill, so to speak?* She didn't laugh. The pun was too close to the awful truth.

Shutting the motor off, she opened her door. Might as well jump in with both feet. *What were the chances of running into her once more?* Pretty slim.

Glory jogged toward her, then slowed as a tall muscular guy caught up with Trudy and grabbed her arm in a tight grip. He said something low, his expression menacing, and Trudy shrank away from him. He shook her and pulled her along as he began walking down the street toward the parkade.

Glory sped up. *Was this Rolf, that Trudy claimed had committed the murder?* If so, he certainly looked intimidating. No wonder Trudy was afraid of hm.

As she got closer, she heard Trudy's protests. "Stop, please Rolf. I don't want to go there right now." The woman pulled back but, strong as she was, it had no effect in slowing them down. Rolf dragged her along, his grip fierce on her upper arm.

"Wait a minute," Glory called, and raced to pass them. She stood in the middle of the sidewalk and glared at the couple. "Trudy," she said, "don't think you can get out of our agreement this easy. You promised to come with me to…" *To what?* Her brain wasn't quick enough to come up with anything that might be convincing.

Rolf stopped and stared at her. "Who are you? Get out of my way."

"No," Glory folded her arms, as her knees trembled. "Trudy promised to come with me."

"Does she look like she's going with you?" He gave a jerk on Trudy's arm and she stumbled against his side, her face pasty white. She pressed her lips in a tight line and shook her head at Glory, who immediately decided to ignore it.

"Just a minute." She raised her voice and glanced around, hoping for some support from the people going by. "Take your hands off her. You have to let her go."

Now some pedestrians were slowing and looking rather than just marching past. Glory took heart. "Trudy, come with me."

A couple of guys going the other way paused, and one said, "Do you need any help here? What's going on?"

"Butt out," Rolf growled in a menacing tone. "Get lost, this is my business."

But the guy didn't leave, just stood there looking at Glory. She gave a tremulous smile. "My friend is coming with me, and this guy is trying to make her leave." Glory wondered in another part of her brain why exactly she was taking such a risk for this woman who hated her guts and had lied about a murder. Because of her, Alex had been put in jail. *Had she lost her mind?* It was a distinct possibility. On the other hand, without Trudy's testimony, Alex might go down for that murder.

More people gathered, and the two guys moved carefully forward. "Do you want to get your hand off her arm?" one of them said to Rolf. "That looks painful."

A car slowed at the curb near the gathering crowd and Rolf glanced wildly around before dropping his hand and stalking off without a backward glance. Glory shook from shock as she took Trudy's hand. "Come on. Let's go, my car's right over there."

~~*~~

Alex worked late. He was so far behind on what was going on with the construction work that he'd spent hours walking the site to refamiliarize himself with the layout, the number of units, the quirks of the topography they were dealing with. Then when Stuart quit for the night, he stopped at the Manx office and read all the engineering reports and recent recommendations from the building inspector. By the time he'd ploughed through most of the plans, it was seven o'clock and his heart was suddenly hammering in his chest.

He had a curfew. It wasn't something he was used to dealing with. If he was at work, he left when he was finished for the day. If the band was playing, he stopped home for a change of clothes and his guitar and carried on to the club. That was before, but things had changed.

He ran for his truck, knowing it was a good half hour into town. He was determined he would not be caught out, not in any way. Not when his mother had pledged the family home.

He pulled up in front of the townhouse with twenty minutes to spare, grabbed his gear and went inside. It was like being back in prison. Now he couldn't leave the house until six the next morning. Sighing, he hung his jacket on the hook by the door, pried off his boots and carried his lunch pail into the kitchen.

He called Glory's cell, but it went to voice mail. Perhaps she had a music class tonight. He should have gotten her schedule from her last night, but he been too busy... Well, he'd been too busy seducing her to think of mundane things like work times and questions concerning where she'd be today. His temperature climbed at the thought and he pulled his mind away to concentrate on other things.

He dialed Saigon Palace, thinking she'd like some Vietnamese food, but they didn't do take out or delivery. He needed dinner and something to put in his lunch bucket tomorrow, so it was back to Chinese or pizza for the moment. He should get organized, stop at a grocery store, something.

By the time he'd eaten, fatigue was setting in. He stripped and stepped into the shower, then called Glory again. No answer.

He'd snooze for a bit. Lying on the bed with a pile of pillows behind his head, he turned on a hockey game and idly watched the action while making a mental list of things he had to tend to. He'd only had one workout since he got home. Maybe he'd leave work tomorrow by five, give himself time to hit the gym. And

Glory, he needed to organize something there, or he might lose valuable ground...

Alex dozed, and didn't hear the tentative knock on his door.

~~***~~

CHAPTER FIFTY TWO

Glory rolled over and slowly rose to the surface of consciousness. Because she worked so early most days, her ability to sleep in had become curtailed. Sleeping late usually meant anything past six o'clock.

She slipped out of bed and tiptoed across the cold floor to her front window. Alex's truck was still parked on the street, that was good. She raced to the bathroom, and then grabbed her housecoat. *Would he be up?* He must be by now. He used to leave for work around seven or seven-thirty.

She cautiously opened her door and peeked out. No one on the steps or the sidewalk to see her early morning romp in her nightie and housecoat. She rapped at his door and it was immediately yanked open.

"Glory!" He pulled her through the doorway and swept her into his arms. "I didn't see you last night. Is everything okay?"

She nodded against his flannel shirt. "I knocked, but there was no answer."

"You knocked?" He held her away as he looked his alarm. "I didn't hear any knock. What time? Why didn't you phone?"

Then his mouth crushed down on hers and there was no opportunity or reason to answer. A few moments later, he lifted his head, his chest heaving even as his hard hand on her lower back pressed her against his growing erection. "You just take my breath away. What time is it? Damn, I have to leave in…"

"Shush," she said. "Listen, Alex. I have some news."

"News?" He looked at her blankly. "I only have a few minutes before I have to go."

"I know. Sit here." She tugged him toward the couch and seated herself on his knee. His hand slid up the inside of her thigh as he pressed his lips to her throat. "Damn, Glory. You're so beautiful. You've got me tied up in knots."

She placed her hands on his cheeks and turned his head to look directly into his dark blue eyes. "Trudy has changed her story."

He stalled, his gaze slowly sharpening. "How do you mean, changed her story?"

"She withdrew her statement about you killing Eddie. And she's given a different version, where Rolf came in and caught them together. He snapped Eddie's neck."

"Ah." Alex closed his eyes for a minute, as the air escaped his lungs. "Fuck. I figured that might be what happened. Damn that Eddie, why couldn't he keep it in his pants for once?" Moisture glittered in the corners of his eyes. "He didn't deserve to die like that."

"No, I'm sorry for your friend. I really am." She leaned against his chest and he tightened his arms around her. "It's sad."

Alex was silent for a moment. "So what now? They have to drop the charges against me."

"Exactly. I've been talking to Mr. Rollins."

"You have?" Faint amusement gleamed in a small curl of the lips. "I don't doubt it. What does he say?"

"He's got your cell phone number. He'll be in touch today as soon as he's sorted things out. They'll have to appear in Chambers to withdraw the charges and cancel the bail conditions."

He nodded, his lips firmed together in a straight line. "The nightmare is over, you're saying. But not for everyone. Where is Rolf right now? Because my guess is he's a dangerous man, especially where Trudy is concerned."

"The lawyer said he'd look after that, too. Trudy is in a safe place until Rolf is arrested and in jail."

"You have been busy," he murmured, one hand sliding inside her housecoat to fondle her breast. "Would you like to organize my life as well? It looks like you're good at it." He pressed a quick kiss to her mouth. "Go home. I have to get to work and I can't leave you here half-naked."

"Very funny," she said and reluctantly slid off his knee. "What about later?"

"Leave your phone on," he instructed. "You obviously don't have a shift at the bagel shop today or you wouldn't still be here. Have you got classes later?"

She nodded. "A couple of after school groups."

"Good, so keep the evening free. That's an order." His grin softened the command. He slid his feet into his boots and grabbed his jacket from a hook by the door. Lunch pail in hand he shooed her out the door. "I'll be in touch."

~~*~~

Mrs. Vecchio had roasted a chicken and baked some potatoes for the family dinner. There was a Greek-style salad of cucumbers, tomatoes, yellow peppers and feta, and a dish of steamed broccoli with a cheese sauce. Her face was flushed from the heat of the oven as she pulled pans out. They clattered on top of the stove. Serving dishes were arranged in a row on the counter.

The house felt warm and homey, decorated for the approaching holidays with candy canes hung in a row across the fireplace mantel in the living room, and a big tree in the corner, loaded with coloured decorations and strings of lights. Ryan said he'd spent two days pinning the lights outside around the front door and across the bay windows of the house.

Glory had helped him set the table in the small dining room, with place mats, cloth napkins, and a pair of candlesticks in the centre of the table. He dug some candles out of a drawer on the sideboard and rammed them into place. Glory gave a startled laugh. "I think you're supposed to carve the bottoms with a sharp knife to make them fit, rather than force them in."

He grinned. "This is faster," he said, just as the front door opened and Alex came in. He'd obviously been home to change, his jeans, boots and work jacket replaced by dress pants and a shirt with an open collar. "Smells good," he called as he hung his jacket on a hook, then caught sight of Glory. His eyes lit up as he examined her tight pants and gauzy blouse. "Nice," he said low. "Very nice." She blushed under the weight of his gaze.

Mrs. Vecchio appeared in the doorway and rushed to give him a hug, pulling his head down to kiss his cheek. "Congratulations, son. It's all over, and you won."

"Thanks, Mum." He pressed his face to her cheek. "You were a stalwart."

"Well, it's over. that's the main thing. No more excitement for a while, I'm hoping."

He gave a ragged chuckle. "I agree." Although when his gaze wandered over to Glory, he raised his eyebrows and gave her a grin. *Maybe a little more excitement?* She smiled back, feeling her cheeks grow warm.

They sat at the table for dinner, the carved chicken arranged on a platter in the centre. Mrs. Vecchio folded her hands and said grace, giving thanks for her son's freedom. They all echoed *amen.*

"Does this mean the legal details are taken care of?" Mrs. Vecchio asked.

Alex nodded. "Pretty much. The lawyer appeared in court this morning with Crown counsel to vacate the charges against me. Then they withdrew the bail conditions. I have to attend at his office after Christmas to sign some paperwork, but he assured me it's all been looked after."

"Well, that's a relief. You can stay out later than eight o'clock, then."

He laughed, and Ryan chuckled. "Not a little boy any more, eh?" he said, his eyes twinkling.

"Don't get smart," Alex said, flexing his shoulders. "I can take you any day."

Ryan pursed his lips. "True. But that's not the only way to win."

They both laughed.

"I heard from Coop today," Alex said as he helped himself to a potato and sliced it open along the top. "He and his bride are coming over to the island for a visit this weekend. They'll be here tomorrow, Christmas Eve. Then they'll be heading back home Christmas Day. He has to be at work Tuesday."

"It'll be nice to see them," Mrs. Vecchio said. "He's a good young man, and I'd like to meet his wife."

The conversation meandered until Ryan said, "Don't know what the future of the band is going to be. Without Eddie, we're handicapped big time."

Glory's ears perked up. "I know someone who plays bass. Don't know if they'll be interested in joining us. I'm still in the band, right?"

Ryan pulled his chin in. "Of course, why would you ask?"

"I don't know. Things have been pretty up in the air since I joined. I just wondered…"

"No, you're definitely in. That is, if you still want to be." He gave her a hesitant look.

"Yes, I love playing." She smiled at Alex, and Ryan nodded. "Great. That's settled then. I know a few guys who play bass, let's just wait and see who we can get."

Glory nodded and took another bite of chicken. "Great dinner, Mrs. Vecchio. I don't know when I last had a home-cooked meal like this. It all tastes good."

Mrs. Vecchio smiled. "Call me Alice," she said. "And you're more than welcome."

~~***~~

CHAPTER FIFTY THREE

Later, Glory parked her car at the curb outside the townhouse and watched in her rear-view mirror as a big black pickup pulled in tight behind her little back bumper. Alex stepped out and came up the side of her car to open the door.

"Welcome home," he said. He offered his hand to help her out.

By the time he got his front door unlocked, he had her coat half off and hanging from one arm. He pulled her inside and backed her up against the door. "I couldn't wait to get you here," he muttered into the side of her throat, one hand on her breast. "That might have been the longest family dinner on record."

She laughed softly, then shut up as his mouth captured hers in a fierce kiss.

"I don't want to rush," he said when he came up for air. "I want us to take our time, because we've got all night."

"Coop is coming tomorrow," she offered.

"Coop can look out for himself," he murmured. "I'm looking after us." He scooped her into his arms and walked slowly down the hallway. "My bed's bigger so we do our workouts here," he said.

She giggled. "Workouts? I hadn't realized this was an exercise programme."

"Of course," he said. He laid her gently on the quilt. "First I take your clothes off, then you work on mine. It's all exercise. Then if I'm on top I have to do the heavy lifting, but if you're on top, I still do all the work."

He laughed deep in his throat and slid a finger inside the hem of her sweater. "Not that you'll hear me complaining. Do you want me to take this off fast or slow?" He carefully lifted the hem an inch. "We can take all the time we want. Although…" As he slowly raised the fabric, his gaze sharpened on the bare skin he was revealing. "Maybe not too slow."

Glory reached for the top buttons on his shirt and their arms got tangled, the clothes revealing a breast, a limb, a shoulder. "Forget it," he said, and lifted the sweater over her head. "This is too difficult."

"For whom?" she murmured.

"For me," he admitted as he peeled her arms out of the tight sleeves. "My patience isn't what it once was. Not since I met you, in fact. You make me impatient, Glory. I want to be with you, by your side, inside you."

She felt a clenching in her belly and concentrated harder to unbutton his shirt, tugging the tails out of his waistband.

"Here, let me." He unbuckled his belt and pushed his pants over his hips. "We just need to get naked and then we can slow down."

She giggled and he gave a ragged chuckle.

Much later, Glory reclined on his shoulder, her arm splayed across his body. Her hand rested in the nest of fine curls in the middle of his chest. She sighed and stretched. "That felt wonderful," she said.

"Oh, God," Alex blew out a breath. "Did it ever. I love you Glory. I want to marry you."

Her heart seemed to stop altogether, then thankfully started again, beating erratically in her chest. She glanced at his face. His eyes were flinty with intent as he gazed at her. He rolled to the side and lifted her chin so they were nose to nose. "I love you. I want to spend my life with you, Glory. I don't want to just have a fling, or sleep with you when you're around. We need our own space, our own home. Somewhere that's safe for you, and convenient to your music classes and the bagel shop." He smiled into her eyes. "What do you think?"

"I don't know." She felt like she was stuttering, but he'd caught her off guard. "I haven't thought about it."

"Could you think about it? Because I'm totally serious." He kissed her gently, his mouth roving over her face to finally stop at her lips where he nibbled for a moment. "You're perfect for me, I knew it from the start."

She laughed and shook her head. "As if…"

"I know," he admitted. "I acted like an ass, but that was because... Well, never mind. But you drew me in like a little magnet. You're lovely and compact." His hand wandered down her back to her butt and lingered there, kneading her flesh.

"My mother likes you," he added. "She says you're perfect for me."

"Does she?" Glory smiled, "I like her, too."

"What about your dad?" He gave her a questioning look.

"He likes you," she said, her lips curling. "He's said so several times."

"Good," he said, his hand exploring further. "I like him too."

"And my mother likes you, we've both seen that," Glory added.

The planes of his face went red as his hand stopped its exploration. "Now, you know what happened that night. I wasn't out of line."

She rubbed her palm against his cheek, feeling his five o'clock shadow emerging. "I know. I trust you, Alex."

"Oh. Okay, then. Maybe we need to move on to a different topic. I can see your nipples puckering and I don't think it's because it's too cold in here. They probably want some more attention."

He lowered his head and she gave a sigh as she fell slowly and completely under his spell once more.

~~***~~

CHAPTER FIFTY FOUR

It was raining Christmas Eve, big drops that landed with an audible splash on the windshields and sidewalks. Glory got to Dad's place late because she'd been over at the Vecchio's visiting with Alex's friend Coop and his bride. They were a very sweet couple, and thrilled to be on the island. Coop had spent time in Victoria as a kid in high school and he remembered so many things. He told stories of when Alex began weight-lifting, when his father had died and their lives changed drastically.

It had all been new information for her. She'd reluctantly said goodbye. Driving her Mini in the direction of James Bay, she perked up again. This was a tradition between her and her father, spending Christmas Eve, and overnight to Christmas morning, together.

She brought some cute items for his stocking that she'd found on the trip north. She had a pair of deer hide leather gloves, hand stitched with decorative designs sewn around the cuffs that she'd found in the general store in Prespatou. And under Dad's tiny artificial tree that sat in the corner by his living room window, she'd placed a brand new hardcopy of *The Last of the Mohicans*, wrapped with a big bow. Dad loved reading westerns, and she knew he'd like this one. Those chapters Alex read to her in that little log cabin had sounded like music to her ears.

She hadn't heard from her mother since the trip north, and didn't know where she was spending the Christmas season. There had been a time when Glory fretted about that and tried to make something happen with Jean over Christmas, but the last few years she'd left it alone. If Mum wanted to see her, she'd get in touch. She always did.

When they went to bed that night, Glory stared out the window for a moment at the rain, listening to it patter on the eaves and wondered what Alex was doing. Then she crawled into bed and breathed a prayer of thanks for surviving the north, the whole trip, and for Alex and his family. They were good people, and had welcomed her as part of them with great ease. It felt comfortable already. Then she prayed for Dad, his health and strength, and gave thanks for him.

~~*~~

The next morning Glory woke to snow. The temperature had dropped in the night and those big fat raindrops had frozen, covering everything with a blanket of white. The Christmas lights up and down the street were on, winking in the brilliance of a muffled sun.

She pulled on her clothes and ran down the stairs. "Dad! Are you up? Did you see?"

Her father stepped out of the kitchen, coffee mug in hand. He grinned at her enthusiasm. "I thought you might have had enough of this stuff," he said, a twinkle in his eye. "Wanna have a snowball fight?"

She giggled. "Let's go out, because it won't last long."

"Okay." They shrugged into heavy coats and mittens, pulling on their boots and stepping carefully down the slippery front steps. The snowball fight lasted about four minutes when Glory gave up in the face of the huge volley of shots Dad was sending her way. They settled in to build a snowman, who stood proudly by the walkway, leaning slightly to the left with two pinecones for his eyes and a stubby carrot nose. Dad came up with an old hat to put on his head, and scrounged around for buttons to press into his tummy.

By the time they stamped back into the house, Glory was starving. "What's for breakfast?"

Dad hung his coat by the door and pried off his boots. "I thought slices of ham, and maybe Egyptian eyes."

"Oh, good." Glory headed for the kitchen and rummaged in his fridge. "Dad, you don't have much food in here. What do you eat?"

"I eat okay," he muttered. "What are you, the food Nazi?"

"No." She turned to look at him. "Do you eat out? Because there's isn't much here. A few vegetables, some cheese. You can't stay healthy if you don't eat right."

"Never mind," Dad said and pulled out a carton of eggs. He grabbed two frying pans from a lower cupboard and placed slices of ham in one to begin warming, and added a bit of butter to the other before turning on the heat. As he cut a square hole out of each piece of bread, Glory sliced a grapefruit and put it into two bowls on the small table.

"I guess we should head over to the Vecchio's around four," she said.

Dad nodded and placed the bread in the pan, breaking an egg into each hole. "That was nice of them to invite us for Christmas dinner, wasn't it?"

"Yeah," Glory nodded. "I think they've been a little lonely since the father died. I mean, we used to be fine, but when you and Mum... Well, it was just different with one person gone."

"I know, girl." He placed a hand on her shoulder. "And I'm sorry it worked out that way. I really am. Yet there wasn't a thing I could do about it."

"I know, Dad. I'm amazed that the marriage lasted as long as it did."

"No, she changed." Dad turned to flip the eggs in the pan. "Jean changed, she wanted to be younger, and trendier and have more fun. Maybe I wasn't as much fun as she needed."

"Oh, Dad. Don't do that. If there's any fault to share out, I think it goes to Mum. But let's not go there.

At least this year, there won't just be the two of us. We'll see the Vecchio's and it will be nice."

~~***~~

CHAPTER FIFTY FIVE

When they arrived at the Vecchio house, Glory immediately caught the aroma of a turkey roasting in the oven. It had been a few years since she'd been to a turkey dinner. She imagined there was stuffing, that gravy and mashed potatoes would be part of the fare.

She smiled at Mrs. Vecchio and gave her a hug. "Thank you for inviting us. This is wonderful to be here at Christmas."

"Oh," Alice waved a vague hand, "that's what Christmas is for. To share." She glanced at Dad, and Glory said, "This is my father, Howard Stephens. Dad, this is Alice Vecchio." As they shook hands, Ryan appeared with Alex right behind him and she continued the introductions.

"Good to see you again, sir," Alex said. "Come on in. Can I fix you a drink? Come into the kitchen, we're just in the middle of the potatoes." He gave a half-grin. "Ryan's peeling, I'm chopping."

By the time everyone had a drink, the potatoes were on the stove simmering in a big pot and sweet potatoes drained and laid out in a baking dish. Mrs. Vecchio sprinkled some brown sugar on them, added dabs of butter and a generous dash of cloves before sliding it into the oven alongside the turkey.

Mrs Vecchio took Dad into the living room and Alex leaned in near Glory's ear. "Come with me," he whispered. "I've got something to show you." He led her down the stairs to the basement.

"My room is down here." He pointed to an unfinished wall and door. "A little rough, but I was pretty young when I built it."

He opened the door and led her inside. It was fairly spacious, with a double bed pushed against one wall, a small built-in closet, and a dresser under the single high window.

"When did you build this?" she asked.

"Grade twelve. It was getting crowded upstairs and Ryan needed his own space, so I started this. Dad helped me lay it out, but he died in the middle of the job. So it got stalled for a while, then I finished it however I could." He pinched the bridge of his nose. "Wasn't easy, but I got it done."

"Anyway." He shook his head and walked across to grab a small package from the top of the dresser. "I wanted to give you this. Here, sit on the bed for a minute."

Glory felt alarm in her chest as she contemplated what was in his hand. It looked like a ring box and if so, he'd want an answer. And she wasn't ready. Nor was she good with being rushed. *What if she reacted the wrong way and lost him altogether?* Panic rose from her stomach and lodged in her throat.

"Sit," he gestured to the quilt. "It'll only take a minute."

With quiet trepidation, she hoisted herself onto the side of the bed and sat there in stunned silence, her eyes squeezed shut. *Oh, God, don't let me blow this.*

When she opened them again, Alex was kneeling on the small carpet by her feet. "Glory," he said. "I know you're not ready to say 'yes' to me right now. We haven't known each other very long, and you probably still have questions about who I am and what I stand for, especially after the last fiasco. But I love you. So, I bought you this." He pressed the blue velvet ring box into her hand. The colour was high in his cheeks and his hand was hot where he touched hers.

"It's not an engagement ring. When we buy one of those, I want you to have the final say in what it looks like. This is a promise ring. I promise to be true to you, Glory. I'm not asking anything in return. This is my promise, given freely. I love you."

She gazed down at the box for a moment, her fingers squeezed tight to hold it in her palm as her heart ticked faster. This wasn't as scary as she'd imagined, so she pried the lid back to look inside. It was a gold ring with a heart-shaped design and a small gem stone, a ruby, set in it. She glanced at him, feeling the sweetness of the gesture soften in her chest.

"It's your birthstone," he said.

She felt a small smile beginning on her mouth. *How did he know when her birthday was?* He'd managed to find out somehow. And he'd sidestepped her nervous reaction to a marriage proposal, with a promise ring.

"It's beautiful," she managed. "I love it. Thank you, Alex."

He was watching her intently, then leaned forward to press a kiss to her lips. "Do you want to put it on?"

"Yes, I'd love to." She plucked it out of the box and he took it from her, sliding it onto her right hand. "This way," he said, "you can still wear it after you get married." He gave her a sly glance and she laughed a little breathlessly.

She admired it on her finger, holding it up to the light. "It fits perfectly. How did you…"

"I kind of guessed."

"Thank you." She gazed into his dark blue eyes. "I love it. I admit I'm nervous about deciding…"

He kissed her to stop the words. "That's okay. We've been through a great deal, you and I, in just a few short weeks. We've got lots of time. I'm not going anywhere." When he kissed her again, it was with intent and it was a long time before he raised his head. "We better get out of here, dinner will be ready."

Alex carved the turkey, Ryan mashed potatoes and Mrs Vecchio made gravy. Glory got her dad to help her set the table, now that she knew where everything was stored in the cramped dining room. They had a wonderful time, a lot of talk and laughter about the trip north, the band fiascos, with a small painful pause over Eddie. But then back to other funny stories.

Harris was more outgoing than she'd seen him in quite a while. *Had Dad gotten a liking for Alice Vecchio, or was he just encouraging Alex where Glory was concerned?* She didn't know, but it was nice to see, and Alice had a glow in her cheeks by the time dinner was over.

Some of the Vecchios neighbours dropped by for dessert in the evening and Ryan's girlfriend Josie arrived. There were homemade shortbread cookies, mincemeat tarts and a cranberry coffee cake with ice cream. Alex and Ryan were kept busy serving the pastries along with coffee, tea and medicinal shots of scotch. Glory was too full to try most of it, but that was okay. There was always tomorrow, Alice told her. And she could take some home.

Glory wiggled her finger and admired the ring. Alex glanced over and gave her a smile that melted her heart. Her whole body grew warm. The more time she spent with him, the better she felt and the happier she became. She glanced at Dad where he was chatting with one of the neighbours and he gave her a wink. Everyone had noticed and admired the ring. Ryan had made some comments under his breath and Alex gave him a couple of shots in the shoulder with his fist, calling him a punk. They'd been laughing.

By the time they were ready to go home, Glory was tired. It had been such an exciting day, with a lot to deal with. For her, the emotional stuff was just as exhausting as the physical effort of work or play. She said good bye to the Vecchio family, shook the neighbours' hands and allowed Alex to follow her onto the step for a kiss. "I'll be home later," he said. "But I can see you're tired."

"Yeah, don't wake me tonight." She leaned into his heavy shoulder. "I'll see you tomorrow."

Dad had already started the truck, and she ran down the steps, free of snow where Ryan had shovelled, and climbed in.

~~***~~

CHAPTER FIFTY SIX

Ryan hit a drum roll and the band fell silent. "That's better," he called. "At least we're showing signs of having a little bit of discipline." This was their third practice since Christmas, and they were just breaking in their new member.

Glory rolled her eyes and Alex caught her. He laughed at her exasperated expression. "Well," she whispered near his ear, "he's turning into a music Nazi. Every little thing has to be done just right."

"Here we go," Ryan interrupted and hit a drum beat for the next number. Alex slid into the rhythm of the song with his guitar and then began to sing. Soon Pete followed, his violin in full swing, the strings on his bow shredding and sagging as he sawed heavily. He'd come a long way in his playing in the last few months.

Glory played her keyboard for all she was worth, then began the chorus. It was her backup singing that made this work, that and Pete's contributions. Things were different in the band than they had been when Glory first joined them. Eddie wasn't here, and Alex still missed him, they all did. His bass sound and deep voice had added a lot to their combined presence on stage. Now that was gone forever.

Pete had begun to sing. Just a little at first, then more full throated backup as he progressed. And he was good, his voice nearly as deep as Eddie's, his timing impeccable.

Since Ryan had said he was looking for a bass player, Glory had recruited her friend, Mercedes. Things had certainly progressed from there. Mercedes had played bass guitar in Glory's high school band. So Ryan let her try out with them at rehearsal, and she was coming along famously. Alex had been surprised by his brother's willingness to entertain the possibility of another female in the group.

However, Mercedes had caught Pete's attention a few times when she'd been in the audience at *Rooster's* the nights they'd played there. He was more than interested in her, and Ryan had decided to bring the girl into the band not just because she was good, but to give Pete a break. Not that the two of them had gotten together. But Pete was obviously working slowly and hesitantly in that direction.

Rolf had been arrested, and charged with the murder of Eddie Marker. He'd been remanded in jail pending trial because of evidence regarding his violent temper. Alex felt a sense of relief. At least someone would pay for that awful deed, and he'd been totally cleared of any suspicion.

He glanced over at Glory as she shifted on the bench. She flipped a page of music on the stand in front of her. She'd promised to marry him. He hadn't told anyone yet, they were still making plans about when it might happen. And no, he didn't think his family was going to be totally surprised by the news.

But he couldn't wait to begin his new life, a life with Glory.

~~***~~

~~*~~

Note to Reader -

I would really like your help. Book reviews are the lifeblood of what I do and your review of my book would mean a lot to me. If you would take a moment or two and leave your review on Amazon.com or wherever you bought the book, that would be wonderful. If you want to send it to me, my contact information is at the bottom.

I honestly thank you.

Last but not least, if you find an error in this book, please email me. This will help me fix things that my editors and I might have overlooked and make for a better read for others. In return, by way of showing my gratitude, I will send you a free copy of the next book with my sincere thanks.

Sylvie Grayson

You can learn more or contact Sylvie Grayson at her website-
www.sylviegrayson.com or email at
sylviegraysonauthor@gmail.com

Prince of Jiran
The Last War: Book Five

Excerpt—

"You nicked me, you bastard." The Prince of Penrhy leaped forward in sudden anger and pinned his opponent to the bare barn wall. Haggskyll just grinned and, with a twist of the wrist, unceremoniously dumped him on his back in the middle of the rubber-plastic mat.

The sun was still low in the morning sky, strings of clouds filtered in pale strands before a light winter wind in the Jiran territory. The fighting arts building near the tribal military barracks was huge and open, with mats spread in uneven patterns across the unfinished brick floor.

Shandro dropped his sword and flexed his fingers in the protective gloves, gulping for breath as the anger drained away, the tension easing its grip on his gut. The politics of the Penrhy tribe sometimes got under his skin in unexpected ways. The struggle to keep their people in a balanced position with the other tribes, the Shafoneurs to the south, Moiselles north of them, and a few that wandered in the vast lands to the west, was only equal to the effort needed to remain on speaking terms with his erratic father, Sovereign of the Penrhys.

He rolled to his feet and ripped the padding off his bare chest. His skin gleamed with sweat, the star tattoo on his right shoulder barely visible in the pale early morning light drifting in from the high windows. He glanced down at his side. Blood oozed sluggishly from a shallow wound over his ribs.

Brushing it off with a flick of the fingers, Shandro glared at his teacher and guard. "That's the second time you've done that," he said with a grimace, his voice echoing off the walls.

Haggskyll was a massive man trained in the fighting arts. He'd been Shandro's bodyguard since his days as a boy in military college at Sommerset, in what was now Adar Silva. Shrugging his thick shoulders, Haggskyll bent to pick up Shandro's sword and handed it to him. "You got me too, and you were getting lax. Best to keep your guard up."

Shandro heard a scuffle and glanced over to the entry. "Who is it?" he called.

Wakeland stuck his head around the door frame, a guard hovering nervously at his back. "Your father wants you in his offices. He said to be quick." Shorter than Shandro, lean and wiry, Wakeland came through the doorway and stepped onto the mats. This man worked as secretary with the prince on all things to do with the Penrhy tribe and Jiran's relations with neighbouring countries.

He grabbed the back straps of Shandro's protective gear. Prying them free, he handed the padding off to

Haggskyll. "The Sovereign's had a delegation in with him since very early. No one knows who they are. They arrived with a great deal of pomp, I might add. Seemed to be important, if only in their own minds. And their clothing was old fashioned, like from Adar Silva years ago."

Shandro felt a shiver of apprehension curl down his spine at the mention of the time when Emperor Aqatain was still in power and the Old Empire controlled the land. Stooping, he pulled the shield from his shins and stepped out of the boots. "You mean, like the Old Emperor's men used to wear?"

He watched Wakeland's face. They'd all been there—Shandro, Wakeland and Haggskyll—in those early days of college before the Last War changed everything. He'd learned much more than his father would ever have imagined.

~~~

"Maa wants to see you."

Chinata turned abruptly at the sharp tap on the classroom door, the drab grey Sanctuary robe swirling untidily about her legs. Her students jumped in their chairs and giggled nervously as Sister One stopped, ramrod straight, just inside the doorway, her stare hard and challenging. Sister One had forever been thus. As Maa's first assistant. she had in all ways been demanding and aggressive toward the other women in the compound.

It was a clear winter day in northern Khandarken.

The Sanctuary, built by Maa as a place of refuge toward the end of the Last War, was peaceful and well protected by the mercenary guards who'd been recruited from the hordes of dispossessed that ranged the surrounding hills. The high walls enclosed fields of vegetables, fruit and nut trees, farm yards and animal pens, everything needed to sustain the encampment and its inhabitants. The women who lived here were strictly ruled by Maa, but in exchange enjoyed a non-violent, protected life with an abundance of food and supplies.

But along with women came children. It had been Chinata's idea to establish the school. The subjects she taught were languages and mathematical calculations. Women with more knowledge in different areas taught other subjects to the varied groups of youngsters who lived within the compound.

China obediently followed Sister One down the corridor from the school house. They crossed the beautiful gathering rooms of the Sanctuary, with their rose-tiled floors and airy views. This was where Maa held assemblies for the women residents, or conducted sessions with the new acolytes who were being welcomed into the Sanctuary culture.

China thought of it more as indoctrination than training, because Maa was a skilled mesmerist and exercised her persuasion on the newcomers through that method. By the time she'd finished a session with them, they always believed what they had been told, even if they couldn't remember the actual words. China held her own very private opinions on much of what the older woman taught.

Sister led her along the paths through the graceful flower gardens, most plants fallow now in early winter, to Maa's office in a small block of buildings near the centre of the compound. She knocked on the door, then bowed imperiously before continuing on down the hallway. China heard Maa's deep voice call, *enter*. She opened the door.

The rooms were spacious and bright from the plexi along one wall which let in the winter light, the entry hall warm and inviting with couches and chairs ranged around the walls. There was a sleeping chamber, bathrobe and work room behind this space, she knew, although she'd never laid eyes on it. Maa sat before a small fireheat, reading on her tomo. She was a tall woman, angular of body and face. Her eyes were deep set and close together below a prominent brow, her jaw wide and angular. Her hair had gone completely white over the years and she wore it short and combed upward so that it stood on end as if she'd had a powerful shock.

Maa flipped the cover shut on her tomo and put it aside. She didn't smile and her glance was piercing as she pointed to a chair opposite. "Have a seat, Chinata."

China bowed respectfully and moved forward to occupy the edge of the cushion. She was never comfortable in Maa's company, although she'd known the woman all her life. But even years ago, when she'd been a young girl in Sommerset, Maa had been a heavy presence in her existence, directing her activities, sharply correcting her actions and seemingly watching every move she made.

Now, China waited. Their leader was taking longer than usual to inform her why she'd been summoned. Maa's small eyes roamed over her from head to toe before she sighed, sat back in her chair and stared into the fireheat.

China had the familiar sinking feeling that she'd disappointed the woman once more.

Finally, Maa turned back to her. "Chinata, I'm sure I don't have to tell you war is coming. The young Emperor has invaded Khandarken and overtaken some areas along the northern border. It isn't enough of course, and he needs more land to establish a new empire for himself."

She stilled at the words. "Are you afraid that he will try to claim the Sanctuary?" It had been a real struggle to build this place out of nothing. A shock of alarm coursed down her spine at the thought that it might be taken away from them just as it was coming into its own—the gardens and fruit trees producing, nut bushes full of seed, the herds of cattle bigger than they needed so they were selling off animals instead of hoarding them against the demands of another cold winter.

Maa narrowed her eyes. China could barely see the irises now, just two slits in the woman's angular face. "That is always a possibility. But there is a way you can help."

"Yes, Maa. What can I do?"

"There has been an offer for your hand in marriage."

"Oh." A thrill wended its way under her ribs. *An offer? From whom?* The thought often crossed her mind of late that she was ready to form an alliance. But who would she choose, stuck as she was in the wilderness? The only men nearby were members of the dispossessed. After the end of the Last War, many men had been too badly damaged either physically or mentally, sometimes both, to fit back into society. They had ended up living in the barren hills and mountains at the edges of the settlement, striving for survival. As a result, the dispossessed were an endless source of labour and trouble in Khandarken.

China shifted in her chair. She didn't voice her questions. It was best to hear the full story when Maa was involved in the conversation.

Maa gazed into the fireheat again and continued as if she'd read her mind. "It comes from Judson Lanser, himself. He is Emperor Carlton's Advisor now and an important man in the new Empire. He wants to marry you."

Chinata hurriedly looked down as disappointment sank like a stone in her stomach. She remembered Judson Lanser from Sommerset. She'd only been ten or eleven when they left, but Lanser had been an old man even then. Why would she want to marry him?

"I don't understand," she stalled. "Why make an

offer now? I haven't set eyes on him for ten years or more."

Maa gave her a piercing gaze. "Lanser knows of your heritage."

She nodded, resignation taking up space in her belly alongside the stone already lodged there. Many people knew of her parentage. Emperor Aqatain was her father, Carlton her half-brother.

"And Emperor Carlton is in favour of this match. He's the one who recommended it."

"I see." She stood suddenly as resolution solidified within. "I will think about it," she said, turning with purpose toward the door.

"Chinata." The voice was harsh and demanding. "I'll expect your cooperation in this. I need your answer tomorrow. The courier is waiting to take your acquiescence back with him."

Find this book on Amazon –
https://www.amazon.com/Sylvie-Grayson/

… also from Sylvie Grayson…
Contemporary suspense, romance and
attempted murder!

Be careful who you trust...

Katy Dalton worked hard to save her money. And
letting her friend Bruno invest it seemed like a safe bet.
But her job disappears and she needs her money back,
everything Bruno has already loaned to Rome Trucking.
When Katy insists he return her money, Bruno stops
answering his phone and bad things start to happen.

Brett Rome is frustrated. The last thing he wants to
do is leave a promising career in hockey to come home

and run his ailing father's trucking company. What he discovers is not the successful business that he remembers, but one that is teetering on the very edge of bankruptcy and a young woman demanding the return of the money she invested.

With the company in chaos, Brett hires her. But danger lurks in the form of Bruno's dubious associates. What secret are they hiding and why are they willing to kill Katy? Can Brett put this broken picture back together, and is Katy part of the solution or the problem?

A thrilling roller coaster of a story... Interesting characters, family conflicts and divided loyalties make this a book that kept me up half the night. Brett Rome is a hockey player with a bright future called home when his father has a heart attack. Worse, the company is in serious financial trouble. Katy Dalton reminds me of Shelley Long on Cheers although she's brunette, not blonde. She arrives at Rome Trucking searching for money she's 'invested' through a friend

Sylvie Grayson has found her niche, you'll love this book...

SYLVIE GRAYSON

LEGAL OBSTRUCTION

Emily moves to a new town to hide her secret, but it follows her. Can Joe protect her from her past?

When Emily Drury takes a job as legal counsel for an import-export company, she does it because she needs to get away to safety.

Joe Tanner counts himself lucky. He's charmed a successful big city lawyer into heading up the legal department of his rapidly expanding business. But why would a beautiful woman who could easily make partner in a high profile law firm give it all up to come to Bonnie? As Joe realizes she has become essential to his happiness, his first reaction is to protect her. But he doesn't know the whole story.

Can Emily trust him enough to divulge her secret? And will he learn what he needs to know in time to stop the avalanche that's gaining speed as it races down the hill toward her?

I loved this book! I've found my new favorite author.

Emily is a fiercely professional woman who is on her own and determined to protect her little family. Joe is a solitary guy who often doesn't deal with problems until they are front and center. But boy does Emily wake him up and does he take notice. Add in a wildcard assistant and a few unsavory characters and I was up all night finishing the book to find out what happens.

...When a police detective falls for his main suspect, life gets complicated...

When Chloe Bowman wakes to find her husband gone, never does she imagine it will take so long to find him, or that in the midst of the search she'll discover she doesn't really know this man at all. She soon realizes she has been left alone with her young son and a time bomb on her hands. Then the earthquake throws everything into question. Lurking in the shadows is the mysterious Rainman who travels under an unknown name.

Police Detective Ross Cullen is already investigating Chloe's husband when he disappears. Although he's powerfully drawn to Chloe, Ross also knows that when one member of a family disappears, the first place to look for the suspect is among those closest to him. No one is closer than Chloe.

But the deeper Ross digs the less he knows, and the more he's attracted to the young wife as she struggles to put her life back together. Can Ross break through the Rainman's disguises to solve the case so he can be with Chloe?

This is the first time that I read a book written by Sylvie Grayson. The Lies He Told Me is an enjoyable read with several charming characters! There's a lot of twists and turns in this story, and it's also filled with mystery, suspense, and intrigue; all this with a touch of romance!

It tells the story of Chloe, her son Davey, and Police Detective Ross Cullen. Chloe discovered she never knew the man, Jeff, who she had married . . . he simply vanished from her life! That's when Ross, who is investigating her husband's disappearance, enters her life and comes to her rescue. Will he be able to help her? Will he discover the true identity of Jeff? Together they embark on a journey of discovery, of lies, and secrets. But with spending lots of time close to Chloe, sparks will flare. However, Ross never intended to fall in love with her.

SYLVIE GRAYSON

Sometimes you
get a second chance...

MY BEST
MISTAKE

Jenny fell for her cousin once before and got burned.
Can she recover, or is this just another big mistake?

Jordie was heartbroken as a young man when he returned to town to find Jenny had married another man. Now she lives beside him, and he'll either go crazy or do what he should have done in the first place - claim her for his own.

Jenny is back and she's angry. Her husband cheated and she can't let it go, her kids won't answer her phone calls and her boss's wife hates her.

But whiles she's off travelling something happens to her boss that threatens them all, and then someone comes after her.

Who can she turn to? With her cousin living right beside her it's becoming harder to ignore the chemistry they have always shared. Can Jordie help put her life back together?

Jenny's in a mess and she's angry -- her husband has cheated, then left her and her children stranded. Now she works for a company where the owner's wife hates her, and she can't get her kids to return her phone calls. She's steaming mad and she's made too many mistakes to think of committing another.

Cousin Jordie has been in love with Jenny since they were kids growing up together. Now she lives right next door. When things start to go drastically wrong and someone seems to be out to hurt her, he's determined to be the one she turns to for help.

I found this a very intriguing story -- Jenny is a multi-layered clever woman who is trying to put her life back together after a bad divorce. Yes, she's made some mistakes, but as things progress, she's determined not to make the same ones again. She's afraid that Jordie might be one of those mistakes. Her job is to patch her life back together. Well written with lots of action and great characters. I'm looking for Grayson's next book.

In the 1930's, can a country doctor and a determined widow save the lives of these abandoned strangers?

After losing her husband to a deadly illness, Julia Butler is determined to look after her family, but this is the 1930's and times are tough for everyone. As the endless string of jobless men trudges past her farm, she does her best to hang on. Then two strangers suddenly appear at her home. They are hiding something that places her family in danger, and nothing will ever be the same.

Dr. Will Stofford has become disillusioned with women. In an effort to heal his broken heart, he leaves his brothers behind and sets up his medical practice in the Kootenays where no one knows him.

Meeting Julia throws his plans into chaos. Will can't turn his back on a challenge and he won't rest until he solves this puzzle and puts things right. If marrying Julia is part of the solution, then so much the better.

If you like western country stories with a dash of intrigue then MOON SHINE, written by Sylvie Grayson, will be perfect for you. I really enjoyed this book! It's well written with charming characters like Julia Butler, her two children, Maggie and Jims, and Dr. Will Stofford.

MOON SHINE tells the story of Julia, a young widow with two young children living on a farm in rural Canada in the 1930's. It's set during the Depression when men had to wander the roads to find jobs to help their families. These times were rough. However, two surprise visitors are discovered hiding on her farm. Danger lurks around her farm.
I really enjoyed this book. It is well written with a strong female main character and a beautiful storyline with hardship and pain as well as love. I found it hard to put down and read it in one sitting. Looking forward to reading more of her work.

Sci-fi/ fantasy from Sylvie Grayson

The Emperor has been defeated. New countries have arisen from the ashes of the old Empire. The citizens swear they will never need to fight again after that long and painful war.

Bethlehem Farmer is helping her brother Abram run Farmer Holdings in south Khandarken after their father died in the final battles. She is looking after the dispossessed, keeping the farm productive and the talc mine working in the hills behind their land. But when Abram takes a trip with Uncle Jade into the northern territory and disappears without a trace, she's left on her own. Suddenly things are not what they seem and no one can be trusted.

Major Dante Regiment is sent by his father, the General of Khandarken, to find out what the situation is at Farmer Holdings. What he sees shakes him to the core and fuels his grim determination to protect Bethlehem at all cost, even with his life.

Ms Grayson has created a fascinating new world with a lot of the same old problems. Sci fi and fantasy rolled into one with a sure hand and enormous imagination
I couldn't help but think a feeling of deja vu. Like I had heard this story before or like it reminded me of something. And then it hit me. It sounded similar to the fall of the Ottoman Empire after WW1. The new countries that came forth. The battles. The new rulers and emperors fighting to keep their territory. And the citizens, adjusting to the new normal.

And then I realized that this story is one of a kind. It has so many unique characteristics- personal relationships are intriguing, names are cool, the plot gets thicker with each page, and I loved the author's style. It became evident that I was addicted to reading the book. I'm going to give this a strong recommendation. It's my kind of book.

Abe Farmer may survive the
Sanctuary, but he won't
escape the Emperor

THE LAST WAR
BOOK TWO

SYLVIE GRAYSON

From the mud and danger of the open road to the welcoming arms of the Sanctuary, from attacks by the dispossessed army to the storms of the open sea, Son of the Emperor takes us on a wild ride into danger and on to the dream of freedom.

The Emperor is defeated yet already unrest is growing in the north of Khandarken. After Julianne Adjudicator's father disappears, she seeks to escape the clutches of her vicious stepmother Zanata, and flees to the Sanctuary. This is the safest place for a woman in a hostile world of unrest and roving dispossessed. But when Julianne seeks asylum, it soon becomes clear all is not as it first appeared.

Then Abe Farmer arrives at the Sanctuary seeking medical help. Abe isn't interested in taking a young woman with them, as he and his injured bodyguard struggle to return to the Southern Territory. Yet when he discovers her fate if she stays, he finds he has no choice.

But the journey becomes more dangerous as they encounter the army of the New Emperor and are caught in the middle of a firefight as they flee toward the Catastrophic Ocean. Can Abe keep her safe till they reach home?

...a whole new world with the same old problems - fantasy at its best...

Really a powerful portrayal of how a society deals with massive upheaval - and at the same time a great adventure filled with action, thrills and even romance. Sylvie Grayson really knows how to tell a powerful tale. Strong plot, string characters that readers get invested in. Amazingly strong world-building. What more could one ask for? Enjoy.

TRUTH AND TREACHERY

THE LAST WAR
BOOK THREE

SYLVIE GRAYSON

When Emperor Carlton makes an offer to Cownden Lanser, can he refuse? Lanser has his own ambitions and Carlton may be offering everything he's dreamed of.

The Young Emperor has been backed into a corner. He holds a bit of land in Legitamia where he marshals his troops, but the skirmishes they've launched to expand his empire have had limited success. Now, his ambitions are aimed at overthrowing everything Khandarken has cobbled together since the Last War.

Cownden Lanser, Chief Constable of Khandarken, is a private man with a close connection to the Old Empire that he doesn't divulge to anyone. Although he's dedicated to his position, things are not what they seem in the rank and file of the police.

Selanna Nettles is a sookie, trained in Legitamia but working near her family in the Western Territory, healing the mine workers. But her life takes a startling turn when Chief Cownden Lanser hires her to attend a set of high-level meetings.

When these three meet up in Legitamia, the result is explosive. Not just for them but for the future of Khandarken. The Emperor makes Cownden an offer that might be everything he's secretly dreamed of. How can he refuse?

The Last War series is a stunning portrayal of a new world created from fire and consumed at the edges... sci fi/fantasy at its best...

Ok, this series is just getting better and better. The increasing complexity of the characters and the development of lead characters is a pleasure to read. The plot, with its twists and turns, intrigue and adventure, is a real joy. If you liked the first two books in The Last War series (and, seriously, that's the place to start before reading this book - it's worth doing) then you will love this book.

Fanny Master is running for her life. Can she trust a criminal enforcer to keep her safe?

The International Head Balls Games are about to begin at Deep Creek. Tension rises with Adar Silva, Khandarken, Jiran and Legitamia scheduled to take part. Damian Stuke, an enforcer for a gamer in the Western Territory, still has nightmares about being captured and tortured during the Last War. When his sister marries the Chief Constable of Khandarken, his life has to change.

Training for undercover work in Deep Creek in the midst of the Games, he encounters a fascinating woman with a small child and a hidden agenda. But as he discovers what she's hiding, his protective instincts kick into high gear.

Fanny Master's her parents are assassinated, and she runs for her life. A member of the Khandarken elite, she doesn't know who is after he, but she'll do almost anything to remain under the radar. That could include using someone else's ident and adopting their child, a child who might be from another world.

As Emperor Carlton ramps up his plans for invasion, the assassin makes a new attempt on Fanny's life. Damian is her only hope. Will he save her from her unknown enemy, or is he still working for the other side?

The Last War has been a truly excellent series so far, and Weapon of Tyrants is staying strong. Exciting, full of intrigue and adventure, wonderfully developed strong lead characters with a great supporting cast, neat world-building and excellent writing. I mean, what more can you ask for? You do need to start with book 1, but it too was excellent so you can't go wrong, and I can guarantee you'll have a ball with this one.

Find Sylvie Grayson at www.sylviegrayson.com to subscribe to her newsletter, for first chance at new books, free copies, and more.

ABOUT THE AUTHOR

Sylvie Grayson has published romantic suspense novels, *Suspended Animation, Legal Obstruction, The Lies He Told Me,, My Best Mistake,* and *Moon Shine,* all about strong women who meet with dangerous odds, stories of tension and attraction.

She has also written *The Last War* series, a romantic sci/fi - fantasy set in a new world she has created. The Last War has ended but the next is about to begin. As Emperor Carlton seizes territory all around him, the newly cobbled countries try to keep him at bay and solidify their strengths.

Ms. Grayson has been an English language instructor, a nightclub manager, an auto shop bookkeeper and a lawyer. She is a wife and mother, and lives in southern British Columbia with her husband on a small piece of land near the Pacific Ocean that they call home.

You can follow her on her website – www.sylviegrayson.com, find her on facebook, or contact her at sylviegraysonauthor@gmail.com

www.ingramcontent.com/pod-product-compliance
Lightning Source LLC
Chambersburg PA
CBHW070537260626
47161CB00002B/420